CONTEMPT
OF
COURT

BY KEN MALOVOS

For Michele
Forever

ONE

EVERYONE HAS REGRETS. Even lawyers. In fact, Mike Zorich thought that lawyers, in particular, have lots of regrets. Some lawyers regret that they are lawyers in the first place and are looking for some other line of work. But not Mike. He loved being a lawyer. No, his regrets were different.

He had probably defended more than a thousand men and a few women who were charged with various crimes, from shoplifting to murder, in his career. Most of them were guilty, but some were not. And it was the innocent ones that bothered him the most. There had to be a few innocent clients sitting in prison right now. But who? How would he ever know? He knew that he could worry and fret all day long but it would not change anything. As the saying of the day went, "It is what it is."

At 54 and widowed, Mike found himself alone more than he wished and he would often reflect on the past. This morning was no exception. But he was not thinking about his old clients. He was thinking about Sheila. His wife had been dead for almost five years. At one level, he still had not accepted that she was gone. There was a lonely feeling in the pit of his stomach that morning as there was every morning. It was 5:45 and he had been awake for about twenty minutes just resting in his bed, his arms behind his head, staring out the window to the backyard of his comfortable suburban home in Carmichael just outside of Sacramento.

His thoughts soon changed to greet the sun pushing itself through the east-facing window. At first it was only a glimmer but it soon made its presence known bringing light to the room and warmth to the bedspread.

Today was a running day. At 6 feet tall and about 180 pounds with charcoal hair, Mike was proud of his body but it wasn't like it used to be. Ongoing aches in his joints had become his constant companion. Slowly he got out of bed and made his way to the bathroom. A headache greeted him the moment that he began to walk. Too much to drink last night. He knew it but he also knew that he wasn't going to do anything about it. It was his way to cope with missing Sheila, his wife of 24 years.

It was bright outside and there was a slight chill in the air on Friday, September 17, as the hot summer was beginning to ease into the inviting coolness of autumn. It was absolutely the best time of the year in Sacramento. Cool mornings, warm days and the soothing Delta breezes in the evening. There was plenty of time for a longer run today as it was much earlier than he usually ran, Mike thought to himself, as he laced up his New Balance running shoes. He wore his usual running shorts and a cotton long sleeved sweat shirt with a zipper in front, over one of his favorite tee-shirts. He grabbed his pocket radio, ear plugs, San Francisco Giants hat, keys and driver's license and headed to his car. He would drive a couple of miles to the American River bike trail. The trail extended about thirty miles from Folsom Dam to downtown Sacramento along the American River to the point where the river merged with the Sacramento River, on its way to the Delta and eventually to the San Francisco Bay.

Things were going well in the topsy-turvy world of Michael Zorich, attorney at law. He liked his current case which had recently heated up after almost two years of no activity because of an agreement by all counsel to try to settle the case through mediation. Unfortunately, the mediation had not worked so it was back to court. The case was sure to keep him very occupied for the foreseeable future. His client was the older of two Darnoff brothers who were involved in a bitter partnership dissolution along with their sister. To top it off, their parents were getting divorced after 50+ years of marriage and after building a very successful wine producing business in Esparto, a small town 50 miles west of

Woodland in Yolo County. Brian Darnoff, Mike's client, was aligned with his father. Brian's younger brother, Jason, was aligned with his sister, Linda, and their mother. Money does crazy things to families, Mike figured. The family split made for juicy headlines in the Woodland newspaper. The early morning chatter at the coffee shops in Esparto was full of the latest rumors.

For Mike Zorich, the case gave him yet again an opportunity to help others find justice. It was the essence of his daily life for the past twenty nine years. Mike loved the courtroom. It was there that he could engage in organized warfare, as he liked to call it, confrontation without fisticuffs. He never was much of a fist fighter in real life. As an adult, he had never really fought anyone, preferring the power of words. Words had been his salvation, both written and spoken. He had achieved a fair amount of success as a lawyer and he savored every minute of it. There was nothing like a happy client, especially someone he had helped through a crisis. That was the satisfaction that he found so often in the law.

It was quiet in the morning especially at this early hour. The sounds from Highway 50, just on the other side of the American River, were just beginning. The automobile was a wonderful invention. It was an absolute necessity but it brought the smog and the noise. Maybe electronic cars will change all of that. Mike imagined what the American River must have been like 160 years ago when the 49ers were hiking on trails like this one, seeking their fortunes at mines in Coloma and the foothills. It would have been quiet. The would-be miners came from the East and a lot of them arrived in San Francisco and took a steamboat up the Delta on the Sacramento River, covering the 90 miles in a day. Arriving at the port where the Sacramento and American Rivers come together, they would set out by horse or mule or stage or on foot and head for the Promised Land, the promise of gold. Others would arrive overland, following the trails of those who had gone before them. Many would not make it but those that did would seek the same gold. Most would find nothing. Only the lucky few would find their fortune. But it would have been very quiet back then.

Even later, when the orphan boys rode their horses from St. Joseph, Missouri, to the terminus of the Pony Express in Sacramento, it would have been quiet. When the Chinese came to build the western part of the Transcontinental Railroad from Sacramento to Promontory Point in Utah, it would have been quiet. It wasn't until the automobile, when all of that changed. Now as the capitol of the ninth largest economy in the world, Sacramento was a huge metropolis. There were factories and ambulance sirens and people and the constant din of cars on the huge interstate freeways. Interstate 5 extended from Mexico to Canada and bordered the western edge of the city. Interstate 80 extended from the east to the west coast and bisected the city. But, no matter, this morning was quiet. It was Mike's alone to enjoy with Mother Nature.

He parked his car in the parking lot at the thirteen mile mark and set off down the trail leaving behind his sweat shirt in the back seat of the car. It wasn't long before he hit his stride and settled into his usual rhythm. He exhaled at every other right footstep. He liked to think of himself as a machine and he easily covered two miles at a decent pace. The blacktop of the bike trail was littered with autumn leaves like leopard spots. The voices from the National Public Radio station were announcing the news in his ears. The usual gang was not there yet, but they would soon be riding their bikes or jogging or walking along the trail. At this earlier hour, there was hardly anyone there. He could see the clear blue water of the American River cascading over the rocks, whenever the trail meandered close to the river.

The first thing he would later recall was the sharp blow to his right shoulder. A very sharp blow. It instantly took him to his knees. It felt like a karate chop. He struggled to gain his bearings. At once, he was on the ground in the low-growing bushes and someone was on top of him. The man was big and sweaty. Beyond that Mike could not see much as he was face down. He felt the sharp pressure of a large rock as the weight of the man bore down on him and his knee and into the rock. The man whispered into his ear that he wanted his wallet and keys. But then he heard the same man say something entirely different.

"Hey, are you all right?" he heard very loudly. "How can I help?"

It was coming from the same person on top of him. That didn't make sense. This guy wasn't the least interested in his welfare. Then Mike heard some other voices, not close, but voices nonetheless.

"It's okay. I've got it. He just tripped and fell," the man shouted. "You okay, Buddy?"

Everything he heard was loud, very loud, and it clearly wasn't directed at him. But he didn't hear the voices of the others anymore. Then he got it. This guy was talking to those people who were further down the bike trail, as if to reassure them that he was there to help. This guy was not there to help. Mike saw the knife, a large pocket knife with an extended blade. The guy was big. He wore a sleeveless t-shirt and shorts and his breath was foul. He must have come up from behind him. Then there were a couple of hard blows from the man's powerful arms, pistons ramming down on his arms and chest. The pain was immediate.

"Gimme your fucking keys, Buddy, and your wallet. Right now."

Mike just froze under the weight. He turned his head to see who was talking to him but he could not get a good view. He did see a ruddy face and a mustache. The awful smell of the man's breath was only overcome by the pain at Mike's knee. And he could definitely feel the knife pressed against his neck. The man's voice had a certain gravelly quality. And a certainty. This was no joke. Mike motioned to his pocket and got his right hand free to pull out his keys.

"I don't have a wallet," Mike said.

The man grabbed the keys. At that instant, Mike summoned all of his strength and heaved upward throwing the assailant off but forcing Mike backwards just a bit. The man was on his feet in a flash and pushed Mike back to the ground. He then took a rock, about the size of his hand, and struck Mike on the side of his head. It really hurt and it stunned him.

"Not such a big guy now, are you Buddy? Not such a big lawyer. What's it like being the bottom dog? Do you like it? Do you like it?"

Mike tried to look again at the brute but liquid clouded his eyes. He rubbed his eyes and saw red all over his hand. Then a kick to his ribs. And another. Mike heard the soft mashing of bones, his bones. The asshole was wearing running shoes but the kicks were hard and powerful. The pain from the kicks exceeded all of the other pain combined.

"Okay big guy. How's it going for you? Not so big today, huh? Not so big today."

Then he took off. The whole deal only lasted a couple of minutes. Mike got a view of his assailant, a barrel-chested Mexican fellow, about age 30 or so with a round face, dark hair and big muscles.

Mike yelled "Help" and tried to run after him but his knee and his head were hurting. And his ribs resisted any movement at all. Nobody answered his plea for help. When he looked down he saw a free flow of blood onto his ankle-high running socks and his running shoes. He put his hand to the side of his head and he felt the blood again. Mike limped along, the best he could. Chasing a guy on a bike is a losing proposition even if you are in great shape, Mike thought. But he wasn't going to do anything when he was like this. Mike stopped. There was nobody else around. His face felt hot. He wiped it with his tee-shirt, which colorfully proclaimed last year's Valentine's Day Run for the Legal Aid Society. He couldn't believe what had just happened. He stopped and rubbed his shoulders. A guy on a bike passed him by and looked at him, puzzled. But he didn't stop. He just kept on heading west on the trail to downtown.

He wasn't sure if he saw anyone other than the guy on the bike. He walked in the same direction as the bike, all the while asking himself what this was all about and why this happened to him. This guy knew he was a lawyer. But why? He wanted answers but there weren't any. He knew that it would be best if he calmed down and regained his composure. It was quiet and he could hear the blue jays in the trees. They sang merrily to themselves. They had no cares and no idea of what had just happened. Too bad they couldn't help or call for someone to help him or even appear in court as eyewitnesses. He looked for an emergency phone on the bike path, but he could not find one. There's never one when you needed it, he thought to himself. He finally made it back to the parking lot at the 13-mile mark of the trail where he had left his car.

The car was gone. "You've got to be kidding," he said to himself. The guy on the bike was nowhere to be seen. There was a water fountain and a bathroom at the end of the parking lot where it met the trail. Mike went in and cleaned his face and his knee. Surprisingly, there was some paper in the towel dispenser. He applied pressure to a gash on his head about three inches over his ear and to his knee while he sat on the toilet. After a while, the bleeding stopped. But to be sure, he pressed the paper towel on his head and went out of the bathroom to the parking lot.

Nearby, a couple of attractive thirty year-old women glanced at Mike as he walked into the parking lot. They were each clad in brightly-colored shorts, running shirts, caps and shoes. They were stretching their legs on the bench of a picnic table just twenty feet from the edge of the black top, where Mike had parked his car. They saw a handsome middle-aged man with an athletic body and dark hair with bits of white, partially covered by a baseball cap. At about six feet, slim body and attractive face, Mike's natural good looks drew their attention. They could see that he was in some sort of pain and they could easily see the blood flowing down his left leg from the knee as well as the red around his head where Mike was still holding the paper towels. Mike sat down on the other side of the concrete picnic table to take stock. The women looked at him, puzzled.

"God, what happened to you? Do you need some help," one of the women dared to ask.

"I'm okay, I think…just got mugged actually."

With that the women drew closer, their instincts aroused and somewhat mesmerized by his baritone voice. "Oh my God. You're not kidding."

"No, wish I was. You didn't happen to see a guy on a bike coming this way, did you? Or someone drive off in a car parked right there?" Mike nodded in the direction of the parking lot.

"No, I didn't. Did you, Nicole?" The other one shook her head. "But we just got here." The two women looked at each other as if confirming their story.

"It was a few minutes ago. He hit me pretty hard and then took the keys to my car. And he took my car."

"Oh no. Is there anything we can do?"

Mike thought for a second. He would really like to get home but that didn't seem likely as the two women were just starting their run. Better yet, he would like to get the guy who took his keys and car and smash him in the face.

"Thanks, but I'll be okay." He paused. "You wouldn't have a cell phone would you? I think I should call the police."

"Yeah, I do."

The woman who first spoke to him walked over to a nearby car, opened the trunk and retrieved her cell phone. She also found a towel and a bottle of water. Mike took off his baseball cap, revealing his charcoal hair and a receding hair line and a distinguished visage. She handed him the phone.

"Here, maybe the towel will help with the bleeding. It's clean. You can keep it. I just have it for emergencies or whatever. Keep the water too."

"Thanks. I really appreciate it. I'll just make the one call."

He called 911 and was patched through to the Sheriff's Department. The dispatcher took some preliminary information and then told Mike to sit tight until a sheriff's car could get there. Mike thought that wise as if he had some other choice. He gave the phone back to the one woman and they both left after offering their sympathies. He sat back on the concrete bench as more bike riders and runners came by. Some of them took a quick glance at Mike out of the corner of their eyes, but most did not pay any attention. Or they wanted to pretend that they didn't see him.

He sat for what seemed to be a very long time before he saw the white sedan with the Sheriff's Department logo on the side ease into the park very slowly from the Arden Way entrance. Mike waved and the young deputy sheriff spotted him and parked nearby. He was probably in his late twenties with dark hair and a fresh face complete with red cheeks. He was way too young, Mike thought. A short while later, an older park ranger, wearing a short-sleeved uniform shirt with buttons straining to keep everything tucked in also arrived in an official vehicle. No doubt he was summoned by the deputy sheriff. Mike sat on the nearby picnic table, his legs dangling over the edge. He had stopped the bleeding with the help of the towel.

The deputy sheriff retrieved a first-aid kit from his car. He sprayed Mike's head and his knee with an antibiotic and put some gauze and tape on both wounds.

"That should hold for a bit and at least keep the blood stopped. There was a lot of blood but the wound on the head. I think your baseball cap cushioned the blow a bit. Nothing will show because your hair covers it all. But you should see someone today. I don't know about the ribs. It could be that he broke some from what you say. I broke some ribs playing football in high school and I had a lot of trouble breathing. You seem to be breathing okay so I don't think it is terribly serious. You should see someone. An x-ray would probably answer the question."

The three of them talked for a while, Mike supplied details of the events of the morning, still feeling the pain in his ribs and forehead and his left leg. Both the deputy and the park ranger were taking notes.

"So he was about 5 foot 7 or 8, maybe 180 pounds, dark-skinned, ruddy complexion, mustache, white tank top, baseball cap in reverse, nothing much else. That about it?"

"I think so. He was built, like I told you. And he had bad breath," Mike said.

"Would you say he was White, Black or Mexican or some other ethnicity?"

The deputy was studying his notes as he asked, barely looking up at Mike.

"Yeah, I think he was Mexican, but I'm not for sure. He had a loud voice, at least it was loud when he was shouting out to other people. He was pretty strong, I can tell you that. He had me pinned down. I wasn't going anywhere."

"But he distinctly called you a lawyer?"

"Yes. I am a lawyer but I don't know this guy and have no idea why he said anything like that, or called me a 'big guy' or 'Buddy' or anything like that," Mike said.

"We've had some incidents lately, kind of like this. Muggers snatch car keys from runners and then take the car. We haven't publicized anything as we don't want to panic the public. We're trying to catch the varmints," the deputy said.

His manner of speaking was tough or maybe he was trying to sound tough. Mike couldn't tell. The park ranger did not have much to add. He was more interested in filling out his official report.

"But we have never had an incident where the guy seems to know who the person is, you know what I mean? Nobody ever reported to us that they were identified in any way, like you were, calling you a lawyer."

"So they just knock people over and take their car?"

"That's about it. Sometimes we find the car a couple of days later maybe missing a few things and a few parts and a little worse for wear. Sometimes the car is gone forever. Kind of depends on the type of car. We have had about three of these assaults in the last few months. The victims seem to be anonymous and unlucky. They just happened to be in the wrong place at the wrong time."

Mike looked at the deputy while he was speaking but he was more interested in the pain in his body.

"Probably drugs, but you never know. Look, you stay here for a bit. I am going to look around," the deputy said.

The deputy jumped into his car with the park ranger and they drove onto the bike trail with red lights flashing after first stopping a couple of hundred yards away or so. Mike stayed perched on the picnic bench holding the towel to his knee. He could see that they got out and did something but could not exactly make out what they were doing or checking out. Mike figured that the red lights were probably to alert any speedy bike riders coming in the opposite direction. He sat on the bench and waited for about ten minutes until they returned.

"Not much that we could see," the deputy said when he returned. "We talked to a few people. One guy said that he saw two cars parked here right next to each other. But nobody else saw anything. I think this was just too early. There are a lot more riders and runners out now."

"Yeah, like I said, I yelled out but nobody answered and I didn't see anyone until I got back to the parking lot," Mike said.

"There was an old bike over in the weeds that we saw. We have it in the trunk and will take a look at it, dust it for fingerprints, you know," the deputy said. "Could have been his bike."

"Okay."

"But I wouldn't expect much from that."

"Yeah, probably no usable prints," the park ranger added, as if he was the leading police authority on the subject.

"Sounds to me like there were two people involved. If the other car was parked next to yours, they might have been following you or checking you out. The one guy might have ditched his bike and took your car. The other guy drove his own car. I can't believe that one guy would have come to the park on a bike and followed you. After all, he knew you or at least knew that you were a lawyer. I would bet that they followed you from your home this morning."

Mike listened and it all made sense. The thought of someone following him was scary. But one thing for sure was that someone was out to get him. Why would anyone be out to get him?

"How far away do you live?"

"About two miles. Most times, I run from my house to the trail, but this morning I just wanted to get here and run so I drove."

"I'll give you a lift home. Why don't you just get in my car and we'll be off."

Mike got off of the bench and walked slowly to the deputy sheriff's car. His ribs hurt the minute he began walking again. He knew that he would be sore tomorrow. But that was not what was bothering him as he opened the passenger door of the deputy's cruiser.

"You know, I had my home key on the car key ring. You think there is any chance he would go there?"

"That's not likely. At least it never happened before with these other ones. Most of the time, they want the car for the radio or compact disc player or the copper in the catalytic converter. I wouldn't worry about it at all"

Mike felt reassured as he put his head on the headrest and tried to close his eyes while the deputy slowly left the park and drove down Arden Way to his house. The odor of cigarette smoke and something else, unknown but equally disagreeable permeated the vehicle, probably coming from the back seat. It was hard to relax but at least he would soon be home and would be able to rest. Or so he thought.

TWO

As they drove along the streets, Mike saw a lot of mothers and fathers taking their children to school and the occasional school bus doing the same. Otherwise the traffic was light. It took about 10 minutes to get to his home. Mike thought again of his car registration in the glove compartment which would contain his home address. The more he thought about it, the more nervous he got. When they got to his house, there was nobody there. No sign of his car and no sign of entry at the front door. The drapes in the front rooms were the same as when he left.

"Looks pretty clear," the deputy said.

"Well, that's a relief. Maybe he didn't think he had enough time," Mike volunteered.

"Either that or he never had any intention of coming here. I had better check around the back and look inside anyway, just to be sure."

The deputy was being solicitous and Mike appreciated it. Mike got out of the car and leaned up against the rear fender, looking out and again admiring the beauty of the fall morning. The deputy went around the side and was back in front in a couple of minutes.

"Do you have a spare key by chance? The doors are all locked, but I would like to check inside anyway."

Mike told him that he hid a key in the back of the house in a rustproof container in a flower pot so the deputy went back and Mike waited at the patrol car in the front of his house. In a while, the front door opened and the deputy was standing on the threshold. His shoulders sagged and he wasn't happy.

"Sorry, but he was here," the deputy said quietly. His face tightened in a compassionate kind of way and there was a warmth to his voice. "He's been all through the house. Pretty much made a mess of things. You will have to tell me if he got anything but it looks as if some of the sterling silver is gone. At least there is an empty silverware box on the floor.

"Shit. I should have figured."

"Like I said, when there has been a mugging on the bike trail, the bad guy usually takes the car and that's it. Nothing more. I think this is the first time on one of these that someone has broken into the house."

Mike felt like someone had punched him again. This time it was a blow to the stomach. A fleeting taste of acid reflux greeted the back of his throat. Mike walked to the front door and looked in where he could see stuff all over the floor. He paused and then finally went in and saw the mess, clothes pulled out of closets and drawers. Some sterling silver was obviously gone from the hutch in the dining room. Mainly, it was a mess.

For Mike, there was an immediate sense of violation and it was even worse than being knocked down an hour ago. The idea that someone was running around his house and looking into his private things was repulsive. The red in his face returned just as it had been that morning on the bike trail.

He remembered how he felt when he went to his parents' home some twenty five or thirty years ago after a frantic phone call. It was a rainy weekday evening. His parents had been burglarized. Everything was on the ground. Every drawer had been opened and left that way. Books were scattered about. A couple of chairs were on their sides. Glasses were broken all over the dining room floor. Some silverware and china were missing. The home in which he grew up and the only home his parents knew as a married couple had been invaded. Thieves and vandals had done a job. His mother was beyond hysterics. His father tried to console her, to no avail. In fact, his father was in need of comfort. And Mike could do nothing but get angrier and angrier. It was the sense of personal violation. How dare they?

And that was just how he felt this very moment. How dare they? "This really pisses me off," he said out loud to nobody in particular. His hands were on his hips as he surveyed the mess in his home.

The deputy was sympathetic. "Look, I am going to send out the Criminal Investigation Unit to do some prints and take a statement. Why don't you clean yourself up and take it easy for a bit until they get here?"

"Yeah, sure."

"But don't touch anything like doors or knobs or anything that has been touched by this perp. Let the CIU people do their thing. Fingerprints could be anywhere. When you feel better, the best thing you can do is to try to put together a list of what you think is missing. The more you can do now, the better it will be."

Despite his youthful appearance, the deputy had obviously seen this kind of situation before. He completed his paperwork, entitling the incident as an "Assault – Penal Code Section 242; Robbery-Penal Code Section 211, Burglary-Section 459 and Grand Theft Auto-Section 487." The deputy walked around the house and outside making notes on his pad. When he came back, he sat on the couch.

"The best I can figure is just like we were talking about at the park, someone was targeting you. I have to ask. Is there anybody out to get you? Someone you work with maybe? A client? Any neighbor you having a problem with? Anything like that at all?"

"Nobody I can think of," Mike answered. His mind was racing but he was just drawing a blank.

"You haven't had any fights recently with anyone? No disputes? Someone on the roads, a young punk in a car who thought you did something wrong? We get a lot of cases of 'road rage.' Someone could have figured out who you were by following up on your license plate number."

"Nothing comes to mind, officer. Believe me I have been trying to think of who this could be. I've represented a lot of guys in the past. It could be any of them I suppose."

"Okay, I will work on it and compare this case with the others and if we come up with anything, I will let you know. You do the same. If you think of anything, you give me a ring and we will track it down. You really need to think about this.

Someone you know or something that happened that didn't go well. It's obvious that someone is sending you a message. They didn't take much from you. If this was a real robbery, I would have thought they would have taken a lot more. Think about it and let me know, okay? I'll bet that some light will go off, and you can give us a clue to follow."

"That works. I'll try to think who it could be. Thanks for everything."

The deputy handed Mike his business card with "Sacramento Sheriff's Department" and a big star on it and started toward the front door.

"The crime scene folks will be here pretty soon. They will have my report but I'm sure they will want you to go over all of this again and ask you a bunch more questions."

The deputy picked up Mike's paper from the front porch and handed it to him without saying anything. He just smiled with a look of genuine concern and left. Mike sat down in the chair in his dining room, staring at the contents of the front closet on the floor. Photographs were thrown everywhere. Albums from the top shelf were pulled apart and lying on top of each other on the floor. He focused on the large color collage of photographs of Sheila and him at their 15th wedding anniversary. "Now that was a party," he thought to himself. Then he saw the vase from Florence which they got on their trip to Italy. Smashed to pieces. It was a joint wedding anniversary present and they both loved it. A little wetness began to form in the corners of his eyes. "Why? Why?"

More of those memories were scattered over the tiled entry room floor. He did not have the energy or desire to pick them up. Right now he wanted to check out the rest of the house to see what else had happened before the Sheriff's investigators arrived. He would make a list of what he found missing as the deputy asked him to do.

Then it occurred to him that the keys to his office were also on his key chain. He phoned his partner, Denny Grantham, and found him on his cell at the office. He gave him a quick rundown explaining that the key to the office was on his key chain. Denny offered instant comfort. But then that was Denny, Mike's best friend.

"Mike, I can't believe it. I'm really sorry for you. You've got to get to your doc and have yourself checked out. The ribs don't sound too good."

"Yeah, I probably should."

"Do you have any idea who did it?"

"No, nothing. I don't have a clue," Mike said.

"I will look around, but it is not likely that he would come here to the office. How would he even know the address or that you even have an office?"

"Well he knew that I was a lawyer. But you are probably right. He wouldn't have gone there."

"Right. Now listen, Ace, you take care of yourself."

Denny's voice was reassuring. The word "Ace" brought a smile to Mike's lips, the first smile of the day. Denny always called people "Ace," kind of his trademark, but he said it in a kind and not demeaning way.

"Yeah, right," Mike said.

"What I should do is get the locks at the office changed just to be sure. I will get someone over here today. You had better do the same at your house. You never know where those keys could end up."

"That makes sense."

"Hey, before you go, Alice wanted to talk to you. Just a minute."

In a minute or so, Alice was on the line. Mike gave her the same rundown he just gave Denny. She was even more concerned about his injuries.

"Maybe I could come and take you to an ER, Mike."

"No, it's not that bad. I'm okay, really. The bleeding has stopped and the ribs are just hurting. I'll call my doctor. I think he's going to tell me to wrap them with some bandages or something like that. I'll manage."

"Well, if you say so. But if you change your mind, just give me a call and I will be right over there. Mike, do you remember that Request for Production of Documents that Robert Cannes sent you a few weeks ago? He has set a Motion to Compel Production of Documents in court asking for sanctions because you did not produce the financial documents that he requested," she said.

Mike recalled the Request for Documents immediately because it was so unusual. Cannes, his opposing counsel in the Darnoff case, knew that he could not produce any financial documents because the judge in the divorce case had issued an order to all counsel directing a stay on all discovery, including document production, while she took control of the case. Her order was specific and quite clear. Cannes was under the same order. Why would he request documents from

Mike, when he knew that the order prohibited it? It made no sense then and it made no sense now.

"That's really strange, Alice. I wonder what the clown is up to. When did he schedule the motion for hearing?"

"That's the other thing. He has an order for a very quick hearing. You have just five days to file a brief with the court and you have to appear the week after next on September 28. He got an order from the court shortening the usual time for hearing of his motion."

"What's the big hurry? Is there anything in his papers about that?"

"No, I don't see anything but I will look further. Are you coming in today?"

"Yeah, I better come in and see what this is all about. It's going to take me awhile to get put back together but I'll be there. Thanks."

Mike hung up. He had a few things to do before going to the office. The first order of a business was to find an old bottle of Tylenol with codeine that he had from a few years back when he sprained his shoulder playing tennis. He saved it for just this type of thing. The bottle was way past the expiration date but Mike figured that they were still good. After all, most expiration dates were just a scam to get you to buy more. Then he took a long and hot shower. When he got out, the bathroom was full of steam. The Tylenol was beginning to ease the pain. After toweling off, he put some new bandages on his forehead and knee. Then he shaved and dried and combed his hair. He found an old stretch bandage in a nearby drawer and wrapped it around his chest. Right away his ribs felt better.

After putting on some casual clothes, he walked into the kitchen and headed for the liquor cabinet. He poured himself a double scotch over ice. Does the trick every time. Little early to be drinking but then this was strictly for medicinal purposes. Just what any doctor would order, he figured as he smiled to himself. He imagined some grubby miners getting hurt on their way to the gold fields back in 1849 and 1850. Whiskey was probably all they had to soothe the pain. If it worked for them, then it would work for him. And it did. His throat felt warm. After downing one, he poured another and then opened the refrigerator to see what there might be for breakfast. He found a package of pre-cooked sausages so he threw three of them into a small fry pan and added a couple of cracked eggs. He thought he would forget the coffee this morning as the scotch was working just fine. He put an English muffin in the toaster and after it browned, he slathered it with butter and some raspberry jam.

He read the Sacramento Bee while he ate, debating whether he should pour another drink. Thinking that he probably had enough, he voted not to imbibe further and put the bottle of scotch away, out of view. Nothing in the news, just the same old stuff. A murder here, a corrupt politician there. Sacramento had plenty of the politician types. Many were ex-politicians now working as lobby-ists, trying to convince their old pals still in the legislature to vote one way or the other. They were paid handsomely. And they justified it all, thinking that they deserved it after getting paid very little for years of public service. At least that was what they would say to themselves. Mike never got into the lobbying scene. He never trolled the floors of the Capitol looking for votes. In fact, he knew little of how the Legislature worked. Sacramento was the capitol of California and home to a completely separate political world than the legal world that Mike knew and loved. Mike's world centered on the Sacramento County Courthouse, which was some ten blocks from the Capitol Building. But it could just as easily have been two hundred miles apart as the two worlds turned on separate axes. But if a corrupt politician was caught with his hand in the cookie jar and the District Attorney felt like pursuing a publicity-laden case, that would be something differ-ent. Then there might be a "perp walk" that would become the headlines for the paper and all of the television stations.

Mike was feeling better now. It was either the Tylenol or the scotch or the breakfast. Or maybe it was the shower. He pulled out the yellow pages from near the phone. He found several locksmiths with nice ads assuring security and prompt service and he picked one. They could have someone out there in an hour. Then he phoned his son, Peter, and left a message on his cell phone just asking him to call back when he got a chance. There was no sense alarming him. He thought of Nancy. Maybe he should call her. Maybe not. He didn't know how he felt about her right now. The lingering images of Sheila were ever present.

Eventually the investigators from CIU arrived and took extensive fingerprints leaving a lot of black powder on door jams and other promising surfaces. They made an attempt to clean up but their efforts were not all that successful. The park ranger called and asked a few questions so that he could finish his report.

After Peter retrieved the phone message, he called back and Mike told him what happened. Peter hurried over. Since graduation from Stanford, Peter was trying his hand at commercial real estate. But the down market meant that he had a lot of time on his hands. Peter was twenty four and stood a couple of inches over his father whom he strongly resembled. He found his father in the living room.

"You all right?"

"Yeah, I'm fine," Mike said. "I'm fine. Take a look around. Maybe you will see something out of order that I missed."

"What's with the knee and the head? You don't look too good to me."

"It isn't too pretty. It will take a while to heal up but both cuts feel much better. I will just stick with bandages for now."

The investigators were just leaving. Peter walked through the house and then helped Mike put the photographs back in the boxes and into the closet, restoring some sense of order.

"This guy sure made a mess in a short time," Mike said.

"Yeah, but I wonder why. Why would he call you a lawyer and a big shot or whatever he said? He had to have singled you out for some reason. You haven't found anything else missing, except for the silverware, right?"

"No, nothing else. Based on my time as a public defender, I can tell you that not much crime actually makes sense. There may be a simple explanation for all of this."

"Maybe but he certainly planned it pretty well, knocking you down, stealing your keys and then your car, driving over here and taking this stuff. Seems like a lot of work just to make a few bucks. When you add the bit about calling you a lawyer, this has to be something else."

"Yeah, I suppose you're right. But the deputy sheriff told me that there were a few other incidents like this on the bike trail this summer, although this is the first one where the bad guy seemed to identify the victim and the first one where he went to a house and took anything."

"This guy had to know you."

"Could be. I just don't know anything for sure, right now."

"Are you going to be okay? I've got a meeting in about twenty minutes that I should really go to."

"Oh yeah, go, go, please go. I'm fine, just shook up. I'll survive. The world goes on and the sun will shine in the morning. Thanks for dropping by."

Mike smiled at his son and gave him all the reassurance needed to get him on his way. After Peter left, Mike sat down on the sofa and closed his eyes. He couldn't help but think about Peter. He loved his son and knew that he would always be there for him. Then he thought about Peter's mother, his very own Sheila. He had a wonderful marriage to an extraordinary woman and they had a loving son who could always be counted on to do the right thing. They had achieved some degree of financial security and shared their lives with good times and similar values.

They were grateful for their blessings until that day about five years ago. The telephone call from the oncologist about the ovarian cancer came on a Thursday afternoon. Sheila was home alone and took the call in the kitchen, quickly finding a chair at the table so that she could sit as she listened to the doctor. She immediately phoned Mike and he came home and found her at the same spot. Her eyes were puffy from the crying and her look was unfocused. There was not much talking that night.

The denial of it all had long since given way to anger and then some level of acceptance, such as it was. There were tests and more tests and a lot more tears. The two of them faced it together. Mike tried to provide comfort but failed in so many ways. Sheila just tried to cope. Her two sisters and two brothers had been some consolation but they had their own issues. Plus the three girls had never been particularly close. It was one of Sheila's regrets. Now it made no difference.

Chemotherapy and radiation followed, along with wigs. There were second opinions from the staff at the UC Medical School in San Francisco. They took a trip to Palo Alto to the Stanford University Medical School. Mike spent a lot of time on the internet, searching for hope. He read quite a few medical journal articles and sent emails to anyone and everyone asking for some insight. Nothing changed. Within two years, twenty months to be exact, Sheila was dead.

But before she died, he made a vow to her that he would always love her and no one else. She had protested and told him that he needed to get on with his life and find someone to make him happy. But Mike would have none of it.

They were such friends, actually best friends. They met when he was in law school in San Francisco. Sheila was an absolute stunner, long brown hair flowing just below her shoulders. She had the kind of figure that made most guys look again. She kept herself in good shape by regular workouts at the nearby gym. But it was her wide brown eyes and incredibly warm face that drew most attention. She had a way of bringing the entire weight of the universe to bear whenever she looked at someone. The recipient often felt as if he or she was royalty. People just couldn't resist her charms and she was often unaware of her effect on them.

When Peter was young, Sheila was home or at his school. She volunteered for everything and usually ended up in charge. Later, Peter's life focused on sports and Sheila was right there cheering at every soccer or basketball game or every swim meet. When Peter went away to college, she knew that she had to do something so she figured that she would try to sell real estate, much like her aunt had done in the Bay Area when Sheila was a child.

For several years, it was real estate all the time, all day long. She was good at it. In fact, she was very good, garnering her share of awards and honors at the end of each year. She was always ranked in the top 5-10% of the agents in her office and had soon gained a reputation as a "top producer." Of course, her comely looks and effervescent personality assisted in no small part.

Mike never saw himself as a George Clooney type, although some might disagree. He always thought he had won the lottery when he started going out with Sheila. And then she agreed to marry him. Mike was madly in love with this goddess and he spent the better part of his life trying to figure out how to be romantic and do nice things for her. It was a new experience but he learned. They had a good marriage. They had the usual arguments but mostly they shared the good times.

Peter was their only child. From the very beginning, Peter was the apple of his mother's eye. They developed a bond that was never broken, to her dying day. He learned his alphabet before he was two, reading on his own at three and a half. The bicycle followed. Everything she did focused on the precocious one and he responded in kind from the earliest age. Mike was part of the equation with his son but in the early years it was only Sheila. She came to know that Peter would always be there for her as so many mothers discover about their sons, especially only children.

Mike came to appreciate his son later, through athletic events like soccer and basketball. Mike would cherish the one-on-one basketball games they would play, even after Peter began beating him. Peter loved sports and he enjoyed unusual athletic gifts. However, for both parents it was Peter's success in the classroom that drew the most pride. The "A's" on his report card came easily, maybe too easily. For Peter, high school was a breeze, filled with activities, advance placement classes and class leadership positions at almost every turn. So acceptance to Stanford came as no real surprise.

But all of that was from a different day.

THREE

MIKE WAS STILL at his house in the early afternoon and knew he needed to phone Nancy, the woman he had been dating lately. He had been putting it off all day. He wasn't sure exactly why he hesitated. He hadn't seen too many women since Sheila's passing. In fact, it had only been in the last six months that he went to a dinner at a friend's house and there just happened to be a single woman there. Until then, the idea of dating anyone was the last thing on his mind.

Nancy had known Sheila. They worked together in the same real estate office. One day he ran into her at the grocery store and she invited him over for dinner. "No big deal," she said. "It's just dinner." They began to see each other a little more. Mike could sense that it might become something more serious. He wasn't sure, it was just a feeling he had.

He called her on his cell and gave her a brief summary of the morning's excitement. She was in the middle of writing an offer on a house in Carmichael. Mike could tell that she was distracted at first but became very sympathetic when she understood what he was saying.

"I can't believe any of this. You were knocked over and cut up and then this jerk takes your car and messes up your house? I am so sorry. What can I do?"

"Not much, really, but thanks for asking. I just have some work to do to tidy up things and get my car back and just sort it all out. It is going to take some time. How about if we have dinner at your place, tonight," he said. "You call me when you know when you are done for the day, okay?"

"That works for me. I've got a lot going on today. In fact, get a load of this. I had a flat tire. I'm waiting for the AAA to come out and fix it. They should be here in about half an hour. Probably picked something up when I was touring this morning. We went to one of those newer subdivisions in Elk Grove and there are always nails on the streets. I had to cancel an appointment," she said.

"Sorry to hear that. That's never fun. How long before they will get there?"

"They said they would be here in forty minutes and it has been at least an hour, so they should be here pretty soon. But enough of that. You had better see a doctor or someone. That knee doesn't sound too good. You have been through a lot. Will you do that?"

"Yeah, okay. I don't know. I don't think I'm actually hurt all that much. More stunned than anything, I guess. There was a lot of blood. The whole thing just pisses me off, to be frank. I can't believe anyone would have the gall. It takes all kinds."

Mike changed into a long sleeved shirt and pants and headed over to his office in his other car, an older Acura that once belonged to Sheila. He never could bring himself to sell it and occasionally it came in handy, like today. It was Friday and he should spend a little time cleaning up his desk, answering mail and getting ready for the next week. But mainly he wanted to see what Robert Cannes was up to, with his motion and urgent hearing. When Mike arrived at his office, he greeted Alice and gave her more details after assuring her that he was all right.

"Well, you sure have looked better," she said with a twinkle in her eye.

"Yeah, I know. I don't feel that bad, all things considered. Miracle drugs, I guess."

Alice was a paragon of order and efficiency. She kept the office humming, always anticipating the next looming deadline with a discreet reminder.

"I'm happy that you were not hurt worse. You look like you'll survive. You just read about so much in the paper these days, people being shot and killed or run over or something," she said.

"I'm just ticked off about the whole thing. Actually, I would like it all to go away somehow. But that's not happening."

"I put that motion for sanctions from Robert Cannes on the Darnoff case on your desk."

"Thanks, Alice. I had better take a look at it today."

"Hey, Ace." Denny emerged from his office at the sound of voices. His wore his ever-present smile.

"Hi, Denny."

"So, did they get anything?"

"Not much. Just the silverware and a few trinkets. Maybe more, I don't know yet."

"The silverware can be easily swapped out at any pawn shop downtown."

"The deputy sheriff told me that he would put out an alert at all local pawn shops."

"That might work. Happy that you are not banged up too much. I changed out the locks and put your key on your desk. If you want another key, let me know. I've got a bunch of extras. Figured I should do it right away."

"Thanks, Denny."

"Didn't cost all that much, really. Maybe we should consider having an alarm installed. What do you think?"

Mike and Denny had resisted having an alarm installed which so many offices in their business park had done. They were not paranoid and could not imagine anyone wanting to break into their office. But this changed everything.

"It's probably a good idea. Hey, Alice, could you make a call or two and check it out? Maybe get us some bids or something."

"Will do."

"So, when did you two get here this morning?"

"Around eight," Alice quickly answered. This was her normal starting time. "I was the first here." She need not have added the last comment. She was always the first to arrive at the office.

Mike studied her for a minute. Denny said he arrived around eight-thirty.

"Well, I was out running on the bike trail at six or so. We had better check to be sure nobody got in here. When you both get a chance, take a good look at the files, drawers, boxes and see if anything has been changed or moved or is missing, okay?"

"Sure," she said.

"I doubt that he came here, but you never know."

Alice returned to her computer as Denny retreated to his office. Denny was about five foot nine inches, a bit pudgy in the jowls and a full head of scraggly blond hair cut like one of the Beach Boys in the 60's. His sideburns were somewhat longer than one would expect for a man of his age. His pants came up just short of his ample waist, the belt holding it all together. He wore a pressed white shirt with a red and white striped tie. He distributed his two hundred fifteen pounds evenly on his oversized leather chair.

The rich aroma of coffee from the lunch room made its way to the outer office. Mike walked down the short hall by Denny's office en route to his own. But first he stopped for a cup of coffee. Mike leaned on the door frame to Denny's office, sipping his coffee.

"It's a wonder that you can get anything done with a desk like that. It's a pig sty."

The state of Denny's desk was a constant source of ribbing for Mike and he could not resist the chance for yet another shot at his partner.

"Nice to know that you haven't lost your sense of humor, such as it is."

Denny looked up at Mike with a big grin on his face.

"Look, I know where everything is. I can find any file you want in two seconds. Go ahead and try me," Denny said. He was half-serious and half-laughing.

"Thank God for small favors, I guess."

"I knew it, afraid to try me. Tell me the truth. You name it and I can put my hands on it in a couple of seconds. You know it."

They chatted and after a while Mike continued on to his office. Mike had long since concluded that all lawyers, male or female, young or old, litigation or business, could be divided into two groups, those with neat desks and those with messy desks. It was either one or the other. Funny thing though is that there seemed to be no correlation with how good a lawyer was with his or her desk. Denny was a good lawyer and he had a messy desk. Mike kept his desk neat and ordered and thought that he was a good lawyer. So there you are, go figure.

He picked up the Request for Production of Documents from Robert Cannes, his opposing counsel in the Darnoff partnership case, which Mike received a few weeks ago. A RFP, as it is often called, is kind of like a subpoena. But it wasn't a request at all. It was a demand. Leave it to the law to disguise something so mundane. Either produce the documents or go to court and explain why you didn't. Cannes wanted him to deliver all financial records of his client, Jason Darnoff, in the statutory time period, which was thirty days. Mike knew right away that he could not do that because Judge Kathleen Newman had issued a Temporary Restraining Order, specifically prohibiting him or any of the other lawyers from transferring or copying any documents belonging to his client.

Judge Newman was the family law judge in the Darnoff vs. Darnoff divorce case, between the parents of the Darnoff boys and their younger sister, Linda. But Mike was not directly involved in that case. It was best to leave the divorce cases to the divorce lawyers. He was only involved because Judge Newman had brought all of the lawyers of all cases under the umbrella of her sweeping Temporary Restraining Order, afraid that actions in the partnership dissolution case might affect the divorce case. Judge Newman had commanded his attendance and had issued her orders. She was trying to bring some order to very involved divorce case and she knew that she could do that only by stopping endless discovery about financial matters. She would exercise all control over the transfer of any information that even remotely touched on the divorce between the husband and wife.

This motion from Cannes should be easy. No judge is going to give Cannes the time of day on it. Cannes knew about the TRO, as temporary restraining orders were always called, because he was one of the very lawyers named in the Order himself. What was Cannes up to? He was trying to cause trouble, no doubt. Mike would write an opposition explaining the obvious, go to court and all would be well.

Some lawyers were just jerks. Cannes was all of that. In fact a better description would be a weird duck, Mike thought to himself. He was not the kind of guy that Mike would accompany on vacation. He was a fixture in the nearby hamlet of Woodland, county seat of the adjoining Yolo County. He was not as well known in Sacramento. He was stern, not given to telling jokes. In fact, he was not given to laughing at all. It was all business with Robert Cannes even when it came to his name. He detested being called Bob and let you know it, if you made that mistake. Even worse, he disliked anyone who did not pronounce his last name correctly. He would always say, "It's like 'can,' as in the city on the French Riviera where they hold the film festival each year." Mike's dealings with Cannes were very abrupt.

Mike quickly prepared his opposition to the motion and accompanying declaration and gave it all to Alice to clean up and put into proper legal format.

"I'll sign it and then please send it off in this afternoon's mail, Alice, so the court will get it in plenty of time," he said.

"Will do. I will ask for the usual return receipt."

"Thanks," he said as he walked back to his office.

He knew that he wouldn't get much else done today. He looked out the window for a long time and then the photos on his credenza caught his eye. There was a big one of Sheila and Peter. A couple more head shots of Sheila and Peter. There was Denny and his wife and Sheila and himself, when the four of them were rafting one summer.

He had met Denny Grantham in law school when they both attended U.C. Hastings College of the Law in San Francisco thirty plus years ago. They met each other in the first year and hit it off right away after they discovered that they were both from the Sacramento area and were planning on returning. They sat near each other whenever they took the same class. And they were roommates for the last two years. Both had good study habits. Law school consisted of studying a lot. As one of his professors told them all at orientation in the first year, "It doesn't take a genius to become a lawyer, just someone who is willing to sit on his fanny and study at his desk for extraordinarily long periods of time each day. This is hard work, ladies and gentlemen, make no mistake about it. But if you are willing to put in the effort, you will all become lawyers."

Those days in San Francisco were not all study. They had their share of good times and their apartment on Gough Street became a popular hangout, as much for Denny and Mike's hospitality as for its proximity to a number of good watering holes for late night adventures. Perry's was their usual gathering spot, when friends came over, but Gabe's Bus Stop was their primary late-night spot for pool and a couple of beers. Denny had a contagious laugh and he could make any place come alive. He would tell a joke and laugh at it and pretty soon everyone else was laughing along with him or at him. It didn't make much difference.

After law school, they came back to Sacramento but went separate ways. Denny had started out right away in civil law, working for a well-known Sacramento law firm located downtown. He focused on contracts and real estate transactions which make up a large part of the business side of civil law. He did not get into personal injury or divorces which make up a whole other part of civil law. Denny learned the intricacies of discovery and depositions and complex business cases that took on lives of their own, sometimes lasting years before final resolution.

Denny came from a large family and grew up in the south area. His father worked for the Department of Education at the State of California and his mother was a teacher in a local elementary school. His brothers and sisters had spread throughout the Sacramento area and the San Francisco Bay Area, each with their own family. He was a likeable guy and made friends easily, always quick with an endearing comment to anyone and everyone.

Within his law firm, he learned how to master the world of office politics. He had been placed in charge of the recruitment committee for most of his time and he liked reviewing resumes and deciding whom to interview or not. Then his committee would make recommendations on hiring which were almost always followed. There was a certain power that went with the job, like giving the thumbs up or down at a Roman Coliseum after the gladiator had fought. His decision could mean so much to an aspiring associate. After paying his dues, he became a partner and soon developed into one of the star business litigators in town.

Mike had taken a different tack. He had grown up in a middle-class Croatian family in East Sacramento. He was the second of two boys and went to Catholic elementary and high schools and then to Sac State for college. His father was a land appraiser who worked for various banks for most of his adult life but he died in his early fifties from a heart attack. His mother lived awhile longer but then she died of diabetes which had plagued her for almost all of her life.

After law school, Mike was hired by Sacramento's Public Defender's office where he was soon mired in a heavy caseload. Criminal law was the mainstay of the courthouse, easily comprising more than three fourths of the trial work load. Those were the good years. The camaraderie among his fellow attorneys was sheer joy. They say that "misery loves company," and that could not have been more true than in the public defender's office. Some of his best friends were former public defenders.

There were a handful of deputy district attorneys who were his friends as well. They were the deputies who understood that he had a job to do and didn't take it personally, when he would cross-examine their witnesses or police officers. It seemed that these old guys were a dying breed. A lot of the new deputy district attorneys were all 'spit and vinegar,' who only saw life through a very tainted law and order prism. They would often earn the nickname of "mad dog" from the defense bar. They were less likely to consider extenuating circumstances. The only saving grace these days was money.

The County of Sacramento, like all other California counties, didn't have any money. The Sheriff, the Probation Department, the District Attorney's office and the Public Defender's office all had suffered cutbacks. The State had cut the number of courts as well. There simply were not enough available courtrooms to handle the number of criminal cases that required trials. With limited resources, deputy district attorneys were forced to make more deals.

Mike still loved to get together with his old friends and relive the "good old days," when life was simpler and more fun. Over a period of twelve years, he tried every kind of criminal case, including two death penalty jury trials. There was the occasional thrill of victory, but mostly the criminal cases ended in conviction, either through a plea bargain or the verdict from a jury trial. If there was one word that Mike lived by, it was fairness. His driving force was the pursuit of justice much like the DNA of every American was to seek life, liberty and the pursuit of happiness. The drive was borne from his earliest days fighting his older brother every day. He hardly ever won because of his smaller size. His mother would always try to separate her boys but it usually didn't work. She would berate Mike's older brother telling him that it wasn't fair to pick on his little brother. She would tell Mike to stop pestering his brother. The tables finally turned when he was about fifteen and Mike passed his brother in height and weight. One day, he popped his older brother in the face and the fighting came to a sudden end. But the many years of losing fights with his brother never left him. He kept searching for fairness.

Then there was Mike's father. He always wanted things to be fair and he passed that lesson on to Mike. Every Friday night Mike and his father shared a special tradition. They watched the Friday Night Fights sponsored by Gillette Blue Blades on television. Mike would dutifully retrieve a legal-size piece of cardboard that came with each of his father's dry-cleaned shirts. He would mark a line down the middle and more lines horizontally to correspond with the ten rounds. Then he would put the names of the two boxers on the top of the cardboard and they would keep score. His father would always say, "Who is the underdog? That's who we're for."

Mike liked that. There was something very noble about rooting for the underdog, giving the little guy a chance. It never occurred to him back then how this tradition with his father would translate into his life's work or how it probably touched his soul. But it did.

The one thing he remembered from his mother was her constant refrain, "If you want something done right, do it yourself." In the end, Mike always knew that there was really only one person in the world that he could count on, that he knew would never fail him. He couldn't count on anyone else but himself. It wasn't a lonely feeling. Instead, Mike found it reassuring in that he didn't have to waste time trying to get people to do his business. He just had to put his head down and do it himself.

After twelve years in the public defender's office, he knew that he wanted something else besides the daily grind of defending the criminal element. It wasn't that he looked down on anyone or that he did not like defending the guilty. It was quite the contrary. He felt a genuine mission helping those who were less fortunate, those who had been dealt different cards in life than he had received. He was proud of his job as a public defender and proud of the friends that he had made. It was just very demanding. It took a lot out of him. And the fact was that he rarely won. The cards were stacked against him. In most cases when the cops arrested someone, they got their guy.

He knew that it was time to do something else, but he did not know what he wanted. By coincidence, Denny was ready to move out of his law firm and start his own practice. The timing was perfect and the two could not have been happier. Seventeen years of partnership had been good to both of them.

At first when he joined Denny, Mike had taken criminal cases because that was what he knew how to do. Over time, he gravitated to the civil cases that made up Denny's workload. He found out that his vast experience in the courtroom was a tremendous asset. Only a few of the civil lawyers had much trial experience. This was partly because of the priority demand on the courtrooms for criminal cases and partly because there were just not as many civil cases as criminal cases. But mainly, the civil cases all seemed to settle before trial. Mike would find that when he suggested that a settlement offer was not acceptable and that they should just go to trial, he was almost always met with surprise. Nobody wanted to go to trial, mainly because nobody had all that much trial experience. Usually his cases would settle on better terms. Mike liked that.

Learning the art of marketing oneself had come naturally to him after Denny gave him some pointers. He focused on real estate law because it had always been interesting to him in law school. In a short while, he took on intellectual property law, mainly because it became so important in California's high-tech market. He still kept his old friendships in the public defender's office and with some of the judges and deputy district attorneys, but time did have a way of mellowing even those relationships. And he still handled a healthy number of criminal cases, especially when there was a paying client. Mike soon became one of those rare birds in the legal litigation world who felt equally at home in the criminal or civil courtroom.

Mike spent that Friday afternoon pushing a few papers around his desk and getting very little accomplished. He returned a few phone calls. He called Nancy to see what he could bring for dinner that night, but she already had that covered. Nancy was his friend. He hesitated to think of her as his girlfriend and did not know what exact title he would use to describe her. Usually, he would just say, "I'm with Nancy Richards" or something else, equally vague.

Mike knew that Nancy had her own challenges and that she did not always empathize with the perils of his job. Nancy and Mike had a good relationship basically. Not perfect, but good. For some reason he just could not get over the hump and think about marriage. Maybe in time, that would happen. Sheila was always on his mind. He really did not want to think about another marriage. At least that was what he told himself whenever the thought entered his mind. She was content to let things be for the time being, especially since her first marriage had been troubled. But he figured that in the back of her mind, marriage was probably lurking.

Nancy was certainly attractive. She was about 5' 5" with a pretty face and big blue eyes and longish brown hair. She caught the attention of almost everyone. She had a good figure and always dressed in a coordinated way. Mike enjoyed her company. Actually, he enjoyed everything about her. Nancy was a hard worker. She really had no choice. Divorced after just eight years of marriage to a good-for-nothing, she raised her son, Brent, by herself. Their older daughter went to live with her father. That was a story by itself, one that Nancy never discussed. Mother and son did not always have much, but they managed. At the beginning, she needed food stamps, as Nancy worked at various office jobs for meager returns. Then she embarked on a real estate sale career and caught the boom of the early 2000's at the right time.

Mike knew not to ask about Nancy's daughter. He knew that they would occasionally talk on the phone or visit at an infrequent holiday. It seemed as if her ex-husband had garnered the majority of their daughter's affection. Maybe someday things would be different.

Her son was a different matter. Nancy loved to talk about him. Brent was off at Chico State University, about ninety miles north of Sacramento, off of Interstate 5. The two were very close and often spoke on the phone. Mike was the second-hand recipient of the latest gossip in college life and could only compare it with his college years and those of his own son just a few years ago. Essentially, all of their college experiences were the same or, at least, it seemed that way to Mike. There were the social issues, the classes, the tests, the professors, the boyfriends and the girlfriends. He loved hearing about it all, mostly because it reminded him of some of the happiest times of his own life.

After Mike arrived, he took off his jacket, fixed himself a scotch and water, his favorite drink, and made a vodka martini for Nancy.

"Here's to the end of a rough week and to being together," he said as he smiled at her warmly.

She reciprocated and sipped her drink once and then slipped on an oversized apron. Opening the refrigerator in search of the halibut and vegetables she bought the day before, she looked back at him.

"It has to be someone you know, right? There have to be a few unhappy campers among all of your old clients. That's the first thing that I thought of. It could have been someone who was not too happy that he got sent off to prison and now he blames you. You have told me a million times that a lot of your clients are just like that."

"Could be, I just don't know," Mike said. "The Sheriff said that they had a few other incidents like this on the bike trail. They don't want to publicize them, for fear of alarming the public. They sounded pretty anonymous, just someone out to make a score. So my deal is different. First the guy called me a lawyer. How did he know that? Then he went to my house and ransacked the place. Wait until you see it. The deputy sheriff thinks that there was someone else involved and they followed me to the park in the morning. I went a lot earlier today than I usually do. I couldn't sleep. So I got up before six and went over there for my run. There was nobody on the trail. But if they followed me, they had to be waiting at my house. Kind of spooky, don't you think?"

"You are lucky that you were not hurt more. He could have done a job on you. I knew a friend of a friend, a woman who was attacked by a mountain lion a few years back on a running trail in Auburn, just off of Interstate 80. She was by herself out running on a Saturday afternoon. That's not the same, but you just never know. You have to keep looking around when you are out there. I know that I wouldn't be out on that bike trail without someone else with me."

"Listen, I am happy to be alive. Changing a few locks and filing a report on my car are not the biggest things in the world. I have my old Acura to use for now. If they don't find my car, I will get something new. That is what insurance is for, after all."

"Well, you sure are pretty chipper for someone who was beaten up in broad daylight. I don't think I would be quite so composed. Maybe you are in denial or in shock. You really need to take your time and let this whole thing come in on you. Better yet, maybe we could get away to Carmel or Napa. Maybe San Francisco. There's always something going on there. A little rest would do you good. You know I'm right."

Nancy had hit on some of the great get-a-way spots in Northern California that they both loved. She just had a way with him and it was very comforting. He knew she was right, but he wanted so much to make light of the events of the day, to brush them off. It was easier to cope that way.

"Those are great places to go. And you're right. I will take it easy, I promise. It is not that big of a deal, really. The guy is gone. I got some cuts and bruises. My car is gone. I can always replace it. I lost some silverware but insurance should cover that. But I like your idea of getting out of town for a weekend. Let's talk after dinner. Now, let's eat, I'm starving."

Mike fixed himself another scotch and water, not being skimpy on the good stuff. Nancy eyed him as she worked over the stove. She knew better than to carry on anymore. There was a kind of finality to his last words. He had given a clear signal to end this part of the conversation. She would return to it later when he was more receptive. She knew that this was not a small deal. Nancy had been stirring some vegetables in the wok while they were talking and while she was waiting for the halibut in the broiler. They sat down for dinner and Mike found a half-filled bottle of Chardonnay in the refrigerator.

"Don't you think you have had enough tonight? You've been through a lot."

"Doctor's orders. This is strictly for medicinal purposes. It helps with the pain."

"What doctor? You haven't seen any doctor today. What are you talking about?"

"It's a known fact. Hard liquor soothes the nervous system, helps ease the pain. How do you think all of those miners in 1850 made it, when they got hurt? Everyone knows that they took to the bottle. In fact, without the soothing anesthetic of the sweet nectar, Sacramento might never have become the gold capitol of the world. Think about it."

Mike was smiling as he looked at Nancy. He poured a glass of Chardonnay for Nancy although he knew that she was unlikely to drink her whole glass. He would likely become the beneficiary of the remainder.

"You've been drinking quite a bit lately, don't you think? Mike, you have to take it easy, regardless of what your mythical doctor is telling you."

Mike was quick to change the topic as he ate dinner.

"Hey, I almost forgot, what happened with your flat tire? All got worked out okay, I hope."

"Yeah, it did. The guy from AAA was really nice. He took the tire off and replaced it with my spare. You know, the funny thing was that he could not find a nail or anything. He gave the tire the water test but there was no leak. So he pumped it back up and put it in my trunk. I checked when I got home and it looks pretty good. Weird."

"No nail? That doesn't happen too often," he said. "How did it get flat?"

"That's just it. He had no clue."

FOUR

It was Monday of the next week and the Honorable Karen Thoreson sat at her desk, working through some files over the lunch hour. She had spent the morning handling a long schedule of preliminary hearings in the old courthouse in Woodland, which is about fifteen miles from Sacramento. As was the custom in courts throughout the state, she was finding probable cause to hold virtually every single defendant to answer for various felonies. This particular assignment was pretty routine and did not require much brain power. Everyone in the courtroom, including the defendant and his counsel, knew exactly what she was going to do. The prosecutor would put on a witness or two, submit a police report into evidence and then announce that he or she had produced sufficient evidence for the purposes of a preliminary hearing.

The defense counsel would engage in some spirited cross-examination but wouldn't put on any evidence at this early stage of the proceedings. It was common defense practice to never tip your hand until the actual trial of the case, something that may happen, if at all, months down the road. Instead, defense counsel would make an intelligent and logical argument that his client should be freed on the basis of insufficient evidence. But in the end, that was not to be.

Judge Thoreson opened her well-worn black binder and began to read from the ritualistic scripts set out for the conclusion of a preliminary hearing. She knew the words by rote but she read out of an abundance of caution, careful not to give the enlightened ones on the Court of Appeal any opportunity to overturn a righteous conviction. It seemed to most trial court judges that the Court of Appeal judges spent their entire waking hours just trying to find something wrong so that they could point it out, in writing, for all of the legal profession to behold. It was a pet peeve of the trial judges but there was a lot more truth in their paranoia than anyone would admit.

"Mr. Jones, would you please stand?" The defendant and his counsel would push back on their chairs to stand and look at the judge, bowing to the inevitable.

"Based on the evidence before me, I find probable cause that Mr. Jones has committed such and such crimes and therefore hold him to answer in Superior Court. Arraignment will be in two weeks. The defendant is remanded."

Her intonation was always the same. Boredom could not begin to describe this work. This type of hearing used to be handled by Municipal Court Judges or "Judges of the Inferior Court," as they were once called. But then the Legislature saw fit to merge Municipal and Superior Courts into one court, and the entire "Municipal Court" nomenclature disappeared over night. It fell to her, a Superior Court Judge, to hear these cases, bind the defendants over for trial and to set the date for arraignment in another courtroom of the Superior Court. It was one of the lowest assignments one could have but Judge Thoreson knew she had to pay her dues before being rewarded with a regular trial court assignment. There was time.

Karen Thoreson was striking in appearance, medium-length, straight blond hair and high cheek bones, she stood about 5'6" and weighed 120 pounds. She had a killer figure and she was well aware of her female charms. Yet she always felt a need to prove herself, partly because she was a woman and partly because she knew that some didn't think she deserved to be a judge. She struggled with the perception that she got where she was by virtue of her looks. Deep down, she herself knew that she was not worthy. She was not worthy to be a lawyer, let alone a judge. But her feelings of inadequacy did not stem from her looks or her charms. At some level, Karen Thoreson knew that she was not as smart as most of the other lawyers with whom she came into contact. She feared being shown that she was wrong or had missed some important legal precedent. She feared being told that she just didn't get it.

Her manner might remind someone of a department store mannequin, although nobody would describe her as plain. Her voice was a tad lower than most other women which gave it a sensual aspect.

After reviewing some files, she retrieved a container of yogurt from her small refrigerator and a power bar from her drawer. This was lunch today. She looked at her computer and saw that she had an appointment with a reporter from The Recorder, a legal newspaper published in San Francisco. The reporter wanted to do an interview for a series of articles that the paper did on various judges in Northern California. To this point, most of the articles east of the Bay Area had focused on Sacramento judges. She would be the first to be featured from the neighboring Yolo County. She was looking forward to the interview and to the publicity.

An earnest young woman was there, right on time. She had brown hair to her shoulders and was dressed in jeans and a long-sleeve shirt and sweater. After Karen asked her to come back to her chambers, she smiled and pulled out a notebook.

"So, could we start with how you got here? How did you become a judge? What was your life like growing up? You can start anywhere. I have done a little research but really want to hear it all from you. I will take notes and put the story together later."

"Oh, one other thing, I really would like to know how you have made it in the legal profession as a woman. What obstacles did you have to overcome? Was it harder than it would have been for a man?"

Judge Thoreson just looked at the reporter, as if she had seen her somewhere before.

"Okay. That works for me. Where did you want to start?"

The reporter looked up puzzled. Hadn't she heard her?

"I was thinking of you telling me about your career and how you got to be a judge. What was it like growing up?"

"Well, I was appointed to the bench two years ago. I used to be a deputy district attorney, but you probably know that. Let's see, starting from the beginning, my father died when I was about four. I have only faint memories of him. My mother was a rock. We didn't have much. I grew up in Rio Linda which, at the time, was a pretty poor area of Sacramento. Still is, I guess. We lived in a trailer park. She remarried a few years later and I was raised by my mother and stepfather. Things got a bit better after that. My mother then had two boys. I guess they looked up to me. I really did not have much to do with them, growing up. I was so much older. My family couldn't afford college or anything like that. We were pretty poor.

"I went to Sac State. Did all right, I guess. I worked at all kinds of jobs going to college. It was the only way. Then I went to Washington Law School at nights, over on J Street in Sacramento. Worked during the day. After that it was the bar examination. Getting a job was another thing. It was very hard to find anything. Finally, I got on with the Yolo County District Attorney. I was there for 15 years. I tried a lot of cases there and put away a lot of bad guys."

The young lady moved in her seat as Karen paused to take a breath. She reached for her glass of water. The reporter looked at her notes. Karen took the opportunity to study her again. She admired the sweater she was wearing.

"Anything stand out that would be interesting to our readers?"

Karen drank a sip of water and looked at the ceiling for a moment before turning her head to look out the one window in the room. Then she remembered where she had seen her before. Not actually her, but the person she looked like. There was that incredible girl in her high school class, who was a cheerleader, class president and got straight "A's" in addition to being "Miss Everything." Karen never spent much time with her. She felt downright intimidated. And now here she was, or at least someone who looked like her. And she was interviewing her.

"Well, as you can gather, I am very proud of my roots. I didn't have much as a kid and I made something out of myself. It's been a tough go, but it has been worth it. I don't think I would trade my life for anything."

"How about your cases?" Our readers would love to know about some of your more important cases.

"Oh, lots of cases, actually. One big one was called the "College Coed Rapist" case. I think your readers will remember that one. It was a serial rape case involving a defendant who had scared the living daylights out of the entire Davis community."

"I think I remember hearing something like that, although it is a bit hazy. Before my time, I think," the young reporter said. "But they are always warning the college women to be careful. So, maybe it came up in that context."

"You're probably right. It was a good fifteen years ago now. But it should stand as a warning for all women," she said.

Davis was a classic college town and home to a branch of the University of California. About 30,000 students populated the school. Bicycles abounded the streets, along with apartment houses and coffee shops. The town possessed a decidedly liberal bent and it was often said that if you did not belong to at least five organizations, all designed to save the world, there was something wrong with you. It had rightfully earned the nickname of the "People's Republic of Davis," for its individualistic approach to the numerous ordinances that the City Council passed each year. The subject matter of the ordinances was usually a protest about the latest incursion by the military into some far-off land or about the protection of some rare species of animals. Left to the citizens of Davis, the world would be a different place, maybe for the better. It all depended on your point of view.

But when someone went on a rampage, selectively raping beautiful young co-eds, the town suddenly found its long-lost interest in law and order. It turned out that this particular evil doer would break into apartments in the wee hours and force himself on his victims while keeping the other member of the apartment at bay. He only struck where there were two people in the apartment and he always wore a ski mask, making identification very difficult.

"So, this guy was devious. Once he got into the apartment, usually through a window, he would first knock the girl to the ground and then overpower any other person there, usually a boyfriend, flashing his ever-present six-inch switch blade. He would tie the guy on a table and carefully place glasses and cups on top of him, whatever he could find, so that if he struggled the glassware would fall off and warn him. He told the tied-up roommate that if he heard one noise, he would cut off the fingers of his girlfriend. That usually did the trick. The tied up roommate would be too petrified to do anything. Then he would drag the woman to the other room and have his will. He would also tell her that if she did not cooperate with him, he would cut off the fingers of her boyfriend. Abject fear overtook any thought of fighting back. His scheme worked well, all too well. Boyfriends and fathers gathered and formed a vigilante force, prowling the neighborhoods at all hours, looking for the "College Coed Rapist," as he was now called by the newspapers."

"I will be sure to check it all out. Shouldn't be that hard to do a search. How did he end up getting caught?"

It was clear that the events that Karen described were creating some excitement with the young reporter. Or was it discomfort? Karen couldn't tell.

"After two years of this kind of torture and at least eight victims later, he screwed up."

A slight smile emerged on Karen Thoreson's face. She glanced at the young lady but her head was buried in her notes as she wrote down as much as she could.

"He was spotted leaving a supermarket parking lot one afternoon in his car, after some curious person wondered why he did not buy any groceries. Instead, he went to his car and sat there for a while. The witness was suspicious. So he sat in his car, just watching. After about ten minutes, the witness saw him drive away and the witness followed behind at a distance. When the suspect pulled into an apartment house, the witness could see that another car has just arrived and a young woman was taking groceries from her trunk up the stairs to her apartment. Putting it all together, the witness figured that this guy was tailing women from the grocery store to find out where they lived, knowing that they were sure to drive directly home after buying perishables at the grocery store.

"So the witness writes down the license plate number and phones the Davis police. They were there in a flash. The guy was gone but the police ran his license plate and learned that he did not live there. Now the cops had a possible suspect.

"They set up a stakeout, both at his house and the apartment house. They had to wait several days, but finally he left his apartment at night and they followed him back to the same apartment house and waited until he was in the process of breaking into an apartment before they made their entry. They arrested him before he could do anything. But he was dressed for the part. He wore black pants and a dark jacket and a ski mask. He carried plenty of rope and a menacing switch blade."

"It all made sense. The cops later figured out that he was scoping out supermarket parking lots and had carefully selected his victims. He found the pretty ones, as they lugged their groceries out of the market and watched as they got into their cars. He would follow the young woman home and would then return some nights later. It worked like a charm."

Karen told the young reporter all of the details. When the case came up for trial, she explained how she was armed to the teeth. She had obtained permission to hire a forensic pathologist for special DNA testing of blood samples from all of the previous rapes and, much to her surprise he had found matches on all of them. A couple of stray fingerprints added to the strength of the case. The defendant had no previous record so none of his DNA or prints was previously available for police comparison. But all of that information was there now. The description of the defendant matched most of the descriptions given by the victims, although his penchant for wearing a ski mask deprived them of a positive identification. Karen did not need it. Virtually all of the victims identified the switch blade knife.

The defendant had offered to plead guilty to some, but not all, of the rape charges, in order to get a better sentence, but Karen refused. It was all or nothing. So, the defendant decided to take his chances, figuring that it couldn't get any worse.

Karen explained how she had slowly and carefully presented her case. She called every witness who had anything to do with the case, often puzzling the judge and the jury as to why it was necessary. The parade of blue uniforms from every case went on for days. Every police officer who had ever visited any scene of any rape was called and asked for his or her two cents. The expert testimony dragged on for days. The sheer enormity of the evidence began to weigh on the jury.

The reporter took everything down in her notes, scribbling quickly and wildly, as Karen recited the facts of her biggest case. She would steal the occasional glimpse of the reporter, relishing the mere fact that she was there taking notes of whatever she said.

She told her how the defendant had mounted a spirited defense that was a direct attack on the reliability of DNA evidence. The guy's public defender found another lawyer in Oakland who had assisted O.J. Simpson's trial team on his case many years ago and had learned all about DNA evidence. He took over this part of the case. He called a couple of experts from Los Angeles who raised questions and attempted to cast doubt on the inevitability of DNA evidence. The presentation was impressive but could not rebut the mountain of evidence and the D.A.'s expert who put the odds of error at something like one in seven million, based on probability studies from research studies. In the end, it was not even close.

"The jury convicted him on all counts," Karen said as she sat back in her chair, a look of smugness on her face. "I got a lot of attention out of all of that. There were articles in several newspapers. I am sure you can check them out. I got a promotion to homicides where I tried a bunch of cases. But that is a story for another day."

The young reporter was writing all of this down, obviously finding this part of the case much more to her liking than the gruesome details of the rapes that were sure to scare any woman. She knew that she could fill in any holes later once she did more research. She had already learned that Judge Thoreson had established quite a reputation as a prosecutor in Yolo County.

Karen asked if she wanted anything to drink but she declined and said she needed to use the restroom and would be right back, if that was okay with the judge.

"Of course, take your time. Today is a good day, not too many preliminary hearings. So we have the rest of the afternoon, if you need it."

Karen Thoreson made herself a cup of tea and sat back in her chair. She thought of what she had told the reporter. She enjoyed the thought of telling her story and was sure that a lot of the attorneys in town would be surprised to learn more about her.

She looked at her credenza where she saw the rapidly-growing files comprising the Darnoff case which had recently been reassigned to her from another judge after two years of attempts at settlement. There were six hardback yellow folders, each about four inches in depth, lurking ominously. They contained pleadings and motions and various court orders, all attesting to the sheer number of parties and attorneys in this case. It was a big civil case, an area of law that she never practiced as a lawyer and which would require a lot of work on her part, to get up to speed. Civil law and criminal law were two different breeds of cat and all of her experience as a deputy district attorney would not be of much help in the civil law arena.

In a few minutes, the reporter was back. She looked over her notes and asked how Karen became a lawyer in the first place. Karen told her how hard it was to get a job.

"I went to Washington Law School in Sacramento, as I said. It is a night school and was established a few years ago for people who were working during the day. I wouldn't exactly call it anything like Harvard or Stanford, but I got a good education. The professors were working lawyers in town who knew their stuff," she said.

In fact, the attorneys who worked in the better-known firms mostly thought of Washington as a factory for the local hacks who made their money by chasing ambulances or evicting tenants. Their answer to any job inquiry from a Washington Law School graduate was always "Thanks, we'll be in touch," which were code words for "Don't hold your breath thinking that we will ever offer you a job." There was a sense of smugness, a sense that she just did not belong. And she knew that she never would belong. But Judge Thoreson did not tell the young reporter any of this. She just thought it as she stared out his window. Then she looked back at the reporter.

"Most of the law firms wouldn't hire me. I don't know if it was because I was a woman or because I did not go to the best law school in the state. I've seen it all. I tried to get on with the District Attorney's office in Sacramento and was told that they had no positions. The only thing I could find was voluntary work at the Yolo County District Attorney's office here in Woodland. I worked for free as an intern. And there was no guarantee of a paying job. Frankly, I took the job because that was all there was. I always did the best I could do at the intern job, even making coffee for a couple of the regular deputies. I learned the lingo and studied the Penal Code as if it were the Bible. It is the Bible for this line of work."

The reporter knew enough not to interrupt her, as the judge was on a roll and she was getting some good stuff.

"Then my luck changed at the D.A.'s office. It turned out that an older deputy was granted a disability retirement on the basis of a bad back and undue stress, so the chief assistant offered me a position as a temporary deputy district attorney. They were not certain if they could obtain permanent funding, but at least I would get paid for a while. I guess I had done all of the grunt work and had impressed someone, so the offer of a job was not a complete surprise. I have never forgotten the good folks at the Yolo County's D.A.'s office and how they gave me my start. About eighteen months later, the temporary position became permanent. I celebrated by taking a couple of deputies out for dinner and drinking some bubbly."

Gazing out the window again, her thoughts turned to something she would never tell the reporter. She wouldn't tell her about the snubs in the Sacramento's law firms, especially the uppity ones who would interview her and brush her off. It stuck in her craw, all right. It was always there. Deep inside she knew she would never measure up. She was not good enough.

"I threw myself into my work, always asking for new assignments. I think I did well. First, I started in misdemeanor trials, then felony preliminary hearings and finally felony trials. At each step, I would seek the advice of those who were older and more experienced. I would ask them how to introduce business records and what to do with the victim who refuses to come to court and how to develop the case with additional investigation. Things like that. I learned how to prepare for the obvious areas where the defense will try to poke holes and how to approach the judges who were more likely to grant defense motions."

Karen swung around in her chair and looked at the reporter.

"I even kept a binder of the lessons I was learning along with a complete summary of each case I tried to a jury. I hoped that over time I would learn to become a good trial attorney. I think I did pretty well."

"I'm sorry but I have to leave pretty soon," the reporter said. "Can I schedule a time to come back and ask you more? This is really interesting and I would like to fill in any holes. Or, maybe I would just call you, if you had the time."

"Oh sure, just call my clerk and set up a time when I have a free afternoon like today. Happy to talk to you," she said as the reporter was picking up her things.

As the reporter left his chambers, Karen glowed with the thoughts of being someone important, someone that had been interviewed for the legal newspaper. Karen Thoreson sat back in her chair and closed her eyes. She thought of what she had told the young lady and, more importantly, she thought of what else she had not told her. She didn't talk to her about her marriage or family. After a few years, she married a good looking county employee who worked as a clerk for Yolo County and had dated for a couple of years. They looked the part, Ken and Barbie. But that was about all that they had in common. Her husband was decidedly lacking in ambition and in common sense. Their marriage was more one of convenience for each of them as they had each reached that stage in their lives when it was the logical thing to do. They had two girls and her husband spent a lot of time at home working part-time while Karen pursued her career. After the kids went off to school, her husband went back to work full-time for the county.

During those early years in their marriage, they learned that they just did not have that much in common. There was some talk of divorce but Karen knew that this was the wrong career move. So she just remained married, hopeful that she could keep her husband interested enough to stay as well. He had his dalliances but she did not mind. In fact, she rather welcomed the idea. It kept him off of her. She figured that this was probably the best she would ever manage. His life was the children, his drinking buddies and golf. So they came to an accommodation that was suitable for both. They lived in quiet solitude, much as many married couples do, trapped in lives that prevented either one from escape.

And she certainly didn't explain about her brother, who was the older of two boys born to her mother after she remarried. He was a good kid but he managed to get into a bit of trouble at school and his grades were not all that great. There were a couple of juvenile arrests for vandalism and for starting a fire in the neighbor's back yard that did not amount to much. Still, she had a certain affinity for the kid. He was likeable and just adored his older sister, looking up to her as some sort of hero. They had a real bond. Karen figured that the kid would work it out.

But by the time her brother was twenty, he had fallen in with a bad crowd and was spending most of his time shooting up heroin in a shack just north of downtown Sacramento. He ended up being sent to prison after he got arrested on an armed robbery. That wasn't all. He had been killed in prison. Karen never spoke about her brother. He had a different last name and no one made the connection to her. And, to be honest, she was embarrassed. Actually, ashamed would be the better word. Here she was trying to make something of her life and her brother got sent to the joint.

But the thing was that her brother was not guilty of the robbery. He was innocent. Karen's mother told her that she was positive that her son was home with her on the night of the robbery. Karen Thoreson had wanted to help but she knew that she couldn't do a thing, as it might jeopardize her career. Her career in the D.A.'s office was just starting to gain some steam, after it was so difficult to even land a job. Besides, Karen had big plans. She wanted to be a judge and it would never work for a judge to have a brother in prison. So she took the easy way and did nothing. She let her brother go to trial and get convicted and go to prison. But all of that was far behind her and certainly not fodder for some reporter doing a profile on one of the area's judges.

No, what was important now was to wade through the stack of files on her credenza and to learn more about the Darnoff case. She had better get this right. There would be some of the Sacramento lawyers appearing in this case and one of them was Michael Zorich.

Before she left for the day, Karen Thoreson picked up her phone and made a couple of calls. It was that time of day.

FIVE

THE WEATHER HAD turned a bit in the week and a half since the bike trail mugging. Scattered rain was accompanied by the usual winds and temperatures in the 60's. Mike thought how spoiled he was to live in California and to complain about the weather. Compared to 90% of the United States, it was great weather – no snow, no flurries, no salt on the road, no shoveling, no intensely cold temperature, no parkas. This list went on. He should have it so bad. The knee was feeling much better and the cut on his head had pretty much healed. At least he did not need any bandage. The ribs were another thing. They still hurt, especially if he moved quickly. But he was able to function to the extent that he needed to.

It was Tuesday, September 28 and Mike was going to appear before the Honorable Karen Thoreson, Judge of the Superior Court in and for the County of Yolo, State of California, where he would explain why he could not and would not follow the Request for Production of Documents from counsel to immediately turn over all financial information of his client, Brian Darnoff. It really was quite simple. Just why Cannes would even do such a stupid thing as to demand these financial documents was beyond belief.

Mike met his client in front of the courthouse and the two of them walked to the courtroom together. Brian was a few years younger than Mike. He was dressed in slacks, sports coat and open dress shirt. His clothes and his disheveled hair gave him a "playboy" look.

"This should be pretty cut and dry, as I see it, Brian," Mike said. "This motion should never have been necessary. I really don't understand why Cannes even sent over his Request for Documents."

His client spoke up. "Great. I really need to get out of here. Sometimes these things end up going forever."

It seemed that most clients just wanted to get everything over, as soon as possible. Mike knew that going to court was never fun so he could understand. Brian took his seat in the audience and Mike sat at the counsel table quietly pondering the coming hearing. He would be resolute when the case was called. He would be standing tall and speaking in slow, measured tones, as he would explain to the young judge that she was required to follow another judge's order and therefore could not comply with counsel's request. His voice would resonate with his 30 years of experience in appearing in courts in Northern California. He had appeared many times in the Old Courthouse, one block from Main Street in tree-lined Woodland. It was a familiar scene. He would be most respectful. But mostly he would just love the whole courtroom scene. This was his thing.

But after he took his place at the counsel table and pulled out his file, he looked up at the judge to see a puzzled look on her face.

"Counsel, I want to review the papers that I have received from each of you before we begin today," the judge said. "I have received your points and authorities, Mr. Cannes, in support of your Request for an Order to Compel Production of Documents, but I don't recall receiving anything from you, Mr. Zorich. Is that right?"

"No, your honor, that is not right. I filed my opposition brief. I attached my declaration to it, your honor."

"Counsel, I don't have it. If you filed it, I should have it. Sally, did we receive anything from Mr. Zorich?"

Judge Thoreson was addressing her clerk who was seated at a desk directly in front of the bench.

"No, your honor, I don't see anything in the file."

"Counsel, do you have a file-endorsed copy of your brief? That would show that we received it. Maybe we lost it."

"I don't, your honor. We mailed it and asked for a file-endorsed copy to be mailed back. We never received that but I assumed that there was just not enough time for you to mail it back."

"Frankly, counsel, I am not sure that we ever got anything in the first place. I know my clerk quite well and if she got it, she would have sent the copy back. I doubt that we ever got anything. We will just have to proceed."

"Your honor, could I just give you another copy of my brief?"

"No, it is too late at this point, counsel. You have to file five days before the court hearing, you know that. It wouldn't be fair to opposing counsel, to say nothing of me. I never read it before now. It's too late. Let's proceed."

"Your honor, I object. I did send my brief to you. Please allow me to present a copy."

"Counsel, I told you that you are too late. If you wanted me to have your brief you would have filed it on time. Let's quit all of this back and forth. Just tell me why you didn't produce the documents in response to the demand from your opposing counsel. Keep it simple."

Mike looked up but realized how futile any further arguing would be.

"Your honor, I have no choice. I can't produce documents when I am required to follow the order from Judge Kathleen Newman telling me not to do so. I have no choice. I was personally named in that order, as was Mr. Cannes, for that matter. Most importantly, her order came before this request from counsel. I have no choice in this matter. If I were to follow this request, I would be subject to contempt of court before Judge Newman."

"So this order from Judge Newman just absolves you of any normal discovery request from counsel, is that it?"

"No, your honor. Judge Newman issued a temporary restraining order, specifically naming each and every attorney involved in the divorce and related partnership dissolution proceedings and directing each and every one of them by name. They were to keep and maintain all documents in their possession. Further, under no circumstances whatsoever, were they to turn over the documents or copies of the documents to any other person. The words 'under no circumstances whatsoever' had been bold-faced and underlined. To ensure there was no misunderstanding, Judge Newman told all of the attorneys to their faces that she meant no one. We all understood that, including Mr. Cannes."

Mike was looking at the judge who was decidedly not interested. Mike saw her studying her notes, looking down in that tell-tale way that judges employ to tell attorneys that they are not scoring any points.

"Judge, it is quite simple. I can't respond to this request. That's all there is to it. Judge Newman is trying to maintain order in the divorce case and she saw fit to impose this order on all financial matters that may have a bearing on the divorce case. It is perfectly reasonable for her to do so. The divorce case is the overriding legal dispute within the family, it really controls everything. She has issued an order and it is my duty and the duty of Mr. Cannes to obey her order. If Mr. Cannes doesn't like Judge Newman's order, he should ask her to rescind it. He has not done so. Instead, he simply sent me a Request for Documents and expects me to comply, when he knows that I am prohibited from doing so."

Mike sat down knowing that this little game by Cannes would soon come to a crashing halt, notwithstanding the failure of Judge Thoreson to read his papers and her decided lack of interest. He closed his file and carefully put his pen into the inside pocket of his suit coat. He felt a hint of smile on his face and quickly suppressed it. No reason to gloat. He also felt irritated that he was even spending his time in court on this stupid motion. Mike knew that he was on solid legal footing. Judge Newman had given him a clear order.

Cannes did not say much when Mike sat down, except to point out the obvious that he had submitted a Request for Production of Documents and that it should be honored. Cannes spoke with a degree of cockiness that even marked the way he sat down. That's odd, Mike thought to himself. What's he got going to be so cocky?

There were at least four other lawyers in court that day, each representing various parties in this complex partnership dissolution action. The three Darnoff children were in their forties and all were interested in obtaining their fair share of the assets from the partnership which was now being dissolved. Actually they were interested in obtaining more than their fair share. Each wanted as much as he or she could get. Their parents had been wildly successful in the wine business, producing high-end Zinfandels and Chardonnays. They had relied on some outstanding wine makers over the years, all of whom had trained at the nearby University of California at Davis. The assets of the wine business had been transferred to the children a few years ago, as an estate planning device. But then there was the divorce and the children had taken sides. So the dissolution of the partnership was probably inevitable.

But now the attorneys sat in various seats and waited to hear the judge's ruling. The words from the bench came as swiftly as they were unexpected.

"You do have a choice, counsel. You always have a choice. We are dealing today with the choice that you made." Judge Thoreson's tone was decidedly unsympathetic. Mike looked at the judge in disbelief.

Every noise in the courtroom stopped, even the squeaks of the old chairs. The clerk put her pen down and the bailiff looked up.

"Mr. Zorich, I want to be perfectly clear. I am ordering you today to turn over the financial documents that were requested by Mr. Cannes. Do I make myself clear?"

Mike paused. He put his hand to his mouth as he coughed once. "You do, your honor. But, with all due respect, I cannot comply with your order."

"This is not a question of you not being able to comply with the order, Mr. Zorich. Of course you can. This is a situation of you simply refusing to comply."

"Your honor, I have no choice."

"I order you to comply by two weeks from today. And to be sure, I shall also issue an Order to Show Cause re: Contempt and order that you appear in this court to either comply or to show cause why you should not be held in contempt of court and punished by this court for your refusal to comply with the discovery request and with this court's order. How much time do you want to prepare before we set the trial date?"

"I'm ready as soon as you like, judge," Mike said as his stomach churned. He was the first to answer. He did not want to grant the judge the pleasure of thinking that he needed any time to prepare for such preposterous charges. He wanted her to know that he was entirely confident and in no need of delay, which was the usual criminal defendant's request.

"Then it will be Tuesday, October 12 at 10:00 a.m. in this courtroom. Counsel, are there any problems with that date and time?"

She was now addressing everyone and, appropriately, they all took out their calendars, telephones or datebooks and searched to verify that the date would work out with their busy schedules. Even if their schedules were not busy, none of them ever wanted to answer a question like that too quickly, as it might appear that they were not in high demand. It all went into the mix. Only successful, busy lawyers need apply. Judge Thoreson looked up from her pad.

"Fine with me, your honor."

"Same here, your honor."

One after the other, they all registered their answers to the question. After a few minutes and after a few mumblings about this or that case, all lawyers were in agreement that October 12 would work. Mostly, all lawyers wanted to have a front row seat at something that does not happen all that often, a contempt of court trial and this one involving a lawyer. Not just any lawyer but someone they all knew. This would be juicy. Even if they were not directly involved, they had to be there and offer their two cents worth. Or they had to be there to watch, kind of like the spectators at the Coliseum in Rome. They would be sitting just to the side of the Emperor, munching on grapes as they took in the proceedings below.

"Is there anything else that we need to do today, counsel?"

Unlike before when everyone wanted to be heard, silence ensued. So Judge Thoreson then stated that she had nothing else and adjourned court. There was an instant buzz in the old courtroom. The lawyers zipped and locked their brief-cases and began talking to each other. None of them knew quite what to say to Mike. He kept to himself. He had a couple of weeks to figure out what to do, how to turn this thing around. He needed a plan and he needed some help.

Mike left the courthouse and walked a few blocks with his client to the parking lot and his car. Mike spoke first.

"Got to love the law, don't you?"

Mike was not quite sure what else to say. There was a period of silence as the two slowly made their way on the sidewalk. Mike knew that his client didn't know what to say either.

"I've got to say, that was a bit different than what I expected," Mike said. "Was this judge for real? How can she possibly think that I am going to comply with this order?"

"That was what I was wondering," Brian Darnoff said. "The way you explained it, you cannot comply because of the other judge's order. That seems pretty simple. What's going to happen? Is she going to throw you in jail for not following her order?"

"To be perfectly honest, I have no idea what she is going to do."

"Being a lawyer isn't all that easy, is it?"

"No, it isn't, Brian. No it isn't. Look, I will do some research and be talking to you this week. Keep me posted on anything happening in your world, such as your brother and sister and your parents."

"Right, how much can I tell you about my wonderful family? You know, I wonder how other families function sometimes. Do they all have massive fights like we do? I doubt it, but I really don't know."

"The thing is, Brian, your family has something that most other families don't have. Money. That is a game changer. It's hard to know how other families operate. But money has a mystical way of letting us all know who we really are, the way I see it. What do you think?"

"You're probably right, counselor. I'll keep in touch."

Brian Darnoff headed to his car with a wave and a warm smile. Mike waved and stood looking as his client got into his car. Mike wondered how he would act if he had a lot of money. Would he be a nice person? Would he be a jerk? Never having had a lot of money as a kid, the gains from his law practice had been intoxicating. He had a bank account that looked pretty good. He would spend a couple of minutes each month, studying his bank statement and his mutual fund account reports. He didn't think that money had changed him but he wasn't for sure.

In a couple of minutes, Mike got to his car. He put his brief case in the trunk and eased the Acura out of the lot. He went down a few blocks to Main Street and then five blocks to the freeway. He would be on auto-pilot once he hit the freeway. He put his radio on a classical station so he could think while listening to a soothing background. His mind was buzzing.

He did not even see the car but he certainly felt the jolt as his car suddenly moved over a few feet to the right. His sore ribs immediately registered the jolt. His seatbelt kept him in position, except for his head which moved decidedly to the right. What the hell? Then another jarring on his left rear side, as his car again involuntarily moved over to the right. There were no cars on the right, so nobody else was in danger. But Mike Zorich was in danger. He knew that much. And he was not feeling all that great.

Somebody was deliberately crashing into his car. Mike looked around and saw a green sedan behind him as his heart jumped up a few beats. He glanced back at his rear-view mirror to get a look at the driver. There was a large man filling up the driver side, both hands on the steering wheel and staring right back at him. It looked like there was a smile on his face and he was hunched over. It was hard to make him out. This guy meant business. Then Mike's car was hit again, this time directly from behind and it jumped forward. With his hands on the wheel, he kept it in his slow lane on the right directly in front of the jerk in the green car.

Now scared, Mike tried to think what to do. His hands were shaking and he could feel a headache pounding at his temples. Should he drive to a police station? Highway Patrol office? Where was an office? There was nobody else on the road, at least nobody nearby. He passed an exit. He certainly was not going to get off and let this crazy guy confront him at a stop sign. So he kept on going, trying to come up with a plan.

And then another bump from the rear and Mike's Acura jumped forward again, except this time it went to the left, into the fast lane. Lucky again that there was nobody else on the road at that particular location.

But just as he was thinking all of this, the green sedan slipped off on the exit ramp and was gone. Mike saw him in his rear-view mirror. Just like that. In the space of a few minutes, someone had tried to smash him and had gotten away with it. No license plate number, no real description, except a large guy in a green sedan. White guy, dark hair. He could have been driving a Ford, but Mike was not certain.

Mike could feel his face getting warm as he pulled over on the side of the freeway to call 911. His fingers were trembling as he fought with his phone to place the call to the Highway Patrol. A lady answered and he explained what had happened and she asked him to come to the office off of Madison Avenue and Interstate 80 and fill out a report. He did exactly that. But first he got out of his car and surveyed the damage. Actually it was not all that bad and the car was certainly drivable. By now he was calming down but this stuff was getting a little rich for his blood.

After he got to the Highway Patrol Office, Mike went in and filled out a report and waited in the front for about twenty minutes. Mike took the time to just sit there and think of what had happened. In a while, his name was called and he followed an older officer, who was in uniform and holding a clip board with some papers, to a small room with two chairs and a table.

"Can I get you some water or coffee? I'm afraid we don't have too much else to offer you."

"No, I'm fine," Mike said.

They got down to business. He talked to the officer and explained it all. There were some familiar questions.

"Did you do something on the road to get someone mad? Anybody out to get you? Have you had any problems with any clients? Or problems with the neighbors?"

Mike had no answers. But these questions were getting old. He told the officer about the mugging on the bike trail and how he was roughed up and how his house was ransacked. The officer said that they would put the information into the computer and certainly be in contact if they came up with anything. But this could just be a case of "road rage," according to the officer. It may have been a single incident, in which case it would be unlikely that they would find out much. Mike was advised to keep his eyes open in case he saw this car or driver again. As he left, the officer had another thought.

"But if you do see someone, you know not to do anything, right?"

"Yeah, officer. I know that. I will call you."

Mike drove back to his office thinking of what had happened to him in the last few weeks. It was clear that someone was out to get him. And that someone could have had something to do with the Darnoff case. Whoever did it knew that he was in court today. But who? And why? First, there was the mugging on the bike trail and the ransacking of his home and now this. Mike thought of everyone and everything that had been happening in his life lately.

He thought of Nancy telling him that it was probably someone who he represented before. But something did not make sense and then it hit him – Nancy's flat tire. If there was no nail, then someone had deliberately let the air out of her tire. Who would do that? Could it all be the same person? And was that someone trying to do something to Nancy? Talk about sending him a message.

To top it off, there was this crazy ruling from the judge. Why in hell would a judge issue an Order to Show Cause to hold him in contempt of court? None of this made sense.

SIX

"Brian, I have a question for you."

Mike got on his cell phone as soon as he parked his car at his office. He figured that he should ask his client what he knew about anything.

"Yeah, shoot."

"When I was driving back from court today, a car rammed me from the side, almost forcing me off the road. I'm just wondering if this has anything to do with our court case. So, my question is, do you think that your brother or sister or any of their friends could be behind something like that?"

"Damn, how are you?"

"Little shook up that's all. Car is damaged, but I can still drive it. It just seemed like it was connected to the court case because I was driving from the courthouse after our hearing, so I immediately thought of your brother and sister."

"Nah, can't imagine it. I have to say that we hate each other right now but that's nothing new. The three of us have a long history of not exactly acting like responsible adults, if you know what I mean."

"Yeah, I get that."

"I just can't believe that either of them would be behind something like this. But they do have people that they hang out with, who might be capable of something like that. In the wine industry, we have a lot of farm workers who help with picking the grapes. While we have been having this fight, we have agreed that Jason is in charge of all harvesting operations. I am strictly working inside with our professionals, so I don't know too much what is going on with our workforce."

"All right, just thought I would check with you. If you think of anything or hear of anything, let me know. This just doesn't add up."

"I will, Mike. In fact, I will ask around and see if I can sniff out anything. I am really sorry that this happened. This isn't in the job description for a lawyer, is it?"

"You'd be surprised what is in my job description, my friend."

Mike called Nancy and told her what had happened on the freeway and in court.

"I've got a question for you. Is your tire okay? Did it lose air when you drove on it today?"

"No, good as gold," she said.

"Just what I thought."

"What do you mean?"

"I'll tell you later."

They did not talk long as Nancy had an appointment but they agreed that they would meet at her place for dinner. When he arrived at his office, he immediately went to Denny's office and explained what had happened, as well as his phone call to his client.

"I'm figuring that it has to be somebody connected with the Darnoff case. That makes the most sense. I wouldn't put it past Brian's brother, Jason, to have one of his regular workers try to intimidate me. It kind of adds up with the mugging on the bike trail. That guy could have been a Mexican."

"Sure it's all possible. Did you ask the Highway Patrol what they thought?"

"Not really. I talked to them about this deal and they figured it was probably a random incident. But there's another thing that bothers me. Nancy had a flat tire the other day and she figured that it was a nail or something she picked up when she was driving through a new housing development. But when AAA came, they could not find a nail. I'm now thinking that someone deliberately let the air out of her tire. And the more I think about it, I think it is all connected. Someone is trying to send me a message and is even using Nancy to do it. You don't think I am getting a little paranoid, do you?"

"No, not at all. These days you can't be too careful. But as long as you are going down that road, who else might be a possibility? How about Cannes? He's a jerk of the first order. Have you thought about him? After all, he's the one who sent you the request for documents. That, by itself, doesn't make any sense at all."

"Yeah, I did think of him. I have a friend checking him out. Especially after today, there has to be some connection to the Darnoff case and Cannes is definitely a possibility. This whole thing is just a bunch of crap. How can any judge treat this motion like it was legitimate or even consider contempt of court? That is weird, too."

Mike explained everything that happened in court and that he was set for an OSC re: Contempt hearing before Judge Thoreson on October 12. He either produces the financial documents that he was prohibited from producing because of the order from Judge Newman or he would be found in contempt of court.

"The deal was that Judge Thoreson was only too happy to issue the Order to Show Cause. She couldn't care less about the order from Judge Newman. And another thing, she said that she never got my opposition papers and wouldn't even let me give her a copy. She said it was my fault so she would not consider them. I know we sent them to her. Alice always asks for a stamped returned copy."

As if by cue, Alice appeared in the doorway to Denny's office where Mike was slumped in the chair facing Denny at his desk.

"Good news. The Sheriff's office called this morning to say that they had recovered your Audi, Mike. They have it downtown and you can pick it up at any time. They said that there was not too much damage, although you will have to get a new radio, apparently. I have the number of the guy who called."

"Thanks, Alice. I'll call him right away. Say, on that Motion to Compel, you did ask for a stamped returned copy of our opposition papers, didn't you?"

"Sure, always do."

"And you got it back?"

"No I didn't. Not yet, at least. Usually I would have it by now."

"Figures. The judge claimed she never got the papers. They got lost somewhere, probably in the mail," Mike said.

"Another thing, Jim Haggerty called back with the information that you asked him for. Here's his number."

Last week, Mike had called Jim, one of his lawyer buddies in Woodland, and had left a message on his voicemail, asking him to find everything he could on Robert Cannes. He knew that Jim would do a thorough job. They had done a couple of cases together and Jim was one of the best prepared lawyers he knew. He trusted him implicitly.

Alice went back to her desk and Mike remained in Denny's office. Neither of them spoke for a while. Finally, Denny broke the silence.

"Here's another thought. Suppose it isn't anyone connected with Darnoff? Suppose it just happens to be someone from your past. Some old client. That is certainly possible."

"Sure, anything is possible. In fact, that is the most likely explanation when you think about it. You know, for a dumb guy, you come up with an occasional brilliant thought."

"That's why I get the big bucks around here, Ace. And don't you forget it."

Mike went to his office and called Jim Haggerty. He was in. And he had a lot to say. Mike didn't tell him anything that had been happening to him lately. He would save that for another day.

"Well, Cannes is one weird duck, that's for sure. He marches to a different drummer. Let's start at the beginning. He is from Louisiana, where he grew up pretty poor in a large family. He was the second to youngest of six kids. His family had to scrape for everything. He got good grades and went to LSU on a full ride and then to University of Tennessee Law School. He met his wife in college. He came to California about twenty years ago because his wife was from here. She grew up in Woodland and had always wanted to live near her family. He probably figured that he was escaping from hell. So Cannes took the California bar examination but failed it the first time. Passed on his second try. He originally did assigned juvenile cases for the county and then got some criminal assignments for public defender overflow. The public defender is really a small contract law firm, so they handled most everything but farmed out the conflicts. Cannes picked up some of those. He kind of stumbled along not making much money, according to what I could find. He's not the most talkative guy in the world but has a pretty good head on his shoulders. Nobody sees him as a dummy.

"Eventually, he got into more civil transactional law, especially when he hooked up with a big wine grape producer in Yolo County. He never had anything to do with the Darnoff family but someone probably recommended him and he was asked to represent the mother, son and daughter in the family feud. He just kept the kids and asked for a divorce specialist to handle the mother. But they are all together. Anyway, the first grape producer got him into his current firm. The firm saw him as bringing some good business and he was eager to get out of his solo practice gig. It looks as if it was a win-win for everyone, although a lot of his partners aren't all that enamored with him. They think he is kind of prickly. He doesn't do a lot with the firm outside of the day-to-day.

"He's married with three kids, two boys and a girl. He can't be all that bad, I suppose. Raising kids is never easy is this day. His wife is stay-at-home. Two kids are out of the house now, just one left who goes to high school. As you know, he is very sensitive about his name. Not sure why he is but he is. Like I said, a lot of guys don't like him. Someone said he has a bit of a mean streak to him. Also, he is a loner and just not that much fun to be around. No particular outside pursuits. Doesn't play golf.

"About the only thing I came up with that is out of the ordinary is that a female deputy district attorney told me he really carries a grudge. She beat him in an assault with a deadly weapon felony trial years ago. He has never forgotten it. She says that it was a slam dunk case with no real defense and she can't figure out why he was so upset. Maybe it's just the thought of losing, or maybe it was losing to a woman, she doesn't know. But whenever she sees him at a bar event or around the courthouse, he will make some sarcastic comment or just disrespect her. The deal is that it has been twenty years. He still won't let it go. Can you believe that?"

"Damn, Jim, when I ask you to check someone out, you do a job. Thanks a lot. I had one case with him, a few years back. It was a partnership dispute and we went to arbitration and I won. Maybe he's pissed off about that case. Who knows? If you hear anything else, give me a ring will you?"

"Will do. Always happy to be of service, my friend."

Sitting in his chair, Mike stared out his window. He figured that he had better start taking this whole thing a lot more seriously. Was it someone connected with the Darnoff case? That made sense, given that what happened today after court. Could it have been Cannes? That made the most sense. But why would a lawyer risk his bar ticket to do something stupid like this? It could it have been Brian's brother or sister or someone working for them. That was possible. The family was obviously taking this litigation very seriously. There was a lot of money at stake. Maybe someone had the bright idea of trying to scare him, get him to back off this case, maybe even withdraw as attorney. That might throw a crimp in the case and give someone an advantage. Definitely a possibility.

Or could it have been an old client, like Denny said? In fact, Nancy said the same thing. There were so many clients. Where to start? Of all of his clients, most were convicted and went to prison, at least the serious felony types. These were the very ones most likely to hold a grudge. There was an element of mental illness associated with a lot of these convicted felons. So that was an additional factor. Who had been convicted of a serious felony who also displayed some sort of mental illness? That would be a good place to start.

Immediately, he thought of the serious sex offenders. They never admitted their guilt, not to him, not to their families and friends and certainly not to the court. No, these guys never pled guilty, always figuring on taking their chances at trial. Sometimes the victims would not want to go to court, out of shame or fear. So the sex offenders would luck out. But sometimes the victims would go to court and would testify. Still, the trials were long and drawn-out. Usually, family members or children of friends, almost always young girls, testified about horrific acts. The defendants would routinely proclaim their innocence and blame the girls or their parents for making it all up. After conviction, there would be defiance and occasionally, but not always, an accusation that Mike has not done a good enough job to expose the lies. So that group of clients was a good place to start.

Then there were the "crazies," the ones who really were paranoid who thought everyone, including Mike was out to get them. Usually they got locked up for a long time and were unlikely to see the light of day.

But there was another group who were going to be released. They were the ones who would be found guilty at trial, do their time and be released to the care of an overworked parole officer. They usually were convinced that the public defender and the district attorney were in cahoots and had figured it all out together, agreeing in secret on the plea bargain for each defendant. These guys figured that it was Mike's job to sell it to his client just as it was the deputy district attorney's job to sell it to his supervisor. Actually, these guys might not have been too far off the mark as there was usually some element of salesmanship in convincing a client to take a plea bargain, even if it was in his best interest. But the client would often resist any such idea and reject the plea bargain. As a result these defendants would go to trial and, after conviction, accuse their defense attorney of "throwing the case" or "not trying very hard," out of pique.

Another group was the most disturbing, the truly innocent ones, any defense attorney's worst nightmare. There had to be some who were convicted but who were actually innocent. They were convicted on misidentification of a witness or on the basis of false testimony from someone with a score to settle. He wondered what it would be like to sitting in prison year after year knowing that you were innocent and then finally getting released. What would you do?

But much of that was a long time ago when he was new and just starting out. Still, he could not escape the memory of some of the faces of the defendants he represented. They had been convicted and sentenced to state prison or county jail or placed on probation. They would look at him as they left the courtroom with pleading eyes, asking for help and proclaiming their innocence at the same time. But Mike could do nothing.

The question today was whether one of his old clients was out to get him. Maybe someone was really innocent. Or, more likely, someone just sat in prison for years, silently brooding about how he would make things all even once he was released. Mike searched old files in his brain trying to think of just who might want to hurt him or get back at him.

A few names popped into Mike's head and then he remembered the "Master Index" that listed all of his cases. A couple of years ago, Alice had suggested that the summer intern could compile a list of all of Mike's old cases, as the intern did not have a lot of work to do. Mike agreed even though he saw little use for such a list. But it wouldn't hurt, he supposed. It might come in handy for checking conflicts of interest or for compiling information on judges before whom he tried cases. Fortunately, Mike had kept his own "working copy files" from his days at the public defender's office because the original documents were stored away at some county storage facility. All of those files were combined with his criminal and civil files that he had gathered since leaving the public defender's office and they took up quite a bit of space in the fourth office that he and Denny had designated for storage.

Alice oversaw the compilation of what came to be known as the Master Index. It contained the full names, nicknames and aliases of all clients he represented, along with opposing counsel, judges assigned to the case, outcome of the case, outcome of any appeal and a summary written by the intern. There was even a place for notes by Mike, but he never got around to going through the old cases and trying to come up with something important to add or a personal reflection.

Mike got up out of his chair and went into the reception area.

"Alice, where do we keep the Master Index, those binders of my old cases that you put together with the intern?"

"On the bookshelf in the conference room. Are you thinking that you might find someone in there who is out to get you?"

"Yeah. I don't have any other brilliant idea."

The Master Index was reduced to letter-sized sheets and placed in two large binders, broken down in alphabetical order. Mike went to the bookshelf and took down the binders.

"I think I'll take these binders home with me. In case I can't sleep, they will come in handy."

"Oh, they are more fascinating than that. Whenever I get a chance, I like to read up on your old cases."

He spent the rest of the day clearing up whatever needed to be done and then went to Nancy's house. She was already there. There were a few packages of food items on the counter. She had just been to the store. She greeted him with a warm kiss.

"You've had a big day. I can't imagine what it must have been like to have some clown smashing your car and you bouncing around. You must have felt helpless."

"Yeah. That's a good word for it. There was nothing I could do."

"How about a scotch? I have a good single malt here – Macallan. That might calm the nerves a bit."

Macallan was one of his favorites. Especially the 15-year old that Nancy was holding. It beckoned Mike like a magnet.

"Great."

Nancy poured a drink in a small glass and handed it to him.

"Darn, that is good stuff. So, what's cooking?"

"I thought I might make some pasta with salmon – s*almone fussili*, to be exact. I got the idea when we went to that Italian restaurant on Fair Oaks Boulevard. How does that sound?"

"Delicious."

"What do you have there?"

"Binders of all my cases. I am following up on your idea that maybe one of my old clients is up to no good."

"Oh good. Tell me about them. You can talk while I am making dinner."

"You really want to hear this stuff? I was just going to go through them tonight."

"No, I would like to hear what you have. Maybe I can help."

Mike took another sip of the extra-smooth scotch. It seeped down his throat like honey on a biscuit. He could feel himself beginning to unwind.

"Okay. I am going to look at the list. Here's one. Johnnie Ray White. He was an average-sized black man about 22 years old. He was convicted of 2 counts of armed robberies on the basis of 2 separate eyewitnesses at 2 separate convenience stores. It all happened on the same night. One witness was 'absolutely positive' that Johnnie Ray was the guilty man who held a gun to the face of his boss and demanded all of his money. The guy was sweeping in the back and hid behind some shelves once he heard a commotion in the front of the store."

The problem was that the other witness on the other robbery was not positive. In fact he was not even sure of anything. My biggest problem was that once the jury heard the first identification the jury would automatically assume Johnnie Ray was guilty of the second robbery which, interestingly, reinforces the first. The two robberies would feed on each other."

"I think I get it," Nancy said.

"I was trying to do the opposite. Let the lack of identification on the second one serve as a reason why the identification on the first one might be mistaken. Unfortunately, they were so similar and happened on the same night and close enough that one person could easily have made it to the second store. There was no way the jury would let someone go who might have done both robberies."

"I guess that makes sense."

"I asked the judge to have separate trials for each robbery so that one would not influence the other, but he turned me down."

"I got the second witness, a guy about seventeen, to admit that the police told him that "they had their man," and that he was in the photo lineup that they presented to him. All of that is now prohibited by most enlightened police agencies. It made no difference, as the jury convicted Johnnie Ray of both robberies and he was sent off for fifteen years. There was something about how Johnnie Ray always proclaimed his innocence. He looked straight at me several times and told me that he didn't do it, just as he told the jury. Who knows, maybe he was innocent?"

"He doesn't sound like someone who would be out to get you," Nancy said.

"He even insisted on testifying, against my advice. He wanted to tell the jury that he was innocent. But he just wasn't all that credible. He has been in prison for a long time. The truth is that the evidence was not iron-clad. Maybe he has been reading about all the stuff in the papers about convictions which were originally based on eyewitness identification and which were later overturned on the basis of new DNA evidence. I doubt that there is any DNA evidence on this case. They just didn't collect that back then. But he could have gotten mad in prison. It's happened before."

"Do you know if he is out of prison yet?"

"Not sure, but I could check. He should have gotten some time off for good behavior and for work credits while in prison. If he isn't out right now, he should be fairly soon. The thing is that I really liked Johnnie Ray and I always wondered about him."

"Okay, who else?"

Mike paged through the first binder, turning pages of former clients that didn't fit any of the categories of likely suspects. He could smell the onions and the salmon from the stove top. He took another sip from his drink.

"Here's one. Billy Wycomb, convicted of eighteen counts of child molestation, California Penal Code section 288, with his own daughters and then with some of their girlfriends. This was a bad actor. He was pretty nondescript, actually. He would just blend in with anybody else in a crowd. As I recall, Billy was out of work and home most of the time, acting as the friendly neighborhood babysitter. He was a large white guy with a red complexion and dark hair. He always wore a wide-brimmed straw hat and the kids seemed to automatically gravitate to his perpetual smile."

"Those are the icky kind that I hate," Nancy said.

"For good reason. Billy turned out to be a very evil man. He wouldn't take any kind of a plea bargain. He said that the kids' parents had gotten together because they were jealous of him and wanted to get rid of him. He loved the children and they all knew it. It was all a big conspiracy. So we went to trial. His family was right there with him. He told his wife and children that he was innocent and they stood by him, except for his oldest daughter, age thirteen. She actually testified against him, because he had done a lot of stuff to her. The mother had practically disowned her so she was living with another relative until the trial was over. Billy's wife had come to court on every occasion and stood by her man. Maybe she wanted it all to go away or for her husband to be found innocent because she could not possibly fathom any other possibility. Maybe she was afraid of him. But I've got to tell you that the idea of the family of a child molester standing by the accused was nothing new in the criminal courts."

"So he went to trial?"

"Yes, he went to trial which went on for about three weeks. The jury sat and watched as each of the girls came to court and testified about what Billy had done to them. The scene each day was more emotional than the day before with tears freely flowing in the audience and among some members of the jury. Finally, Billy himself testified and denied every accusation, blaming the parents of the children for making it all up. He had no explanation as to why his own daughter would join the cabal. The D.A. didn't have to do much on cross-examination. Billy just made it worse on himself, the more he said. I knew that the chances for any kind of verdict other than guilty would be extremely unlikely, but I tried my best to protect his rights. The jury returned its verdicts of guilty on all counts and Billy was sentenced to prison for over a hundred years."

"So, he's he still in prison?"

"Probably, but I'm not sure. After the trial, I filed the Notice of Appeal on his behalf. There were some serious legal issues as to the admissibility of all of the evidence. The first stories of the girls didn't match the stories they gave in court. I argued that someone had obviously coached them. Remember that big child molestation case in Los Angeles where it was finally shown that all of the children at a day care center had been coached to blame the defendant?"

"Yes, I remember that. It's been quite a few years now."

"Same thing here. Billy got a hearing in the Federal District Court on a writ and he was sent back for a new trial. By then most of the girls didn't want to testify again. Either they were lying the first time or they were too embarrassed, now that they were older. So the D.A. made a deal and Billy got a reduced sentence. He could well be out by now."

"Okay, but why would he blame you?"

"He thought I should have argued more or better to get the testimony of the girls thrown out. I went to talk to him when he was in the county jail after he was sent back by the federal court. He told me that I was the reason he lost the case and why he spent time in the joint. I remember the exact words he used. He told me he would have won if he didn't end up with 'half a real lawyer and a God-damn public defender.' Then he began making a lot of noise and the guards came and removed him. He wouldn't talk to me anymore, not that I had anything to say."

"So this guy is a real possibility. What else?"

Mike went back to the binders while sipping his scotch.

"Oh, here's one. Arthur Scheffler. He was a notorious member of the Aryan Brotherhood or 'AB' as it was known, a white supremacy prison gang. I remember him very well. He was a big guy, blond hair with a lot of Nazi tattoos. He was downright scary. He had a long record and had spent quite a bit of time in Soledad State Prison and Folsom, before I even met him. I represented him for an assault with a deadly weapon and attempted murder of a black man at Huck Finn's, that bar in Old Town. The case for the prosecution was pretty strong. There were a couple of eyewitnesses at the bar who saw him beat the guy up and Scheffler was taken into custody right away by some burly bouncers. Scheffler denied having anything to do with it and instead claimed that he was set up by some 'black dudes from L.A.' who were out to get him."

Nancy began setting the table.

"Keep talking. I can hear you. I'm just finishing up on the vegetables. Aren't you getting kind of hungry? We're just about ready."

"Yeah, I am."

Mike got up and came into the kitchen.

"The thing is that he insisted on calling about a dozen witnesses from prison who would testify on his behalf about the blacks who really did the beating and who would also testify to his good character. I told him that this was a bad plan. Prisoners would not make the most attractive or believable witnesses. I could pretty easily see that his plan for calling everyone from prison was just a way to accommodate some order from the AB leadership to give some people a free ride to Sacramento, kind of like a day on the town. It was very unlikely that they knew anything about this killing. At least, Scheffler couldn't say what it was that they would say. So I had nothing to argue. Naturally, the judge turned down the request for the transportation of the prisoners and Scheffler was mad as hell, both at the judge and at me. He figured that I was part of the establishment out to see that he got convicted."

"So, he got convicted?"

"Yes, but first he tells me that I should bring a writ of habeas corpus and get his witnesses. When I said that wouldn't work, he called me a son-of-a-bitch. Said I was nothing but a tool for the D.A. He kept claiming that he had his rights."

"I told him that he did have his rights. And I told him that I was doing everything I could to protect his rights and see that he is given a fair trial. I tried and the judge turned down our request to have these guys transported to the courthouse. I told him that he would have this issue on appeal, if he were convicted. I said that the appellate court may agree with him and he would be given a new trial. But for now, we have to deal with the cards we were dealt."

"Did he testify or have any other witnesses?"

"No, he wouldn't testify. I think he was afraid that the D.A. would go after him for perjury. Go figure. He was convicted in fairly short order and was carted off to Folsom Prison to begin yet another term in the joint. I'm not sure that he is still there. He's probably out by now. The deal is that the AB is a pretty big operation. Even if he is still inside, they have a lot of guys on the outside to settle scores. I could easily be a target for someone who is given an order from higher up. I just don't know.

"Okay, dinner is ready. Let's go back to that later."

"You got it. The fact is that there are a lot of options. Going through old cases is like looking for a needle in the haystack. It could be anyone or none of these. All I can do is to go with what we have. Right now I don't have much, just some stupid things that can't be a coincidence. It just can't be a coincidence."

Mike had finished his second scotch and sat down with Nancy. At first, they ate in silence. Then he asked about her day and she gave him a quick summary. He had a glass of white wine from a nondescript Sonoma winery and Nancy did the same. Mike was no longer thinking of his old cases. He was thinking of something entirely different. He reached for the bottle to pour another glass and her voice interrupted his thoughts.

"I hate to be a nag, but shouldn't you be watching the booze?"

"Yeah, I suppose. But I'm perfectly sober."

That was a lie. Mike could feel the buzz and he knew that she was right. But it was the warm embrace of alcohol that had seen him through many a dark night, ever since Sheila's agony and death. He saw the scotch as his old friend, the one friend that he could always count on to deliver him from the pain.

"You just cooked a great meal and we are having an intelligent discussion. What could be more normal than that?"

His logic didn't really add up. Nobody was talking about what was normal or not. He sat there silently for a couple of minutes.

"The deal is that I have bigger fish to fry at the moment. I have a showdown with my favorite judge in Yolo County over a possible contempt charge. I have to focus on that. The one thing that I do know is that I don't have the answers. I'm not even sure I know what to say in court. I think this judge has her mind made up."

"Is there anyone who can help you? How about Denny? He's pretty experienced," Nancy said. "You need someone. You can't do this all by yourself."

Mike and Nancy watched some television and they nestled together for a while. A little cuddling soon became something more. In short order, the two of them came to resemble a couple of hormone-crazed teenagers left alone without any parents. They quickly rid themselves of various articles of clothing and retired to Nancy's bed.

SEVEN

NANCY WAS RIGHT. He knew that he needed some help in the courtroom with the contempt of court charge. But Denny couldn't help him as he had no criminal law experience. He needed someone who was well respected and who knew criminal law as well as civil law and someone who could defend him on this kind of charge. He thought right away of his old friend, Jim Haggerty, who was both a civil and criminal law attorney in Woodland, specializing in appeals but with plenty of trial experience earlier in his career. Plus there was the added advantage that Jim practiced in Woodland. Maybe that fact might equalize any hometown advantage that Robert Cannes had in the Woodland courthouse. Mike set up lunch with Jim for the next day. Then he dropped by Denny's office and told him what he was about to do. Denny agreed right away that he needed someone with criminal experience. Further, Denny offered that he was probably too close to be perfectly objective.

The next day Mike and Jim met at a sandwich shop downtown on J Street. Jim said he had to be in Sacramento for a morning calendar and they could meet for lunch after court. That saved Mike from a trip to Woodland. Jim Haggerty was tall and thin and his face resembled a wrinkled piece of leather. There were lines of laughter and sadness but mostly there were lines of age. Jim Haggerty had been around a long time. He was kind of a good old bear who was always there, plugging along. Mike always liked him, as did virtually all of the local lawyers. Actually, "respect" would have been a better word to describe how people thought of Jim Haggerty. After placing their orders at the counter, they found a table and Mike brought him up to speed, filling in any details that he had not already told him.

"That's about it," Mike said. "The deal is that I need your help. I need someone who can persuade Judge Thoreson to get off my back and to set this whole thing straight. You're the man, Jim. No question about that."

"Not sure of that. But let me get this straight, you're saying that all of this was a big surprise, huh?"

"Right. I had no clue that this judge would go this far. It should have been an open and shut case. Motion denied. That simple. But, no, she orders me to comply with this stupid Request for Production of Documents and then, assuming I am not going to comply, issues an OSC and sets a trial date. I still don't get it. Something is not right here. Have you had much experience with her?"

"No, not at all. Doesn't she just do the criminal stuff? I'm surprised she is even handling this type of case."

"She is clearly out of her league. The case got re-assigned to her a couple of months ago. It had been stayed by the first judge when all of the attorneys asked if they could have some time to try and mediate a settlement. But that didn't work, because this is all tied into the divorce case. That is what is driving the litigation. As soon as Mom and Dad have settled their differences, the rest of this should follow. So it makes a lot of sense to put a stay on all discovery in this case. Judge Newman got it right. But now we are back in court in front of Judge Thoreson. If she is going to fall for this crap from Cannes, there isn't much I can do."

Jim jumped into his BLT when it was delivered and was quiet. Mike knew that Jim was not the most warm and fuzzy guy in town. He had been practicing law for a long time. He had heard it all and most of what he had heard was a bunch of crap. Most criminal defendants were guilty of something. He was there to ensure that their rights were protected and that they got a fair trial and a fair appeal. As a result, his emotions did not really enter into the equation. He took life as it came along without much recognition one way or the other. Mike actually liked that aspect of Haggerty and sometimes wished that he himself could be a bit more stoic.

"Tell me everything that happened starting from the beginning," Jim said.

Haggerty sounded a tad condescending as if talking to a nephew at a family gathering. Mike chose to ignore it.

"I will, but before that let me tell you what happened after I left court. Some nut rammed me from the back three times on Interstate 5, after I left Woodland. He took off on an exit before I could get any license plate or better identification."

"You're kidding. That would make life a bit more exciting than normal."

"Oh, it was exciting all right. Very exciting. I gave a report to the highway patrol but they were not too encouraging. My car was okay, damage was not too bad. I'll have to take it to a body shop, but I can drive it. I will tell you that it is a little bit unnerving to be rammed from the back and have your car go out of control on you. It wasn't really out of control, but you know what I mean."

"Yeah, I know."

"The deal is that is not all. I got mugged on the bike trail a couple of weeks ago. I figured that was just a crack head or heroin junkie, but now I am not so sure. My house was ransacked. Plus, someone let the air of the tire on the car of my girlfriend, Nancy. I am getting to the point of wondering if all of this is connected."

"Could be. How are you doing with all of that? Sounds pretty wild to me."

"I'm okay. I just need to settle down. I'm fine, really. I will deal with the car later. It's just that having been mugged on the bike trail and then this. You know, you can become paranoid after a while. Ha-ha."

There was a silence as Jim just stared blankly at his sandwich.

"You've got me. Are you reporting all of this stuff to the police?"

"Sure. More or less."

"What do they say?"

"Nothing. They haven't exactly set up a task force to solve the mysteries in the life of Mike Zorich, if you know what I mean. But the problem is that there is the Sacramento Sheriff and the California Highway Patrol. There are two separate incidents and two separate agencies."

"You know, we don't have to talk about this now if you don't want to."

"No, let's do it now. There's no better time."

Mike took a sip of coffee and sat back in his chair. He paused a bit before beginning.

"Well, first off Judge Thoreson says she didn't receive all of my papers. That was strange because I know they were filed. At least I mailed them and they have always been filed before. So I felt like I was in a hole, right from the start. Then she asked me if I had complied with the request for documents and when I told her that I did not, I explained why. She asked a few more questions. Really, she had her mind made up. There was not much I was going to say or do."

"What about Cannes?"

"Cannes was his usual stuffy self. He did not have to do much. He just recited the company line and everything fell in place for him. He is not an easy guy to like. He's just what you told me, a loner. Plus I wouldn't be surprised if he had something going on with the judge."

"Yeah, well there is the Woodland brotherhood. I'm part of it, I guess. A lot of the judges eat lunch at the same place and it just happens that a lot of lawyers end up there too. So, your thought of them talking to each other is not that far-fetched. I'll try to keep an eye out and see if Judge Thoreson and Cannes have anything going on. I can ask around about that too. Problem is that you could never prove it."

"I don't have to. All I have to do is to imagine it. Good enough for me."

It was a fact of life that in California's smaller counties, there was a clear and distinct hometown advantage for the local practitioners. They met with the judges far more often than their bigger city counterparts. They would bump into each other at all kinds of events, so it was hard not to keep everyone happy in the little family.

The more Mike talked, the worse he felt. But nothing was going to be resolved this day. The two continued to discuss the day's events and the background of the case. After about forty-five minutes, Mike paid their tab and left.

"I would appreciate any help you could give me, Jim," Mike said.

"I'm going to look into things, maybe get the court file from Woodland. Could you have your secretary make a copy of everything you have on the Darnoff case and send it over to me?"

"No problem. I'll do it today."

"You should also think of any of your old criminal cases when you were a public defender. Maybe someone stands out who would be out to get you. That is just too obvious a possibility that we cannot forget that."

"Believe me, I have already started doing that but nothing is jumping out at me. There were a few that might be possibilities but those were just guesses."

"Do you have any kind of overall list of your old cases? Maybe we could run them against the Department of Corrections list of prisoners to see who has been released in the past year or so."

"Good idea. I do have a list. We call it the Master Index. I haven't checked to see if any of them were released from prison. I'll get the names and have my secretary do a search, like you said. Can't hurt," Mike said.

"Okay, give me a few days to read everything. Let's get together at the end of the week and figure out what to do on your contempt hearing. We'll figure out something."

"Works for me," Mike said.

Mike got his Audi back that afternoon after Alice gave him a ride to the Sheriff's Department. The car was none the worse for wear. It was missing a radio, like they said. Mike figured that he could remedy that pretty quickly. That afternoon he went to one of the many specialty shops on Arden Way and had a new Bose radio/stereo system installed in his car. He was back in business. He asked Alice to run a check with the California Department of Corrections and Rehabilitation or CDCR, as it was affectionately known, to see which of his old clients had been released from prison. It would take some time.

The next morning, Mike got up leisurely, made coffee and opened up the newspaper. A headline on page three of the Regional Section caught his eye. "New Forgery Charge for Ex-Con." The article went on to explain that Johnnie Ray White, released from prison last year after serving twelve years for a couple of robberies, had been arrested for forgery. Bail has been set at $200,000.

What do you know? Johnnie Ray was back in business, Mike thought to himself. The same Johnnie Ray White that Mike just picked out from his master index. Mike remembered back to a time early in his career and how he represented the young black man on the robberies mentioned in the article. It was a big trial for him at the time as he had not had much felony trial experience. There were two eyewitnesses but Mike knew that he could cast some doubt on them because one of them was so shaky. Most jurors were aware that eyewitness testimony had come under a lot of scrutiny these days because of high-profile cases on television. Mike reminded them in his closing argument of some of the more notorious cases. Johnnie always protested his innocence, which was nothing new. But this was different. He constantly made Mike promise that he would call this witness or would argue this point or would do something else.

"Mr. Zorich, do you believe me? Do you believe that I am innocent?"

"Johnnie, that is not my job. I am not your judge and I am not your jury. I am here to do the very best I can to defend you."

Mike knew that he was giving his stock answer and wanted to do something more, such as tell him that he did believe in him. But he knew from experience and the constant tutoring of his supervisors that this would not be wise to do.

"Mr. Zorich, it's important. You have to believe in me. I didn't do any of this stuff. I didn't do it, really."

After he was convicted, Johnnie begged him to file an appeal and to get him out of jail. Mike promised that there would be an appeal and a good appellate lawyer working on his case. Johnnie and his mother hugged each other with plenty of tears all around. With that Johnnie Ray White disappeared into the holding tank. There was something about the young man that always stayed with Mike. It was the protestation of innocence. Oh sure, they all say they are innocent, but Johnnie Ray White was different.

He visited Johnnie a couple of times at the Mule Creek Correctional Facility near Ione, just south of Sacramento, but Mike always wondered if there was something else he could have done. Maybe he could have done a better cross-examination of the neighbor. Maybe he could have made a more powerful final argument. And he knew how much better of a criminal defense lawyer he had become. Now he would certainly do a better job.

But that day he had other thoughts. How long had Johnnie Ray been out of prison before he got picked up on the new beef? Did he have anything to do with Mike? Was he pissed off that Mike did not do a good enough job for him years ago?"

The next day Mike drove to Jim Haggerty's office in Woodland. The two had talked a few times on the phone but now it was getting more serious. They plotted and planned. They asked questions of each other, each attempting to ensure that they had probed the depths of the facts and the law in preparation for the next skirmish in court. This was a time to carefully hone the legal arguments.

Haggerty did well at this. He spent considerable time working at his computer, using the legal research software that made life so easy. Books had become a thing of the past in almost all law offices. He accumulated all of the cases on contempt charges in California and from some of the larger states. Surprisingly, there were not all that many. He studied what little there were and tried to find analogies for use in persuading the court of his position.

"You know, I did have one other thought and that was to contact Judge Newman to see if she would either withdraw her order or at least have her contact Judge Thoreson to get her to back off of her OSC. So I called her," Haggerty said.

"Good idea. I hadn't thought of that. But that is why I am not representing myself," Mike said.

"Unfortunately, she is out of the country and will be for at least another 30 days. Maybe if we had tried before we might have got some kind of response. Of course you didn't know that Judge Thoreson was going to rule the way she did. But I wouldn't worry about it. I doubt that Judge Newman would make much difference. It sounds like this judge had her mind made up."

"Yeah, I agree. She was emphatic that Judge Newman's order made no difference."

"Still she's the one who could either revoke her order so you could turn over this stuff to Cannes or better yet she could talk some sense into Judge Thoreson. Maybe not all that kosher, but that would do the job, if Thoreson is even capable of understanding what a mess she's created. Judges are always talking to each other so it wouldn't be all that unusual."

"It's always possible that Judge Thoreson knows exactly what she is doing. That she wants to hold me in contempt."

"Okay, I'll bite. Why?"

"I don't know. It's just that she was so smug. And Cannes was so smug. The two of them have to know that a judge can't issue an order that contradicts another lawful court order from another judge. That's pretty basic."

"I get all that," Haggerty said. "But right now, I don't see that we have many options except to go to court and try ourselves to beat some sense into her brain.

We have just got to go in front of Thoreson and fight it out. But let me ask you this? Have you ever appeared before her before?"

"Yeah, I did. I was retained by a family from Woodland a few years ago. Their name was Cardoza. Their son got picked up for a series of burglaries. The evidence was not all that strong and I felt that he was innocent. I remember that pretty well. But he was convicted and he appealed. The Court of Appeal reversed the conviction. I know that the D.A. over there wasn't too happy with me. But they never tried him again."

"Why the reversal?"

"Judge Thoreson let in evidence of prior similar acts by the defendant. But the thing was the prior acts weren't similar at all. They were just some old things he had done. One was an assault on a guy at a bar in downtown Woodland and another was some high school fight that got out of hand. Both were misdemeanors and happened at least five years before the burglaries. I argued like hell that they should not be admitted because they did not go to credibility and they were old, but she let them in anyway. I was on solid legal footing. It didn't take the jury long to figure out that Cardoza was a bad guy and should be convicted."

"Was the opinion from the Court of Appeal published?"

"It was. There was some pretty strong language in there from the justices on the Court of Appeal. They hit her pretty hard. They said that this was pretty basic and that the result of allowing the evidence before the jury was a waste of precious judicial resources."

"Interesting. So at a minimum, she is no fan of yours."

"Right. And to make things worse, we have to fight two of them, Cannes and Thoreson. The deck is kind of stacked, don't you think?"

"Look, Mike, we have to do what lawyers do. We don't measure the odds, at least we don't make bets. We make the arguments and do our level best. You know that."

They spent another hour preparing the direct examination when Jim would be asking Mike questions. They tried to anticipate any question that Cannes would ask by cross-examination. They felt good about their preparation and couldn't wait to get before Judge Thoreson and to set her straight.

EIGHT

MIKE KNEW THAT the person at the store was someone he knew, but he just couldn't place him. It was about six p.m. on Friday and Mike stopped to pick up a few things for dinner. He was eating alone tonight so he picked up some fish, a loaf of bread, milk and the usual assortment of vegetables. But as he was waiting in the checkout aisle, he saw the man in another checkout aisle. Who is that guy, he thought to himself. And then it hit him – James Montoya, the witness in the Martinez case. Mike hurried along to his car but as he opened the trunk, Montoya was right behind him.

"Mr. Zorich, you remember me?"

"Yes, I remember you, Mr. Montoya."

"You still think that guy you got off is innocent?"

"Mr. Montoya, I am not the judge and I am not the jury. That is who decides whether someone is guilty or not. I am not the one to answer your question."

"Boy, you are smooth. That's for sure. Kind of golden-tongued. You know, there was no need for you to tear into me, like you did. Someday you are going to get yours, Mr. Lawyer, just you wait and see."

"Mr. Montoya, are you threatening me? I don't think your boss at the parole office would like to hear what you said to me."

"Nah, I'm not threatening you. I'm just saying. You got a guilty guy off. What you did wasn't right. You're Mr. High and Mighty. Someday you'll get yours. Mark my words."

Montoya turned and went to his car. Mike did not know if Montoya had followed him to the store or if he just happened to be here. It was not his neighborhood as Montoya lived downtown, a good 10 miles away. Mike headed home and thought about the case that brought the two of them together. James Montoya, the parole officer, was a witness to an alleged burglary. He said he saw Arthur Martinez carting off a television during the early evening. He came to court and positively identified Martinez. But Mike, who was representing Martinez, was quick to ask Montoya why he was so sure of his identification. Mike remembered his cross-examination of Montoya as if it was yesterday. It was one of his more memorable efforts in the courtroom.

"Mr. Montoya, I represent Mr. Martinez in this case and I have just a few questions to ask you. Sir, as I understand it, you are quite positive of your identification of Mr. Martinez. In fact, there is not the slightest doubt in your mind, is that correct?"

"That is correct."

"In fact, it doesn't make any difference to you, if Mr. Martinez was not even in Sacramento that evening does it?"

"I am certain of what I saw, that is all I can say."

"Sir, did you ever ask the detectives what Mr. Martinez said about his whereabouts that evening? Did you ever ask about anything that Mr. Martinez might have said?"

"No, I did not."

"Would it be correct to say that you did not really care what Mr. Martinez said?"

"Yes, it doesn't matter to me."

"So if the detective told you that Mr. Martinez was with him, that very same detective, at a softball game and could not possibly have been at your neighbor's house that would make no difference to you at all?"

"Well, I guess it would, if the detective was positive that he wasn't there."

"Sir, did you ask the detective anything, anything at all as to what Martinez said or where he claimed to be that night?"

"No I did not."

"And why didn't you, sir?"

"I didn't think of it. Nobody said anything about that."

"Now, can you tell me about the weather that night? Was it rainy, cloudy, cold, warm?"

"It was pretty normal and clear outside. That's what I recall."

"Clear. So it was easy to see, is that right?"

"Yeah, that's right."

"And at some point, you spoke to a police detective, is that right?"

"I did, yes."

"That was the next day, right?"

"Yes."

"And did you give the police detective a description of the person you saw that night?"

"I did."

"And when you gave the description, were you careful to tell the detective the truth?"

"Yes, of course."

"And you were pretty certain of your description, were you not, sir?"

"Yes, I was."

"Just as you are sure here today in the identification of Mr. Martinez, is that right sir?"

"Yes."

"In fact, you are absolutely positive about your identification of Mr. Martinez, isn't that right, sir?"

"Yeah, that's right."

"And the description you gave was 5 feet 6 inches tall and about 180 pounds, is that right?"

"I don't remember. Whatever it says is right."

"Mr. Montoya, I am looking at the police report right now. And it says that you described the individual you saw that night as five feet six inches tall, weighing about a hundred eighty to two hundred pounds, Latino, no scars on his face, black pants and a short-sleeve dark shirt. Is that what you told the detective?"

"If that is what it says, that is what I told him."

"Sir, do you remember today what the man looked like?"

"Just like that."

"Mr. Montoya, did you ever ask the detective, how tall Mr. Martinez was or how much he weighed?"

"No."

"Would you like to know that sir?"

"No. He is the man. I am positive."

"You are positive. Of course you are Mr. Montoya, you already told us that. Do you know sir that Mr. Martinez is 5 foot 11 inches tall and that he weighs about a hundred fifty-five pounds?"

"No. It doesn't matter."

"Why doesn't it matter, sir?"

"Because he's the one. That's why."

"And you are absolutely positive about your identification, isn't that right, sir?"

"Yeah, that's right."

"Sir, if the man you saw was shorter or larger than Mr. Martinez, wouldn't that matter?"

"I don't know."

"Now, Mr. Montoya, did you go down to the police department and look at some photographs a couple of days later?"

"Yes, I did."

"And did you see the photograph of Mr. Martinez?"

"Yes, I did."

"Yes. According to the police report, you were shown a total of five photographs and you selected the one of Mr. Martinez, is that correct sir?"

"Yes."

"Mr. Montoya, did you know whether or not the police already had arrested Mr. Martinez when you were shown his photograph?"

"I don't remember."

"Sir, you do remember that the detective told you that they caught the guy and wanted to know if you could identify him?"

"Yeah, I remember that."

"And when you were shown the photographs, you were told to take your time and the guy they arrested was one of the five?"

"Yeah, I remember that."

"And when you selected Mr. Martinez, the detective told you that you got the right guy?"

"Yeah."

"And you were told that you would be coming to court one of these days, is that right?"

"Yeah, that's right."

"Did you tell the detective that you were not positive when you selected the photograph of Mr. Martinez?"

"No, I didn't say that."

"Sir, didn't you tell the detective that you were not sure if you could select a photograph of the man you saw?"

Mike was looking at some papers in his hand as he asked the question.

Montoya paused. "Yeah, I might have said that. What does it say in the report? I don't remember what I said."

"In fact, Mr. Montoya, you told the detective that it was very dark that night, did you not sir?"

"I don't recall that."

"Mr. Montoya, I am just reading from the report. Did you not tell the detective that it was very dark that night?"

"I might have."

"Didn't you tell the detective that because it was very dark, it was hard to see?"

"I don't remember what I said."

"And did you not tell the detective that you were not sure if you could identify the man from photographs?"

"I might have."

"Sir, as you sit here today, can you tell me how tall Mr. Martinez is?"

"No."

"Well, let's ask Mr. Martinez to stand up. Mr. Martinez, please stand. Now, sir, you are looking right at him. Go ahead and tell me your best estimate of his height?"

"Well, he is skinny."

"How about his height?"

"I don't know, he is tall, I guess."

"And you told the detective that the man was 5 foot 6 inches tall and weighed about a hundred eighty to two hundred pounds, is that right?"

"Whatever it says."

"Well, if that is what the police report says, then that is what you said, right?"

"Yes."

"And Mr. Montoya, you are absolutely positive about your identification, isn't that right, sir?"

"Yeah, that's right."

"Mr. Martinez, you can sit down. Thank you. Mr. Montoya, can you tell me what color tie I am wearing today?"

Mike had carefully placed his files in front of his tie.

"No, I can't. I can't see it, because you are blocking it."

Mike remembered that Montoya looked quickly at the jury, pleased that he had got one over the lawyer.

"Can you tell me what color it is based on when you saw it a few minutes ago?"

Montoya's mood changed. "No."

"Mr. Montoya, how long have you been looking at me, while I have been asking you questions?"

"I don't know. Seems like a long time."

"A long time. Sir, if you cannot remember what color tie I am wearing when have been looking at me for a long time, are you sure you can remember what the man looks like that you saw that night?"

"Yes."

"But you do agree with me, that you can look at someone for a long time and not even remember something about that person, right?"

"Yes, I guess so, if you mean your tie."

"Yes, that is what I mean, Mr. Montoya. And do you agree with me that your memory of who you saw was better the day you saw him than it is today?"

"Probably."

"Sir, do you agree with me that you told the police the truth when you gave them the description of the man you saw?"

"Of course."

"Do you also agree with me that the description that you gave the police detective was an accurate description of the man you saw?"

"Yes."

"And do you agree with me that the description you gave is different as far as height and weight are concerned than the height and weight of Mr. Martinez?"

"I don't know about that. Like I said, it was dark that night."

"It was dark that night? I thought you told the jury that it was clear that night and that you got a good look at the man?"

"Now you are trying to confuse me. I know something about my saying it was dark. You said so yourself."

"Yes, I was quoting from what you told the police detective the next day when you gave the description."

"Right, that it was dark. It was dark."

"It was not clear, is that right?"

"It was not clear."

"You understand Mr. Montoya that we all make mistakes from time to time, do you not sir?"

"I suppose."

"Well, have you ever made a mistake?"

"Sure, plenty of them."

"And you just made a mistake in saying today in court that night was clear when it was actually dark, right?"

"I might have."

"And you told the detective the day after that it was dark? In fact, you told him that it was very dark, correct?"

"Yes."

"And you understand that there is nothing wrong with making mistakes. In fact, it is perfectly normal?"

"Yes."

"And you trust your memory better back that night than today, is that right sir?"

"Sure."

"So if you said something different today from what you said that night or the next day, then you would trust what you said back then over what you said here today, right?"

"Yeah. I guess."

"And you agree with me, sir, that if Mr. Martinez, my client, was not anywhere near your neighbor's house that night, you would have appreciated it if the detective told you that, is that right, sir?"

"Yeah, I suppose."

At this point, Montoya was hoping that he could just go anywhere and get out of the courtroom. But he knew that he was stuck.

"And you agree with me, sir, that Mr. Martinez is not 5 feet 6 inches tall and does not weigh a hundred eighty to two hundred pounds?"

"I don't think so. I am not for sure on that. I don't know what he weighs."

"Well, do you know how tall he is?"

"No, I don't."

"If he was not five feet six inches tall and does not weigh a hundred eighty to two hundred pounds, then it is possible that you have made a mistake, right?"

"Possibly. But maybe I just got the description wrong that night. I don't know."

"But you just told me that your memory was better that night than today, right sir?"

"Yes."

"If there is a mistake it would not be what you said that night, but what you said today, right?"

"Yes."

"You know that the police make mistakes, every now and then, right?"

"Yes, I suppose. No, I take that back. I don't know about the police."

"And it certainly is possible that you have made a mistake, is that not a possibility, Mr. Montoya?"

"Yes, I suppose."

Montoya just glared at Mike. There was no mistaking the anger in his eyes.

"Thank you, Mr. Montoya. I have no further questions of this witness, your honor."

Mike recalled how satisfied he was with the cross-examination. But he also recalled how upset Mr. Montoya was that day. He was glaring at Mike during most of the questioning and he was clearly upset with how he was being treated. Mike remembered very clearly how Montoya left the witness stand. He walked very slowly past the counsel table and stared at Mike. He was seething. The humiliation was complete. Mike did not set out to demean the man but that was the way it turned out. Later that afternoon when Mike was leaving the courtroom, he went to the elevator bank and there was Montoya. He had been waiting for him and it was clear that he was not a happy man.

"You know, your guy is guilty. No matter what you say to me or try to get me confused. He did it."

"Mr. Montoya, I have nothing to say to you. You can always talk to the D.A. if you like."

"You think this is all a lot of fun, don't you? You love making people look bad. Well, let me tell you something, I was telling the truth. Your guy is guilty as hell. You are scum – just another lawyer willing to say or do anything to get a guilty guy off. I hope you rot in hell."

Mike remembered that trial as if it was yesterday and he wondered if Montoya would ever let it go. He got his answer today when he saw Montoya at the grocery store.

NINE

MIKE WAS UP and at it early on October 12, the day set for the hearing. He barely looked at the newspaper as he ate some breakfast. One egg and a piece of toast were all that he could handle this morning. Then he was off to pick up Jim Haggerty. He thought things were looking good, as he steered his Audi A-6 onto Interstate-5 and made their way to Woodland and the Yolo County Courthouse. It was about a twenty to twenty-five minute ride. They both were upbeat. There was not much to say between them as they were already "all talked out," as his father used to say.

Parking a few blocks away, they walked briskly to the old courthouse and climbed the stairs, only to be met with a line about ten to twelve people. Everyone was being processed through the x-ray machines and the mandatory inspections. When it was their turn, they both "failed" the super-sensitive x-ray test and had to be manually checked for contraband by a young deputy sheriff who appeared to be too young to have ever seen actual street duty.

They sought out Department One and entered the courtroom. Judge Thoreson was droning on about some trespass and harassment case with a man and woman standing docilely before him. After scolding the woman, she told them to leave and sin no more. They picked up their papers and departed. The judge then announced that she would be taking a short break before the next case. Mike saw his client, Brian Darnoff, sitting quietly by himself in the left corner. He spoke to him for a few minutes and Darnoff wished him well. He also saw Jason and Linda Darnoff in another part of the audience. They were staring straight ahead. He studied them for a while trying to imagine either of them doing some bad stuff. But it just didn't register.

Some twenty minutes later, the judge appeared again. Black robe in place, she looked around to see who was attending today as she ascended the bench. The clerk called the case and there was the usual mumbling and shuffling of papers as the attorneys pushed their chairs up to the table and gave the judge their attention.

"The record will reflect that we are in court this morning, Tuesday, October 12, in the Darnoff case and specifically for an Order to Show Cause re: Contempt proceeding against Michael Zorich. Will all counsel please state your appearances?"

Attorneys for the mother and father identified themselves and attorneys for the other parties and entities did likewise. They were all there to see what was happening, not that they had a direct stake in today's proceedings. After Cannes and Haggerty identified themselves and their clients, the judge carried on, reading from her notes.

"First of all, Mr. Haggerty, has your client given the requested documents to Mr. Cannes?"

"No, your honor, he has not."

"Mr. Cannes, have you received the documents from any other source?"

"No, your honor, I have not."

"All right. Then, I guess we are ready to proceed with the Order to Show Cause. As you both know this is a different kind of case. A rare one. At least I don't have these kinds of cases every day. As I see it, it is quasi-criminal and Mr. Zorich is like a criminal defendant. He is presumed to be innocent. It will be the duty of the opposing side, specifically, you, Mr. Cannes, to prosecute and prove the contempt of court beyond a reasonable doubt. I will be sitting as the sole determiner of facts and law, without a jury. Mr. Zorich need not testify and cannot be compelled to do so. I don't imagine that any of this is a surprise to anyone. Are we ready to proceed?"

"Yes, your honor," answered Cannes.

Mike thought that Cannes answered that question a little too quickly. Haggerty rose slowly from his seat, adjusting his tie and buttoning his jacket, ever so slowly. He carried himself well in court. White-haired and stately, carrying a couple of extra pounds, Haggerty presented a fatherly figure. The wrinkles in his face corresponded with his years of court room experience. He exuded confidence and credibility. Jurors would hang on his words. If only judges would do the same.

"Yes, your honor," Jim said.

His deep voice almost vibrated off the plaster walls in the old courtroom. It was a rich voice and it immediately attracted the attention of anyone who was not paying attention. Haggerty paused for effect and cleared his throat.

"I am ready to proceed. But I have one matter to take up with the court first. With all due respect, your honor, we would at this time move to disqualify you on the basis of your involvement in this case. This is certainly not personal. But it would not seem that you can avoid the appearance of impropriety by sitting on the very case in which you issued the order in question. It is not that I or anyone is actually accusing you of any bias, but rather we are confronted with the question of appearance of impropriety, which, by itself, may well be grounds to set aside anything that might happen here today. No point in proceeding through a trial, only to have it thrown out on this basis alone without regard to the facts. Again, no personal accusation is meant by this motion. I have prepared a short brief on this matter with citations to authorities in support of my position."

Jim handed a copy to the judge and another copy to Cannes. The judge stared down from the bench. Certainly she had to expect this. She looked at the brief for a few minutes and then turned her attention to Cannes.

"Counsel, do you have something to say to Mr. Haggerty's motion?"

"Judge, I believe that you can be fair and, in fact, I further would think that these types of trials should occur before the judge before whom the contempt occurred. Nothing new here, Judge. This is very typical. You, as the judge before whom the contempt occurred, are the very best judge to decide this matter. If we follow Mr. Haggerty's suggestion, you would have to appear as a witness in another courtroom. There is no precedent for that."

Haggerty was back on his feet, deliberately buttoning his suit jacket before he began speaking, as he did every time he stood to address the court.

"Judge, this situation is uncommon, not normal. There is nothing typical here. You are being asked to find someone in contempt of court and you are the very person who is bringing the allegation and who saw the alleged contempt occur. Surely, the Court of Appeal would be most concerned with the appearance of impropriety in these circumstances. Again, no personal accusation is meant by this motion. Really, your honor, you should assign this matter to some other judge and allow the court process to happen. It is a legal question and this proceeding should not be affected by any other factor."

In Mike's mind, Jim was going a bit overboard with the "making nice" part. The judge gets the point or, at least, she has heard enough to understand our position that we are not trying to impugn her personally. But Mike was no longer his own attorney. At that point, Cannes spoke up.

"Your honor, if it would help I could take some time this morning to look over counsel's brief and check out his cases. I would need an hour or so."

"No, that won't be necessary, Mr. Cannes. As you might imagine, I have thought of this very issue. I find no authority for a mandatory recusal of myself. I do not see the need to grant your motion. That doesn't mean that in certain circumstances such a motion might not be appropriate. But, I don't think it is appropriate here. I harbor no ill will towards Mr. Zorich. I am doing my job and I would imagine that Mr. Zorich believes he is doing his job. I don't know. I can be fair and impartial and see no reason as to why I should be disqualified. The motion is denied. However, I will say this. If anyone feels that there are new facts that they wish to present, I will always reconsider my order today."

As far as Mike and Jim were concerned, this was an expected development. After all, if Judge Thoreson thought that she should not be sitting on this trial, she would have long ago disqualified herself. She did not. So it stood to reason that today she would take the same position.

"Mr. Cannes, you may proceed."

"Your honor, I will prove today that you issued a valid order and that you had jurisdiction over the person charged with contempt, Mr. Zorich, at the time of the order. I will prove that Mr. Zorich had full knowledge of your order. Further, I will prove that he deliberately disobeyed the order. There really can be no question about the facts, as they are known to us all. Most importantly and as I have already shown in my brief, disobeying a lawful order of the court is punishable by a fine of five thousand dollars and/or a sentence of six months in the county jail."

The words, "person charged with contempt," were jarring, but not as jarring as the words "six months in the county jail." Certainly neither Cannes nor Judge Thoreson actually believed that this "offense" was worthy of jail time, under any circumstances. But Mike had to admit to himself that Cannes correctly recited the legal parameters of the sentence that could be imposed, in the event of a conviction. Zorich knew in his heart that there could be no conviction so it was all a moot point.

Court proceedings were then interrupted when Judge Thoreson was given a note which told her that she needed to take a plea of guilty in a criminal case. It was a case set for trial that day and the district attorney and defense attorney had come to an agreement on a plea bargain. The presiding judge was too busy to handle it himself. So Judge Thoreson sent the attorneys in the Darnoff case out into the hall and dutifully attended to the criminal case. The delay only added to the tension.

The rest of the morning consisted of battling between two lawyers, Cannes and Haggerty, both of whom were arguing legal points and rules from cases of long ago. They debated the meaning of the term "valid order," in the context of a contradictory and pre-existing order from another court. The arguments went on for over an hour and a half. Shortly before lunch, Judge Thoreson announced that court would be adjourned for the lunch hour and that it would reconvene at two p.m. She explained that she was going to a judges' meeting and could not get back any sooner, at least not with any real guarantee. In lieu of having lawyers sitting around waiting for her, she thought the better idea would be to give a set time that was generous and one that she knew she could achieve. With that she left the bench.

"Everything about normal, I guess," Haggerty told Mike as they headed out of the court house.

"I suppose. But she seems to be very comfortable in this case. She is not the least bit likely to back off, is she?"

"No, probably not, Mike. We will have to do our best, but I am not picking up any signals of any last minute reprieve."

"So, then what?"

"Just what we discussed. She will find you in contempt of court, order you to produce the documents in two days and order you not to do it again. She will probably have her order sent on to the Disciplinary Section of the State Bar so that they can take a look at it. Maybe the State Bar will decide to take some action, but I think we can defend that pretty well. So I would not lose sleep over that possibility."

"I can live with that."

"She might decide to fine you, say a hundred dollars, kind of like the sanctions that are usually given out for being late or for failing to comply with discovery requests. I just don't know."

"Well, I can live with that, too."

"But nothing beyond that, if that is what you were thinking."

"Yes, that is what I was thinking. Jail."

"No way."

By then they arrived at one of the many lunch spots located close to the court house, all of which catered to the attorneys and their clients who were looking for a little respite from the morning's events.

After lunch the attorneys returned to court. The judge was a bit late. Cannes introduced a copy of the order and his own declaration in which he stated under penalty of perjury that he had properly requested the documents and had not received the documents. Further, he noted that the court had specifically ordered Mr. Zorich to comply and he refused. Cannes offered to testify to all of these facts, if necessary, but thought that he might just save everyone some time by using his declaration instead.

Then it was Mike's turn. He got up to testify when Haggerty called out his name. Mike moved slowly from the counsel table and took the oath from the clerk. He sat down and looked up at Jim.

"Mr. Zorich, please explain the situation with regard to the divorce case."

With that open-ended question, Mike was off to the races. "Judge Newman issued a Temporary Restraining Order and it was directed personally at all of the lawyers involved in the Darnoff matter, including the lawyers in this courtroom."

Judge Newman, a woman of about 65, had been sitting in the family law department for a long time, longer than most could remember. She had issued a Temporary Restraining Order, upon the request of Mrs. Darnoff's attorneys, who were trying to get to the bottom of Mr. Darnoff's financial dealings, so as to determine the value of the couple's estate for purposes of an appropriate property division. Mrs. Darnoff was convinced that her husband and his attorneys were going to destroy all evidence of their financial dealings or at least enough evidence to make her job of proving that the assets were all obtained during the course of their marriage and not before, most difficult. She knew her husband well.

"What were the parameters of that order?"

"None of us were allowed to copy, transfer, distribute or otherwise dispose of any financial documents connected to our respective clients, without the court's specific order. She said that her order would remain in effect until she determined that it no longer served any useful purpose in the divorce action. And she said that anyone wanting this information was to apply to Judge Newman and, upon noticed motion, she would rule."

As Mike spoke, he saw his son Peter enter the courtroom and take a seat. He was a little surprised to see Peter. Even though they had spoken about this case a couple of days ago, Mike wasn't sure that Peter was serious about coming to court to see him.

"To your knowledge, Mr. Zorich, did anyone ever file such a motion?"

Haggerty wanted to emphasize the alternative approach that could have avoided this whole hearing before Judge Thoreson and Mike smiled to himself at the question.

"No, nobody ever did."

"Specifically, did Mr. Cannes file such a motion?"

"No he did not."

"By the way, Mr. Zorich, was Mr. Cannes himself a subject of this Temporary Restraining order?"

"Yes, he was. He was personally included in the order, along with every other lawyer who had any remote connection to the Darnoff case."

"Tell me, Mr. Zorich, how long had the Darnoffs been married?"

"I am not sure but I think it was close to 50 years. It was certainly more than 40."

"Do you know how many financial documents they acquired during that time?"

"I don't know the specifics. But there were many partnerships and real estate dealings. The family made its money in the wine business and then got into real estate development."

"Can you be a bit more specific of the quantity of documents that we are talking about here?"

"Counsel for Mrs. Darnoff has estimated that his client is in possession of over thirty banker size boxes. I am sure that Mr. Darnoff is in possession of that number at a minimum. Probably more, as he was the manager of much of the business. In addition, the various partnerships have documents that are kept by the children who are managing partners or serve in some similar capacity. I would think that there are probably around one hundred banker size boxes all together, but I don't know for sure."

"Mr. Zorich, to this point have you transferred any financial information regarding the Darnoff case to anyone, including counsel?"

"No, I have not."

"Why not?"

"Because to transfer these documents after a specific court order not to do so would put me in contempt of court for violating Judge Newman's order."

"Other than the Temporary Restraining Order, was there any other reason for not transferring such information?

"No, there was not. I am sure that normal discovery in the divorce case would have meant a request from counsel for Mrs. Darnoff, asking for all of the financial information from Mr. Darnoff. But that never happened."

"So what you are saying is that counsel for Mrs. Darnoff had not even requested this information in the divorce case?"

Jim was pointing out the absurdity of a lawyer in a secondary case trying to get information that was unavailable to the lawyers in the main case.

"Yes, that is correct," Mike answered.

"Mr. Zorich, how many business entities are connected to the Darnoff family dealings?"

"I believe that there are five."

"What about counsel for the corporation and other entities, have they requested this financial information from Mr. Darnoff?"

"Other than Mr. Cannes, no."

"So Mr. Cannes is the only attorney in this whole operation who has requested the financial information?"

"Yes, that is right."

One could never do with enough repetition on the right point, Mike thought to himself as he answered.

"And is Mr. Cannes directly involved in the divorce case?"

"No, he is not. He is only involved in one case, the partnership with the children."

"One final question, Mr. Zorich, do you know if Judge Newman is even aware that an attorney is trying to disobey her order by demanding the production of this financial information in direct violation of her order?"

This last question should hit home as it was the simple fact that to obey Judge Thoreson's order meant disobeying Judge Newman's order.

"I don't believe that she is aware, Mr. Haggerty. We have not had a hearing before her since this hearing was scheduled. It is possible that someone told her. I don't know. I have not had any communication with her. And you told me that you tried to get a hold of her and that she is out of the country at this time."

"Objection, hearsay, your honor."

"Sustained."

"Thank you, Mr. Zorich. I don't have anything else, your honor," Jim said as he sat down.

Mike thought to himself of his situation. He was between a rock and a hard place, between the devil and the deep. He wondered about the former deputy district attorney who was now sitting as the judge in this courtroom. He did not think that Thoreson would want to be seen as indecisive or as soft, particularly not as soft. Mike stared out from the witness chair and caught Peter's eye in the back of the courtroom. He gave Peter a quick smile.

"Thank you, Mr. Haggerty. Mr. Cannes, do you have any questions?"

All lawyers have questions so this question to counsel was always a bit comical. Cannes rose from his seat in an almost circling fashion, kind of like the lion moving toward his kill. His head was slightly down, studying the weave of the carpet. He had no notepad and both hands were at his side.

"Mr. Zorich, let me start by asking you this question. Judge Thoreson is in fact a sitting Superior Court judge, is she not?"

Mike thought that question a bit odd.

"Yes, she is a judge sitting in court."

"Judges issue orders from time to time, do they not?"

"Yes they do."

"In fact, Judge Thoreson issues orders from time to time, does she not?"

"Yes."

Mike could now see where this was going.

"In fact, Judge Thoreson has issued orders in this case, has she not?

"Yes."

"Now, I'm just looking at the order in question wherein you were ordered to turn over to me all financial records of your client Brian Darnoff. Do you agree with me that it was a lawful order? Again, I am only looking at this order and no other order."

"I suppose, but you cannot look at this order without considering the other order of Judge Newman."

"Mr. Zorich, I will get to that order. For the time being, could you please humor me? I am only asking about this order by itself. I am looking at this order in a vacuum, so to speak. Do you agree with me that it was a lawful order?"

Haggerty was on his feet.

"Your honor, objection. This question is irrelevant to today's proceedings. You cannot look at the one order of this court without looking at the other order of the other court. Also, he is asking for a legal opinion, which is inadmissible."

"I will allow it, counsel. Objection overruled. Proceed, Mr. Cannes."

"Thank you, your honor. I repeat, Mr. Zorich, looking at Judge Thoreson's order in this way, do you agree with me that it was a lawful order."

Try as he might to avoid the question, it was becoming increasingly difficult. Mike hesitated and looked down from the witness chair.

"Yes, I agree, putting it the way you say. But that is like asking if my blue car is really red, if I put aside the blue paint for the moment. It makes no sense."

Mike enjoyed his little analogy, which he thought of in the moment. It did not allow Cannes the pleasure of a clean answer. But Cannes was undaunted. Mike could see that Peter liked it too.

"All right, we have established that the order was lawful if seen by itself. Now let me ask you this. Did you obey this order of Judge Thoreson?"

Cannes was going to persist in this little word game, no matter what. Mike paused for a moment.

"No I did not because Judge Newman ordered me not to. If I followed Judge Thoreson's order I would be in violation of Judge Newman's order. Judge Newman issued her order first."

Mike wanted to emphasize this last point as it was an important point of law.

"Okay, as I understand it, you are saying that Judge Newman ordered you not to follow Judge Thoreson's order, is that right?"

"No, I didn't say that, Mr. Cannes. Judge Thoreson's order had not yet been issued. Judge Newman ordered me not to turn over Mr. Darnoff's financial records to anyone."

Mike was getting a bit peeved, but he did not want Cannes to have the satisfaction of knowing that.

"So she did not order you to disobey Judge Thoreson's order, right?"

"Correct, because Judge Thoreson's order had not yet been issued."

Cannes had a way of making himself even more unlikeable than he already was.

"But you interpreted her order to mean that you could not follow Judge Thoreson's order, right?"

"Yes, I interpreted her order that way. I don't know how else you could interpret it. I can't provide the documents, period."

"So, this is about your interpretation of some other order, is that correct, counsel?"

"Interpretation or not, Judge Newman ordered me not to do the very thing that Judge Thoreson is ordering me to do. I was faced with an impossible choice. If I obeyed Judge Thoreson, I am in violation of Judge Newman's earlier, valid order."

"But you do agree, that different people, even different lawyers, can interpret orders differently, do you not? Again I am just asking as a principle of human experience, in a vacuum, if you will."

"Objection, your honor. Mr. Zorich is not here as an expert psychologist on whether people interpret things differently," Jim snapped.

"I will allow it counsel. Please repeat the question, Ms. Reporter."

The reporter did as instructed and Mike paused.

"No, I don't believe in this case that there is any other logical interpretation."

Mike was adamant and refused to be drawn into Cannes' hypothetical question.

"That is all, your honor."

"You may sit down, Mr. Zorich."

Cannes sat down without looking at his papers which were scattered on the desk in front of him. He was very satisfied. Always good to end cross-examination on a good note and he at least got Mike to admit that he was relying on his interpretation of an order as opposed to a specific order. That was something. If and when this case goes up on appeal that would be something else for Mike to confront. And it would be something else for the justices on the Court of Appeal to think about.

Mike was a bit flushed. It is a very strange experience to be questioned in court or even at a deposition. There is a feeling of being out of control, not knowing what will happen next. As a lawyer, Mike knew that once a question was asked, the chances were that he would have to answer it. So being questioned was a little like sitting in the arcade at the state fair waiting for the next shooter.

Judge Thoreson studied the papers in front of her on the bench, with her head down for a minute or so.

"Anything else, counsel?"

Judge Thoreson was not looking at anyone. No one responded.

"Mr. Cannes, please explain to me why you think Mr. Zorich is in contempt of court."

Judge Thoreson did not need the answer to the question. She already knew. But the question implied a search for truth, an honest attempt to determine whether Mike was guilty or not. It would look good in the transcript on appeal. Besides, she needed to throw one down the middle to Cannes so that the record would be very clear. Cannes, quick to the punch, supplied Judge Thoreson with all of the information she needed.

"Your honor, an order is an order. You have the right to issue orders. You have the right to expect them to be obeyed. This is not just disobedience by a party appearing before him but this is defiance by a member of the bar. That is another thing altogether. As Mr. Zorich said, he based his actions on his interpretation of another order."

Cannes emphasized the word "interpretation," as he paced behind the table situated in the bowels of the courtroom.

"Attorneys have heightened duties. They are members of the Court for crying out loud. They have to follow the law and that includes this court's orders. Their duty is not to interpret but rather to follow orders of the court. At the end of the day, your honor, there is absolutely no excuse for this conduct. I ask that you find Mr. Zorich in contempt of court and that he be dealt with accordingly."

Mike jumped ever so little in his seat as he heard the words "dealt with accordingly." He didn't like to hear that and the last thing he expected was to be "dealt with accordingly," assuming that meant a fine or, God forbid, jail. But the thought did cross his mind.

Judge Thoreson gave Haggerty the last word, but it was more like the final words of a man about to be executed. The words did not resonate with the court. Judge Thoreson did not even offer eye contact to the lawyer. Instead she was busy writing on her pad of paper. For all Mike knew, she was simply doodling. But Mike then thought otherwise, figuring that she had begun writing out her order before Haggerty had the opportunity to make his final comments in a last heroic attempt to save the day.

Jim finally stopped and simply said, "I have nothing more to say."

Judge Thoreson looked up after a couple of seconds.

"Mr. Haggerty, was there any evidence that your client had asked Judge Newman for clarification of her order or whether he had requested that Judge Newman modify her order so that he would not be subject to another court order in another court?"

"No, your honor, I don't believe that there is any such evidence. As Mr. Zorich said, I don't believe that Judge Newman is even aware of your order."

A silence followed. It seemed like half an hour but was really only a few seconds. The judge's voice was strained.

"I find you in contempt of court, Mr. Zorich. Your explanation for not following this court's unequivocal order is not persuasive. You are remanded to the custody of the Sheriff of Yolo County forthwith to serve five days in the county jail. Deputy, please take custody of Mr. Zorich."

Mike's body shook and his face flushed red. His throat was dry as he asked himself if what he just heard was true. Haggerty was on his feet.

"Your honor, I must object most vehemently to your order."

"I understand, counsel," the judge replied, in a matter-of-fact tone.

"Your honor, five days in jail is completely inappropriate, even in light of the court's findings."

Haggerty was just about shouting at this point.

"I understand, counsel. That is my order."

Judge Thoreson stood and was gathering her papers and the case file, preparing to leave the bench.

Mike could scarcely believe what he just heard. "You are remanding me to jail, you have got to be kidding," he said to no one in particular.

There was a commotion in the back of the courtroom. Then Mike heard a very familiar voice.

"You can't do that. He didn't do anything. You can't do that."

Peter was yelling while an officer was making his way in his direction.

"Bailiff, please take charge of that individual and escort him out of the courtroom immediately. Ladies and gentlemen, there will be no talking of any kind while this court is in session. Am I clear? The next time something like that happens, someone is going to jail."

Mike turned to see the officer pushing Peter out of the courtroom. Because he was seated in the back row, it wasn't very far. He strained to look at Peter to see what was happening. But all he could see was the back of his son as he left the courtroom. His client, Brian Darnoff, sat in his seat looking totally perplexed. Meanwhile Haggerty was focusing on the matter at hand.

"Your honor, could you at least set bail on appeal. We most certainly will seek review before the Third District Court of Appeal."

Now Cannes was on his feet.

"We object, your honor. There is no need for bail."

The minute he uttered the words, Cannes realized that he had overreached. No need for bail, when an attorney is being sent to jail? Cannes knew that his automatic trial lawyer response was a little much. In fact, it was ridiculous.

"No, counsel, I will allow bail. Bail is set in the amount of five thousand dollars on appeal. That is all. Court is adjourned."

With that the judge hit her gavel rather loudly on the bench and immediately departed from the courtroom. Mike was still sitting in his chair in something of a daze, never really expecting it to come to this. He recalled reading about the syndrome, so often experienced by those waiting to be executed, of the constant expectation of a reprieve, a pardon. It did not happen. What he had expected that morning as he climbed the steps to the courthouse turned out to be true. Exactly true.

Now he was enshrouded in the warm glow of anger. He was furious that this lame excuse for a judge would take such an action against him. Putting him in jail? Mike was not going to take this sitting down.

Still he was more than uncomfortable at being asked to place his hands behind him and to feel the cold clasp of the hand cuffs as they snapped tightly around his wrists. He darted one glance back at his son who was no longer in the courtroom. Then he adjusted his eyes straight-ahead on the door to the court-room, where the prisoners entered and exited. He was now one of them for the first time in his life.

"I will call Denny and get bail right away," Jim said. "You won't be tied up all that long."

Mike was amused by the words "tied up," but said nothing. Cannes looked on with a steady stare as if daring Mike to look at him. There was just a hint of a smile on his face. Mike noticed. Jim Haggerty was packing his bags.

Mike was ushered into the holding tank where he was told to take a seat among a group of other defendants who were either going to court that day or had already concluded their business. Either way, dressed in a suit, he was clearly out of place. A few looked him over and one even asked why he was locked up. Mike said nothing.

TEN

THE SHORT DRIVE to the Sheriff's Department in the back of a cruiser was more humiliating than anything else. Mike looked around to see if anyone was looking at him. He was convinced that the entire local bar was out on the streets that damp October morning, just waiting to catch a glimpse of the respected counselor. They were not out there, but that did not diminish the expectation that they were, not one bit. Mike kept reminding himself that he had done nothing wrong. He repeated it again and again in his mind, hoping that it would stick.

At the entrance to the county jail, Mike was told to exit the vehicle, which he did promptly. His anger was giving way to subservience. He was escorted through the doors which automatically opened into a foyer, consisting of several old, wooden chairs next to a large counter. A grizzled sergeant who was on duty that day stood behind the counter. The sergeant was staring at the well-dressed criminal as he walked toward him.

"What have we here, Bob?"

The deputy who had taken charge of Mike in the courtroom looked up abruptly.

"Judge Thoreson found him to be in contempt of court, five thousand dollars bail. He's an attorney. I don't have any paperwork yet. I am hoping that you can handle it all with your usual stuff, okay?"

"Sure."

The clang of the heavy steel door was sharp and loud. Mostly it was loud. It echoed throughout the waiting room where Mike Zorich sat on a stiff wooden bench. His head was down and he could see dark blood stains on the bench, unmistakable even to the untrained eye. The linoleum under the bench was worn where countless shoes rested for hours on end. Mike Zorich, age fifty four and prominent trial attorney in Sacramento was being booked into the Yolo County Jail. For all intents and purposes, he was a common criminal who had committed a violent crime and was now being brought to justice. But this was not the case at all.

Things went very well, in the eyes of the sandy-haired desk sergeant, a veteran of 28 years at the department. He wished all bookings went as smoothly as this one. It was rare to see any attorney, especially a well-known attorney, being booked into the Yolo County Jail. This one was clean-shaven and wearing a handsome blue suit with a nicely-starched white shirt complete with silver cuff links. He was obviously nervous but he gave no trouble to anyone.

Usually the sergeant was given the initial arrest report from the arresting officer, but not this time, because there was no paperwork. So he asked a clerk at a nearby cubicle to obtain a "rap" sheet from the State Office of Criminal Investigation and Identification. Then he opened his computer to the initial criminal booking page. Calling out Mike's name, he summoned him to his desk.

"Name?"

"Michael M. Zorich."

"Age?"

"54."

"Height?"

"Six feet."

"Weight?"

"175."

"Color of hair?"

"Black going on white, I guess."

"Color of eyes?"

"Brown."

"Any scars or distinguishing marks?"

"No. Wait, yes, I do have one. Here, look."

He extended his hand to show an old injury on his fourth finger of his left hand. The sergeant studied it for a minute and wrote something down. Mike couldn't see what he wrote.

He glanced around amazed at the busy activity of the booking area. A lot of people were coming and going. Doors were constantly being opened and closed. The fingerprinting followed some more questions so that the sergeant could complete his paper work. The CII rap sheet confirmed his lack of a prior record.

The booking process took about fifteen minutes. After answering questions and waiting for the process to be completed, Mike was led to a small room containing a wooden table, two chairs and a phone. Left alone he dialed his law partner, Denny Grantham, and got him on his cell in his car. Denny was already making preparations to post bail, having heard from Jim a bit earlier that morning. Finding the cash would be no problem and that was preferable to wasting ten percent on a bond and a bail bondsman.

Denny hustled over to a branch of the Bank of America, where he obtained a cashier's check for five thousand dollars. Then he drove over to Woodland where he presented the check to the desk sergeant. Mike sat in the room by himself with nothing to do for the hour it took Denny to get there. Then it was another fifteen minutes before they let him go.

"Thanks, man. I appreciate it."

"No problem. Just as you figured, I guess. But I was still surprised that she remanded you jail," Denny said.

"Yeah, me too. I figure that she planned to put me in jail all along. She and Cannes are pieces of work, you know? Cannes was really smug today. He knew that he had me on the ropes. He was walking around that courtroom like he owned the place. Maybe he does, who knows?"

"So, how are you feeling?"

"Pissed off. I would like to punch someone out." Mike paused. "Have you seen Peter? He was in the courtroom and then got taken out by the bailiff when he shouted out."

"Yeah, he is still here. I saw him as I drove up but I didn't want to delay any longer. Let's go find him."

Mike could not prevent his hand from trembling and figured that Denny noticed it. Trying not to be conspicuous, he was at a loss for words. Getting thrown in jail over something like this had a crushing impact on a decent, hard-working person just doing his job. His job happened to be under the watchful eye of the law. As with any lawyer practicing in the courts, he was especially vulnerable to the whims of the judge who ruled with just about unfettered discretion.

"Dad." Mike heard Peter the moment he emerged from the building. "I can't believe what I saw. That was so unfair. You didn't do anything wrong. She had it in for you. I can't believe it."

"Things happen, Peter. It's the wonderful world of the law."

"Does this happen all the time? I just come to court to see you and the next thing they are arresting you and taking you away."

"No, it doesn't happen all the time. In fact, this is the first time. You just happened to be here. It's not every day you get to see your father hauled away in handcuffs."

"I had no idea that a judge could do that. You were just representing your client. How could she do that?"

"Peter, as a wise man once told me, there is no one more powerful in our society than a sitting trial judge. Once they get the black robe, they can pretty much do what they want. Whether it sticks on appeal or not is another question. Even if it is thrown out on appeal, that all takes time. But right now, appeal doesn't do me a lot of good."

Denny was standing by and taking in the whole scene between father and son.

"Hey, guys, I have to go."

"Fine," Mike said, while staring off a bit, as the three walked to the public parking lot near the county jail. "I suppose I should too. How are you doing, Peter?"

"I'm okay. I am just happy that you are okay. That was some excitement. I still can't believe it."

They all got into their separate cars and left. In about thirty minutes, Mike and Denny were walking into their law office.

"I don't want to do that again," Mike said.

"I can understand that. Neither would I. Getting hauled away could not have been fun for you."

"This is not going to be that easy. Cannes has it in for me and he has the judge's ear. Judge Thoreson was in her own world up there. I have to figure out some way to turn this thing around," Mike said.

"Well, appeal is the obvious thing to do. But are you thinking of something else?"

"What I would like to do is to inflict some pain on her, if you want to know the truth."

"Yeah, I bet. In fact, I will go along with you and do my thing."

Denny knew that Mike was joking. But there was no laughter from either of them. It was obvious that Mike was mad. The color in his face was a giveaway.

"Well, short of that, why don't you win on the battlefield? Let's put together a winning brief on appeal and have him and that Judge Thoreson taken down a peg or two," Denny said.

"That all takes time. Appeals are not the surest bet, as you know. Only about 20% of appeals in civil matters are ever granted, if that much. So I could spend a lot of money and time and end up losing. And to top it off, the appellate court could end up publishing the decision. You just never know about an appeal."

"That is all true, but you have to try. You have to give it a go, Mike. When you think about it, you have no choice."

Back in Woodland, Robert Cannes could not suppress a decidedly different mood. After court, he returned to his office. He missed all of the action at the jail, but he could imagine just what was happening and it was all good. As he walked up to the back door of his office, he had a rare smile on his face. He put his briefcase in his office and emerged to find his secretary returning to her desk with a cup of coffee which she offered to him.

"Thanks, but I won't need that. Just got a big win in the Darnoff case. A very big win. I am going to take a couple of days off. Give me a ring if you need me. Otherwise, I will see you the first of next week."

He left before she could say much of anything. She stared at him as he walked out, shocked at his announcement that he was taking time off. Robert Cannes went home and met his wife who was packed and ready to go. As he put their overnight bags into the back of his silver BMW 528, his mind raced with the happenings of the Darnoff case. He and his wife were off for the weekend to a swanky golf resort in Napa. And he was feeling good. He was feeling very good.

He had managed to get his opposing attorney found in contempt of court. Mike Zorich had been hauled off to jail right out of the courtroom. How sweet was that? He could not imagine a more deserving person. Zorich and Cannes went back a long way. Seven years ago Cannes lost a case to Mike. It was a private arbitration held before a retired judge.

Cannes represented two partners in a law firm who wanted to get rid of their third partner. So, they dissolved the law firm and kicked out their third partner, represented by Zorich, only to have the arbitrator rule in favor of Zorich's client. The arbitrator, a graying retired judge from San Francisco County Superior Court, found that the dissolution was not proper. Cannes' clients had simply not followed the law. They figured that they could just do what they wanted to do but they needed to obtain the consent of the third partner. It was pretty basic.

The problem was that Cannes had advised his clients every step of the way. They counted on his legal advice only to be told by the retired judge that they were wrong. Cannes had misread the Corporations Code, because he really did not understand all of the intricacies of partnership law. It really was sloppy work and Cannes eventually saw it for himself.

During the hearing, the arbitrator's questions and comments made the outcome predictable. At the end of the hearing, the arbitrator left the room after announcing that he would take the matter under submission. It was only the two of them. It had not gone well for Cannes and he knew it. As he was packing his briefcase, Mike looked at him and said "better luck next time, my friend." Cannes shot him a glance, his lips closely bound together, as if he was about to spit on Mike. They did not talk as they walked out and went their separate ways. But Cannes never forgot that little incident. He saw Mike Zorich as a big jerk and an ungracious one at that.

In four or five days, the award arrived in the mail. The retired judge had issued a well-reasoned and somewhat lengthy "arbitration award," which had the effect of a final and binding court ruling. Cannes had lost on all counts.

All Mike had to do was to petition the local court to convert the award to a judgment and, presto, he was in business. He could enforce the award. The award was not appealable under California law so, there would be no delay. The loss to Cannes' clients had been swift and complete.

Within two days of receiving the award in the mail, Mike was on the phone telling Cannes that he was going to ask for attorneys' fees from the retired judge, but would not do so if Cannes simply sent over a tidy check for $30,000. This was a bitter pill to swallow for anyone, to say nothing of Mr. Robert Cannes. To lose and then to pay the other side's attorneys' fees is adding insult to injury. But Cannes sent over the check, paid out of his own checking account, fearing that a larger award might be entered against his clients if Mike pressed the point. Cannes would be reimbursed by his clients. Main thing was to get this case over.

Cannes' clients naturally asked Cannes why he advised them as he did. Cannes could only admit to himself that he did not really understand partnership dissolution law as well as Zorich, who had the intelligence to write a commanding brief pointing out all of Cannes' failings for the world to see. But to his clients, he had no answer. Oh, he complained about the retired judge and argued that Zorich had to have some kind of an "in" with him. But this lame explanation did not account for the simple fact that Cannes had agreed to use this retired judge for the arbitration and, in fact, Cannes was the one who originally recommended him.

The further problem was that Cannes in his usual haughty manner had written letters to Zorich, promising to "destroy" his client in cross-examination. He told Zorich in one memorable letter that Cannes' bite was much worse than his bark. He recounted his record of winning cases and promised to do the same in this case. He even got to the point of offering to settle only on grounds of complete capitulation by Zorich and the payment of Cannes' legal fees. It was pure hubris. Zorich had refused and had pressed on to the arbitration hearing where he won a convincing victory.

The whole question of paying the attorneys' fees to Zorich was like adding fuel to the fire. The clients simply refused to reimburse Cannes and dared him to sue them. In the end, Robert Cannes was left holding the bag for the thirty thousand dollars. Most people don't forget things like that. Robert Cannes was no exception.

To make matters worse, Cannes later learned that his two clients had actually called Mike Zorich and asked if he would be willing to take an attorney malpractice case against Cannes on a contingency. Mike was inclined to take the case realizing how much money was involved. But on reflection he declined, figuring that he might be taking the whole thing a bit too far. Still, the mere thought of going back to court against Cannes had been most tantalizing.

Robert Cannes could feel the sting even today. He winced every time he saw the letterhead or the pleading paper with the words "Grantham and Zorich, Attorneys at Law" on the top. That little phrase repeatedly stared back at him whenever he did anything on the case. It was as if he was reliving the old arbitration case.

With the developments in court on October 12, he had achieved some measure of comeuppance. And he was savoring every minute of it. Cannes was packing the trunk of his car. He and his wife had planned this little trip down the road to Napa, checking into one of the cottage units adjacent to many privately-owned condominiums at the Silverado Country Club. It was just what he needed. His phone rattled with the usual ringtone and he immediately checked to see who was calling. It was Judge Karen Thoreson. He stepped out of the garage of his home to ensure better reception.

"Good morning, Judge."

Cannes answered, all the while wondering why the judge was calling him.

"Robert, how are you?"

Not waiting for an answer, the judge got to the point of the call.

"I am a little worried about the proceedings on the OSC. Throwing an attorney in jail is not something I do every day. I guess I wanted a little assurance that you have my back all the way to the appellate court."

Judge Thoreson was referring to the need for an appropriate and strong response to the inevitable appeal of the contempt order that Zorich was sure to bring. It would be brought nominally against the judge asking the Court of Appeal to overturn the contempt of court proceeding. Judges never appeared in such cases. Instead, it was up to the opposing party, Robert Cannes, to defend the court order.

Cannes knew right away that this phone call was wrong. Just like the other phone calls from Judge Thoreson, Cannes knew that there was no way any judge should be talking to any attorney about a pending case outside of the other attorney's presence. This call was completely and totally unethical both for the judge and for the attorney. It was obvious that Judge Thoreson was worried. Cannes hesitated to say anything.

"Judge, with all due respect, I don't think we should be talking about this case."

"I understand, Robert. But the case is over now so I don't think there is a problem. I just want to know how it stands on appeal, that's all."

Cannes knew that the case was not over. It was still pending in Judge Thoreson's court even though there was a strong possibility that Zorich would take it up on appeal. He hesitated a bit longer not knowing exactly what to say. After an awkward moment, Cannes figured that he had no choice. Besides, nobody would ever know. Judge Thoreson wasn't going to tell anyone.

"Well, there's no real problem, judge. I have it covered. I think we will do fine on appeal."

"That is not exactly what I need to hear, Robert. I need to know for sure. I do not want to be reversed again by the grand gurus on the Third District."

"What else can I do, judge? I will write a strong brief. I will argue the case personally. You have a tremendous presumption in your favor in support of all rulings at the trial court level. You will likely win, judge. But I can't guarantee it. No. No lawyer can guarantee his results."

There was a silence as the judge did not respond to his comments. Cannes was not giving Judge Thoreson the kind of comfort she wanted. But really there was nothing else to do.

"Think about it, Robert. Think about it. I need to know for sure."

"All right, Bye."

With that the call was over. What was Cannes supposed to think about? He would do his best. The more he thought about it, the more perplexed he became. First, he was worried that he had just taken part in an obviously unethical phone call. Second, this call was very strange even if it was from a friend. He and Judge Thoreson went back a long way, all the way to the time when the young prosecutor stopped by his office one day, unannounced, and introduced herself. A bit unusual, he thought at the time. But soon they had become friends. Cannes got to know a little something of the workings of the law enforcement system and it never hurt to know someone in the district attorneys' office on a personal level. You never knew when you needed a favor.

Cannes figured that Judge Thoreson was an ambitious type and he was right. Some years later, she called Cannes and asked him to write a letter to the Governor on her behalf for an appointment to the bench. Cannes obliged and Judge Thoreson had been especially gracious to him ever since. The two had become pretty good friends over the years although it was strictly a business friendship.

A few minutes later he was driving the 50 miles down Interstate 80 to their hotel in Napa. His wife was sitting next to him but they hardly talked. He was lost in his thoughts and they were not good thoughts. She knew to leave him alone when he got like this.

Why had Judge Thoreson called him? What was he supposed to do? Cannes had to prepare for the legal challenge to the judge's contempt of court finding. He knew that Zorich would fight him and he relished the fight. Cannes would win that one too. He knew it. Then Zorich would have to explain to his clients, to the bar association and to the world that he was found in contempt of court and the finding was upheld by the Court of Appeal. Cannes would just remain quiet, smug in the glow of his achievement. But it would take work. That was not the problem. The problem was Judge Thoreson. Her phone call didn't make sense.

After about an hour they arrived and checked in. He asked the front desk to make reservations for them at a favorite restaurant in St. Helena. But first, he thought a phone call was in order. He walked out of the hotel and he pulled out his cell phone and dialed the number for Tom Summers. He hoped that the reception would be all right.

"Is Tom available?"

The usual pleasantries upon making a call were becoming a little too much for Cannes this autumn afternoon. He waited for a minute or so and Tom came on the line.

"Listen, Tom, this Darnoff case. Any updates on Zorich?"

"Well, I gave you what we have. Don't think there is much more to it. Not a lot on Zorich out there, as you might guess. He hasn't been in any trouble, as far as we can see."

"So, nothing else?"

"Not really. We have newspaper clippings on old cases. He did file one case against a client for non-payment of his fees. Hard to know what happened with the case, as it was dismissed before trial. He probably settled. Other than that we haven't found a thing."

"Look, Tom. Zorich was just found in contempt of court and booked into jail. He made bail and is out. He is sure to bring an appeal or a writ and take this to the Court of Appeal. If you find anything on that, I need to know. I have to win that case."

There was a pause, as Tom Summers reflected on what he heard.

"Okay, Robert. But I am not sure what you mean. How would I find anything on that?"

"I don't know, Tom. I can tell you this. Mike Zorich is the biggest asshole in the world. He just struts around the courtroom like he knows everything. He needs to be told the facts of life. Judge Thoreson is the one who found him in contempt and she wants me to do everything I can to support her order. So, I just thought I would give you a call to see if you can help me. That's all."

Tom did not know what to say.

Cannes broke the momentary silence. "How is your guy Bolger working out? Okay?"

"Yeah, sure. What do you mean?"

"Nothing, I was just thinking. Maybe he has some ideas. He's been around. The point is that Judge Thoreson is pretty worked up over this whole deal. She means business."

Summers couldn't tell if Cannes was speaking for Judge Thoreson or was using that as a cover and was speaking for himself. And he couldn't tell what Cannes was asking him to do, although he began to get an idea. The mention of Bolger had triggered a light bulb.

"Okay, Robert. I'm on it," was all that he could come up with, not quite knowing why he even said that.

"Tom, I have to win that case," Cannes said. "It means a lot to me, personally. It means a lot to Judge Thoreson. Just do what you can. Thanks."

Tom Summers was more perplexed than he liked to be. "What to do?" He was not dense. He got the message from Robert Cannes. But then again he was a licensed private investigator. He did his job with pride. He enjoyed his reputation and he enjoyed the money that he obtained from the local members of the bar.

As for his part-time employee, Frank Bolger, Tom Summers generally liked what he saw. He brought a genuine energy to his assignments. But then again, he barely knew the guy. He had checked him out before hiring him and found the prior record but every one deserved a second chance. Tom was used to that. Bolger wasn't the first ex-con he had hired. After all, just who exactly did he think he would attract to his office in the first place? The pay was not exactly in six figures.

Tom Summers himself was caught up in a major construction defect case, currently set for trial in just two weeks in San Francisco Superior Court. He was meeting with counsel every day. He would be testifying as to defects he discovered and information that he passed on to other experts. This was a big case and Tom was at the center of it. The fees from this case were huge and the attorneys' appetite for meeting and preparation appeared to be endless. All of this was well and good for Tom, as it meant that his meter was running all the while. The checks each and every month were sizable.

But this also meant he had little time to oversee Frank Bolger. It was a good thing that he had one of his trusted lieutenants to take care of Frank, to see that everything was in order.

ELEVEN

IT WAS ABOUT a week later and Frank Bolger went to the closet in his studio apartment in midtown Sacramento and looked for a sweatshirt to put over his long-sleeve tattered blue shirt. As he passed the thermostat on the far wall, he glanced at the temperature. Fifty-nine degrees wasn't going to work today, even if Frank needed to save on his electricity bill. So he moved the dial upwards. He sat down on the bench-style seat at the small table and ran his fingers through his thinning hair as he took a sip of beer from the open can. At forty-eight years of age, 5'10" with a large build and nearly bald with longish and unkempt sideburns, Frank would never be confused for a Hollywood movie star. But then he did not much care how he looked. He could scrub himself up and make a decent appearance if he had to. It was just that he never had to.

The old RCA television was blaring from its perch on top of the countertop. It was just more about unemployment rising and layoffs. Same old stuff. The economy is in the crapper. Nobody is doing anything about it. Another depression is about to happen. Frank made the customary visits to the blood clinic to collect his weekly stipend. On a good month he could get two hundred fifty dollars. Plus there was the general assistance grant for another two hundred dollars. Every now and then he would pick up some odd job, such as moving furniture, delivering newspapers on a substitute basis or washing dishes at some restaurant when they had a big crowd. Scrapping it all together, he made out all right. His expenses were not much.

Ever since Desert Storm, he hungered for the thrill of the chase, the rush of the action. He had spent twelve months in Kuwait as a military policeman. Mainly, he directed traffic in a small village not too far from the Iraqi border. He heard stories of the real combat from returning soldiers. Occasionally, there would be a convoy to a nearby hamlet, but Frank had managed to avoid much real shooting. He never fired his .45 handgun or his rifle. And for this, Frank was genuinely disappointed.

But then his time was up and he came home. There was nothing much to talk about and this suited Frank just fine. He would say he did not want to talk about the war, leaving the listener to think that things must have been unimaginable, that Frank had suffered beyond comprehension. Frank liked that. The impression was far better than reality.

After the war, Frank went to school, but limited means and a limited I.Q. meant a limited education. The VA did not offer much. A couple of years at De Anza College in Cupertino, about 50 miles south of San Francisco, had convinced Frank that formal education was not going to do it for him. He needed something else. After a bit, he took the State civil service examination to become a correctional officer and failed it. Two years later he tried again and, miracle of miracles, he passed. His prior military police background in the army helped him make up for the scores on his tests which were lower than the State really liked to see.

But there were no jobs. Frank waited. Eventually, the benefit of passing the state examination paid off and he answered an ad for a job in Sacramento. He got on with a private security firm mostly focused on big warehouses in the industrial section of town. So he moved to Sacramento and found a place an apartment complex on the corner of 26th and J Streets in midtown. It was frequented by other working stiffs and their families. His apartment was one of the older ones and run down. Hot water was always an issue.

Then his troubles began. With increasing frequency, Frank would drink too much. Then something bad would happen. Usually, Frank would get into a shouting match with some well-dressed patron at a bar over politics or sports or religion or some other topic of the day. If that was all it was, Frank would walk home. No harm, no foul. But, on occasion, it was worse.

One incident with a young macho type landed Frank in jail. A couple of weeks behind bars and some counseling were the order of the court. The counselor, located in a converted wood-framed home not too far from his studio, met with him for about two months. The counseling was not effective. There were a lot of questions about Frank's early years starting with his mother, his father, his brothers and his one sister. He didn't know his father, who left home when Frank was five. His older brothers served as his father and they didn't do a very good job. His mother was working all the time, trying to support her brood of five. She was diagnosed with a serious heart condition at fifty two, undoubtedly helped along by her two-pack a day cigarette habit. Her overworked body just could not handle the stress and the medication. Her last months were not pretty. Frank could barely stand to be with her and this led to huge guilt.

Another late-night drinking bout had led to a yelling match with the woman upstairs. Next thing, Frank was throwing his shoes at her door, except that she opened the door and caught one right in the face. The Sheriff was called and Frank was arrested. So much for his job. The judge at the courthouse gave Frank credit for time served, fifty hours of public service and a small fine. But losing his job was a disaster. It validated his time in the army. It validated him as a person. It gave him some status. But all of that was gone now and Frank was not dealing well with the consequences of his actions.

Now he would have trouble paying the rent on his apartment. So the allure of a quick drug deal and instant riches was too much. A low-life that Frank met at one of the nearby watering holes suggested that Frank show up around eight p.m. at 7th and K Streets and pick up a package for delivery. Only trouble was that the man he met was an undercover officer. The criminal justice system moved with amazing speed and before he knew it, Frank was in Folsom Prison. Folsom had its own mystique. Gone were the days when Johnny Cash visited and recorded his famous song. Gone also were the days of notorious gangsters and hangings in the old cell block. But it was still Folsom State Prison, the mere mention of the words putting a shiver up most backs. Frank served a little less than three years after time off for good behavior and work credits.

Folsom Prison was more than just another entry on his resume for Frank. Frank learned all about the wonderful world of prison gangs and how they ran "the joint," as it was affectionately called. He met up with the AB, the Aryan Brotherhood, when he was there. The AB was the natural group for Frank and they were all pretty good guys as far as Frank could see. In any event he felt that he could talk to them a whole lot easier than most of the other inmates. They offered him all of the protection he needed and he did what he needed to do to keep in their good graces.

Once out of prison, Frank moved in with an old buddy in south Sacramento and registered with his parole office. The living arrangement did not work out so Frank found a studio apartment near 15th and G Streets, with the aid of a general assistance welfare check. From there it was a short walk to several bars. He caught on with one of them as an occasional bartender and dishwasher. It paid some bills and allowed him to meet some folks. When he was sober, he would donate blood at the blood banks like he did before. Frank spent his free time walking the streets and camping out at another pub in midtown, watching football and baseball games at the end of a gummy, wooden bar. The bartenders were a lot younger but seemed to like Frank.

At some point, Frank could not exactly recall, but maybe a year ago, he met Tom Summers after striking up a conversation with him one night at some bar and extolling his military police service for the army. Tom Summers was cool. He was a private investigator. Frank had asked about working at Tom's office and Tom had said he would give it some thought, but Frank knew it was a big brush-off.

Then about a week later, there was a phone call. The excitement that came when he retrieved a phone message from Tom Summers pulsed through his body. Frank phoned him back right away. Tom had a small job for him. Tom told Frank to expect a visit from an old friend, Art Scheffler. Frank had met Art at Folsom. Art was one of the lieutenants who gave orders. They had hit it off and Art had gone out of his way to be sure that Frank was comfortable in prison. Tom explained that Art worked for him and did a few jobs off the record, so to speak, and that he thought Frank would be perfect for a new case he had.

A couple of days later, Art met Frank at the Lucky Horseshoe bar in midtown. Art explained that he wanted Frank to do some snooping. Frank was overjoyed. He was going to be a private investigator, like Colombo. Actually, he was not going to be an actual P.I. He was going to be a gofer. As a convicted felon, Frank had to fly under the radar. But Tom Summers always had a soft spot in his heart for the down and out so Frank was the latest recipient of his generosity. Frank's job was to get all of the dirt he could on Mike Zorich, attorney at law. This was right up his alley. Search court records. Search newspaper archives. Make discreet inquiries. Go through the trash. Whatever it takes to deliver the goods and in return Frank would pick up a few extra dollars.

"So what's the point of doing all this?"

"Not to worry, Frank," Art said. "Your job is just to follow orders, to do what you are told to do. Get it?"

"Yeah, I get it. Just wondering, that's all."

"Well, I can tell you that this Mike Zorich is a guy who is not all he is cracked up to be. He was my public defender awhile back. I know the guy. He just sells his clients down the river. So I figure that it won't be hard for you to get some stuff on him, know what I mean?"

"Yeah, I guess so."

"Okay, that's the spirit. You get whatever you can and report back to me. I'll give it to Tom for his client. Stay in touch."

"Right."

Art left and Frank followed as soon as he finished his beer. Getting online to do any kind of search was a little beyond Frank's scope. He hired it out to a smart young college student, known to him only as Jack, a guy he met at a local gym, where Frank got to use the equipment for free in return for some clean-up work every couple of days. Never suspecting or caring much, the impoverished student was only too willing to check out every available website for information on Frank's target for a fee. And Zorich had been a gold mine. There were the usual articles on local lawyers, but Mike Zorich appeared to be one of the more prominent local lawyers.

"Mike Zorich elected President of the County Bar Association," was the lead on a couple of articles in the local newspaper and a legal paper going back more than 10 years ago. "Murder suspect found not guilty," screamed another as it detailed the successful efforts of his deputy public defender, Mike Zorich. That one went back even further. "Robber goes to jail," was the more common type of article with bare mention of the attorney for the culprit. The headline could just as easily have been "kidnapper" or "burglar" or "rapist" as the articles recounted the twelve-year career of a deputy public defender in Sacramento County. Then there was the obituary of his wife. "Sheila Zorich, wife of a prominent attorney, died last Thursday after a long and courageous battle with cancer. At her side were her husband, son and other relatives." The article went on to detail her many civic activities.

All of that ended a while ago. After that, the newspaper articles were few. Jack also supplied a credit report for Mike Zorich. Frank was happy to get the information from Jack his internet wonder. He did not know how Jack was able to get the information and he didn't care. He could handle the court registry himself especially something as simple as the "Plaintiff/Defendant Index" of all cases in this county and the nearby counties. Unfortunately, there was not much there. He retrieved property records for anything owned by Mike Zorich in Sacramento County and the surrounding five counties. Mike owned two homes, one in Carmichael and another in Kyburz, on the road to South Lake Tahoe, probably a summer cabin.

He eagerly read the stuff from his college student friend and managed to find the money to pay him off at $10 per hour. Fortunately, the total cost was not all that much and Frank would be reimbursed. The irony of Frank being an employer when he had so little money was not lost on him. He had no other choice. "It takes money to make money," he heard once and it was probably true. He needed to impress Art Scheffler and Tom Summers and he knew that this was the only way to do it.

His own efforts were not productive at all. The late night trips to Mike Zorich's home and searches through the garbage accomplished nothing. The stakeout of Zorich's law office was even less fruitful. He found nothing and saw nothing. This was not going well. What to do? Frank could not afford to lose this job. He figured that he had better meet with Art Scheffler again. So they met at the old Lucky Horseshoe Bar. They both got beers and sat down at a scratched and dented table in one corner.

"I haven't heard from you for a while, Frank. I was beginning to get worried."

"Yeah, I've been doing this thing for you guys on Zorich. Not sure that I have all that much. You got my stuff, right?"

"Yeah, we got your stuff. It's not terribly impressive. The usual newspaper clippings, his property, that kind of thing. The guy looks like he's a boy scout. That the way you see it?"

"Yeah, I guess so."

"Listen, Frank, we're going to need you to do something a little different. It's not just that we need stuff on him anymore. We need to send him a message. We don't like this guy, see? And, most of all, the boys in the joint don't like this guy. Understand?"

"Yeah, I suppose."

"In fact, the man says that we are going to need to rough him up a bit. Seems as if our guy Zorich has made some enemies along the way and it's time to make things even. You got a problem with any of that?"

"No, I don't think so. What do you want me to do?"

"Just like I said. We have a couple of ideas. But I'm sure you can think of some on your own. It doesn't take a genius to figure this out."

Frank said nothing. He took a drag on his beer and looked around.

"So, what's the problem, Frank?"

"Well, I'm okay with snooping around like I have been doing, but anything more than that, I don't know. I'm not too happy with getting caught and going back to the joint."

"Frank, I need to explain something to you. I'm not exactly asking you. You're one of us. Understand?"

Frank knew that "once an AB, always an AB." There was no question about that lesson. He learned it right away in prison.

"Yeah," Frank said, although he didn't care for the tone of the conversation.

"When we need to get some work done, we do it and we don't ask questions, see? I'm telling you that you need to do what you are told to do and not to ask any questions. Got it?"

"Yeah."

"Look, we even have some help for you. A couple of the boys can help out. In fact, any of the old guys from Folsom are good to go. Just ask them if they work for me. You know who I'm talking about, don't you?"

"Yeah, I do."

"Okay then. That's settled. We'll be in touch, Frank."

Art got up from the table and left. Frank stayed there for a while and then shot a couple games of pool. He understood what to do. He understood all too well.

All of that was a few months ago. But today Frank sat in his apartment on that cold October day and wondered how far he had come since then. Once the AB gets a hold of you, there's no letting go. That's for sure. And Art Scheffler was nobody that he was going to argue with. Not on his life.

When Scheffler called him again that afternoon, Frank knew that he had no choice. Scheffler explained that they needed to be sure that a certain order from the superior court was upheld on appeal.

TWELVE

AFTER VISITING THE Yolo County Jail and being treated like a common criminal, Mike was anxious to get back to the business at hand. On the following weekend he went to his office. The air was cold and Mike wore a long-sleeved flannel shirt under a jacket. He would be alone that Saturday as Denny told him he wasn't coming in over the weekend. Mike thought he would clean up his desk when the phones weren't always ringing. He liked the quiet of a Saturday. He could get so much done.

But the minute Mike inserted his key into the door to the office and stepped in, he knew something was wrong. Things on the reception desk directly in front of him were just not right. Mike went to his office and looked around. At first blush, things seemed to be normal. The usual files were on his desk. He kept a pretty neat desk, unlike Denny. It was a point of pride, even though Denny had given him a little poster which he hung in a corner of his office, "A clean desk is a sign of a sick mind." Everything seemed in order. His pictures of the children and of Sheila were in his bookcase where they always were. The picture of his parents was there too. He stopped for a minute and stared at the picture of the couple taken many years ago. Then he picked it up.

His father and mother were both deceased but not far from his mind, especially his father. Timothy Zorich was a significant human being both for Mike and for anyone else with whom he came into contact. He spent his life as a bank appraiser, just as his own father had done. He would tell stories of Mike's grandfather making appraisals during the Depression. He always tried to give top dollar to his many clients but he also recognized that values had been utterly destroyed. He had a manner about him that people respected. And Mike's father carried on the same tradition. Fairness was the watchword. That and a firm handshake, both of which Tim had handed down to Mike. Where Mike got his temper, he didn't know. But there was no question that he could get mad.

Then he noticed. His computer was gone. Everything else was okay. It was Saturday around noon and he was by himself. He could not fathom what had happened. Practicing law was not supposed to be like this. His mind raced as he thought of what he had to do. But he did not even want to go there. He wanted to try and figure this whole deal out, try to make some sort of sense out of it. "What was going on? Who was doing this?"

Interestingly, Denny's office was not disturbed, at least not to the extent that his was. A few files were thrown around but whoever did this was aiming directly at him. Someone wanted to send him a message. It took a while for him to settle down, but soon his rational side took over and he breathed a bit easier. Replacing the computer and its contents was the big thing. Fortunately, all of the data on his computer was stored off-site and he could retrieve it, with some time and effort. Buying a new computer was not hard, given all of the deals available online these days. Assembling everything the way he had it before would be another issue. Hopefully, he hadn't lost anything. Lacking anything better to do, he gave Denny a ring on his cell phone.

"You won't believe this, but we have been burglarized. Someone broke in and took my computer. For the most part, they left your stuff alone. I haven't a clue."

"Good God. Have you called the cops, yet?"

"No, I thought I had better let you know first. I'll call them although I don't know what kind of help I will get on a Saturday afternoon."

"Damn. I should have had that alarm system installed by now. They put me off for a couple of weeks but I should have insisted that we get that thing installed. If we had it, the alarm might have scared off any intruder," Denny said.

"Yeah. It might have. But whoever did this might just have easily figured out how to defeat the alarm or have taken the computer before anyone could respond. Who knows?"

Mike put things back on his desk and credenza as he waited for the Sacramento County Sheriff's Department to arrive. Surprisingly, it did not take long. Two young deputies exited their white cruiser, parked directly in front of his building. One male and one female both clad with thick belts carrying a gun, cuffs and pepper spray.

"Any possible suspects? Anyone you think might have done this?"

"Funny you should ask. I don't have a specific person in mind, but I've got a story to tell you."

Mike gave an orderly explanation, still trying to figure this out in his mind. He spared no details, at least not anything that he thought could help the Sherriff's Department. The rest of the conversation was pretty much the same along with the mandatory personal information details. The one deputy was not very encouraging. She said that they always experienced a rash of office break-ins when it gets darker earlier in the evening, usually for stuff that could be easily sold. It could all be a simple "rip and run," for all she knew.

The deputies listened attentively and took copious notes. They agreed that there was likely some sort of connection with all of the other events that Mike related. They said they would get a copy of the report of the mugging on the bike trail and burglary of his home in September. They would ask the CHP for their report of the car smashing on Interstate-5 in October. They would give all of this to the detective bureau and hopefully someone would be in contact with Mike on Monday.

About two hours later after dusting for fingerprints by the Criminal Investigation Unit, the deputies departed and Mike settled back into his black leather chair. His mind raced to the image of Cannes, that slimy excuse for a lawyer. He must have something to do with this. But why would any lawyer get involved and run the risk of jeopardizing his license to practice law? That kind of stuff just doesn't happen anymore. His mind returned to the case that he and Cannes had several years ago. But that was old hat. He thought of the old cases that he had reviewed when he went over the Master Index, Johnnie Ray White, Billy Wycomb or Arthur Scheffler. Or someone else? It could have been any one of them. Or someone with the Darnoff case.

He knew that he had to finalize the brief for the appeal of the contempt order. Jim Haggerty had dropped off a draft of the brief and Mike was eager to read it and add his two cents. He spent the better part of the day doing that and discovered that Jim was a very good writer. The arguments were powerful. It was clear that there was a lot of work still to do but he would work with Jim and they would end up with a great brief. Mike made a few corrections and some suggestions on the draft and left it on Alice's desk with a note asking that it be delivered back to Haggerty first thing Monday morning.

On Tuesday, Mike spoke with Jim on the phone and told him about the burglary of his office. They made arrangements to meet that afternoon. When he got there, Jim was in his conference room.

"We need to prepare like hell on this appeal," Haggerty said. "We need to think of every possible argument and we need to work hard to be sure that we cover all of the possible questions that the justices on the Court of Appeal might throw at us."

"I think you have done a great job, Jim. I really do."

"We are asking the Court of Appeal to stop the proceedings in Judge Thoreson's court and are asking them to issue an immediate stay of all proceedings, while they figure it all out. I think our chances are reasonable. Frankly, most appeals are denied. But this is a little different. The Court of Appeal doesn't often see a contempt of court case with an attorney involved. They have to be interested."

Haggerty had more to say.

"We have to make a first-class argument to the court. It has to be thorough and it has to be convincing. The problem is that there is not a lot of law on this point as we said in our brief. That is a good thing and a bad thing. We can always argue that the absence of law is a good reason to establish some law and clear up this type of issue for the future in the event that others find themselves in this situation."

Jim was fired up and Mike loved it.

"All of this is well and good, Jim. The problem is that I don't have my files and my legal research. They are on my computer. It is going to take a while to get back up. This burglary at my office really hurt."

"The beauty of the law is that it is not in your files. It is in the books, all of which are available on the internet. I have almost everything we discussed on my computer. We will just use my stuff."

Mike paused and settled with that thought. It was true. He sat down at a computer in Jim's office and got to work using the Westlaw computer research that so many attorneys used. Preparing the points to be made on argument went reasonably well. Mike surprised himself with his legal output and began to fancy himself as a legal orator like Johnnie Cochran. Actually, he loved oral arguments.

The loss of his legal research files was not that big of a deal. Who knows, maybe he needed to change his stripes. He could become an appellate specialist. He brought up all of the issues that needed discussing and then deftly answered the comments from opposing counsel in his rebuttal brief. When he finished, he was satisfied he had prepared a compelling argument.

Haggerty was complimentary of Mike's work and their combined output became a formidable brief. They framed the question succinctly and clearly. "How was he, or any attorney, supposed to respond when under a direct order from a Superior Court Judge to do one thing, he is given a direct order from another Superior Court Judge to do the opposite?" He was in the horns of a dilemma, no way out, the classic Hobson's choice.

They finished the brief and filed it with the Court of Appeal. Surprisingly, the Court issued an order for a hearing before they even received any opposing brief from Cannes. All of this was quite unusual as, customarily, the Court would wait to read the opposition brief before setting the oral argument. They set the date for December 6 and informed Cannes that his brief was due in ten days. It was clear that the Court of Appeal was taking this whole thing very seriously.

The rest of October and November was a time of great expectation for Mike. He had not seen Montoya again and had heard nothing of Johnnie Ray White since he got locked up again. His car was not getting bumped when he went driving on highways. Nobody had let any air out of Nancy's tires. Mike had been able to restore virtually everything on his new computer that he had before. His Audi was humming along just as it had before. Cannes was not sending over any more motions. The Darnoff divorce case was mired in interminable legal wrangling between the lawyers representing the mother and father. Judge Newman had ordered depositions to take place and the pace of litigation had slowed until the depositions had been completed. Some sense of normalcy had returned to his life. Mike spent as little time as possible thinking about all of this, hoping for the best. He was an optimist and he knew that things had to get better. He was wrong.

THIRTEEN

IN ORDER TO get his mind off of the Darnoff case and off of everything for that matter, Mike and Nancy decided that they should spend some time in November at Mike's cabin in Kyburz. There had been an early storm in the mountains. There was some snow along the road on Friday, November 12 as they drove along Highway 50 to Kyburz. But it was not so much as to require chains. He drove slowly and carefully following a safe distance behind the car in front. The trees alongside the highway were dusted in white. The sky was a perfect blue. The sweet aroma of winter was everywhere. The American River was largely motionless at this time of year but still sparkled when he could catch a glimpse. The whole scene was straight out of a fairy tale.

After a period of silence, Mike realized that they had not spoken in a few minutes. He looked at her. Nancy had a serious look about her.

"What's up?"

"Mike, I don't know if there is a good time to talk about us, what with everything that has been happening. But I want to talk to you about us. I am not sure that it is true that 'two can live as cheaply as one,' but I am willing to give it a go. What do you think?"

There it was, out there for the two of them to discuss. Nancy had a very disarming way of getting right to the point. It was pretty clear that she had been thinking about this for some time.

"Funny you should bring this up. I was thinking of where we were going myself. I guess that is a possibility. I love my house. It means a lot to me to say nothing of the memories. It would be very hard to leave it. I know you feel the same way about your place."

"There is a solution. We could sell both houses and get a new one just for us. We would make our own memories. You know, we are not the first ones to face this situation."

"That's creative. Do you really want to take it up a step?"

"I think so. Brent is launched. My career is what it is and the market will come back. It always does. I am more worried about you. Peter seems to be doing all right. What you had with Sheila was special and I would never see myself as a replacement. But that doesn't mean that you don't deserve more."

"You are right. I deserve more."

"I just didn't want you to think that I am here to replace your old times. I'm not. I certainly know how you must feel. Sheila was a special person. Everyone at the office loved her, but you know that."

"I do know that. And I know that this conversation is entirely too serious. Can't we think of something else to talk about?"

"Is someone trying to avoid the topic?"

"No. I am open to us living together. I am. It's just that I haven't really thought about it so I need some time to figure things out. Okay?"

"Yes, Michael, that is okay."

She rarely used his complete first name. But when she did, it meant that she was serious. He could tell that she wasn't all that happy with his response. But the idea of selling his home and moving to a new place with her was a little too much to digest at the moment. He liked her and she was fun, but moving in together? Mike didn't even want to think about it.

They arrived at the cabin and Mike spent about an hour getting all systems in working order, a fire in the fireplace, checking the propane, turning on the water and the electricity and getting some warm air into the cabin. It was cold and it took a while before they felt comfortable. He unpacked the car while Nancy got started with dinner. Mike poured drinks for each of them and he sat down in a worn out and saggy chair. There was music in the background from an old CD player. During dinner they talked more about the cabin than anything. It was understood by both of them that they needed to let the topic of their relationship assimilate for a while before they returned to it. They finished a bottle of Grgich Chardonnay, a premium Napa wine, Mike had packed especially for the trip.

They went to bed without a lot of conversation. Mike had trouble going to sleep. But this time it wasn't that he was trying to figure out who his mystery assailant was. Instead it was all about Nancy. He tried to figure out how he felt about her. He stared into her closed eyes listening to her soft breaths for a while. Then, growing impatient that she was not awake as well, he began to stroke her shoulders and breasts. She gradually awoke.

"Oh, hello. It's you. I was just dreaming of you. Funny coincidence," she said.

"Maybe I brought it on, with the careful massage that I was giving you. What do you think?

She took off her nightgown and climbed out of their cozy bed. She was so sexy. She danced the dance of the hidden veils, using her nightgown and whatever else she could find. After a prolonged time in front of him, she climbed on the end of the bed and gradually moved closer to him, continuing her sensual movements. Her arms were moving slowly and sensuously. Her smile was provocative. Soon they were making love. And then she was asleep nestled beside him. But sleep evaded him again. He tried but it did not come easy even with the relaxation of a spent body. Eventually he drifted off.

It was the smell that woke him. It was the distinct odor of something burning. Mike bolted upright in bed and looked at Nancy. She was sound asleep. He shook her and asked if she smelled something. She came to her senses quickly and she nodded her head vigorously.

"We need to get out of here" he said. "Grab some clothes. It's cold outside. Let's go."

There was panic in Mike's voice. Utter panic. Nancy stumbled out of bed and landed on the floor. She picked herself up and looked for some clothes in the dark. Mike got the light on and he felt the warmth from the next room. The warmth was not normal. He grabbed some pants and a jacket and looked at her.

"Just grab whatever you can. This is not good."

He was yelling. They went to the back stairs which were attached to the adjoining room, away from the warmth that Mike sensed coming from the front of the cabin. Down the stairs they went, tripping over each other until they landed on the ground. They saw some flames and a lot of smoke right away. It was dark, so the smoke was not immediately obvious to anyone driving by on Highway 50. By the time the fire was obvious, it was too late.

They got outside and looked back at the red and yellow flames which were getting bigger each minute. Smoke was everywhere. They were coughing and choking. Neighbors gathered and offered them blankets and warmth. Mike would later try to recall the sheer terror that he experienced at the thought of being trapped in a house on fire, but words were not adequate. Nancy could only say that it was like a dream. She moved as quickly as possible to get to safe ground. It was only later that she really understood the enormity of the peril that they had escaped.

The cabin was totally demolished. The El Dorado County Fire Department arrived in due time but to no avail. Fire hoses were stretched across the river to douse the last of the flames. Very fortunately the fire had not spread to any of the nearby trees, thereby avoiding a calamity. The cabin stood on a piece of cleared land as Mike had followed the instructions a few years ago to create a large clear space around any structure. California had certainly seen its share of forest fires and the federal forest service had published very strict guidelines. This area along the American River was wetter and greener than most and the increased moisture at this time of year helped to prevent the spread of the fire.

They both cried as they watched the firemen work with their hoses. The lights in all of the nearby cabins shined brightly. A large group of people had assembled close by. It took a good four hours before the firemen left. Mike and Nancy spent what was left of the night at a neighbor's house, huddled together in an uncomfortable bed thanking God in heaven that they had been spared. The new day was already breaking through the thick trees that lined the American River. Neither of them got any sleep as the horrific events in the early morning had overwhelmed them. After a short while, they went downstairs to the main room and were greeted by their neighbors who had some coffee brewing and some clothes that would make do for the time being. They also had some bacon and eggs, but Mike and Nancy hardly had an appetite. All of them looked at the burnt cabin and walked around still smelling the smoking embers in the forest.

Fortunately their car was not damaged except for the strong odor of smoke that permeated everything. The two of them drove into Placerville and bought some clothes. They hardly said a word to each other. The shock of the events of last night would not soon go away. Then they drove to the El Dorado County Fire Department to meet with the inspector as they had been asked to do the night before. An older gentleman who had not been at the fire that night greeted them. He invited them into his office and sat down at his desk. Mike and Nancy sat opposite him.

"We will know later today or tomorrow the likely cause, but I can bet right now that it was arson. We found the likely point of origin. It seemed to start on the north side away from the highway."

The senior fireman said more, but Mike and Nancy were too shocked to pay much attention. Arson? How could that be? Then they were met with what had become an all too familiar question.

"So, do you know anyone who might be out to do this to you? Seems very strange to us that only your cabin burnt," the inspector said.

"Well, it just so happens, that a few unusual things have been happening in my life," Mike said.

He told the fire inspector his tale of woe and the inspector seemed to be most sympathetic. As he spoke, Mike could feel the anger swelling inside of him. He knew that his face was getting red as had happened recently. The idea that this fire could have some connection to everything else in his life was just too much to even consider. But there it was. It had to be.

"Listen, there is a question of jurisdiction."

The older man's voice interrupted Mike's thoughts. Mike glanced at Nancy but she was just staring straight ahead. Maybe she was rethinking her plan to move in with Mike. Maybe she was asking herself what she had gotten into. Mike could only guess.

"All we have here is the fire. That is very serious and we will conduct a complete investigation. We do not have the ability or the resources to investigate these other crimes. You need to have the Sacramento County Sheriff's

Department on top of this. I suggest you go there and raise hell and see if you can't get those guys to put everything together."

"Right."

They exchanged pleasantries and left. Mike knew that the veteran fireman wanted to do more. He agreed that his hands were tied. How could he expect this man to figure it all out? He couldn't. He needed to get someone to do something.

That afternoon they returned to Sacramento. As he drove, he was developing a pounding headache. There was too much to think about. It was the same questions and the same lack of answers. "Who did this? Why?" The answers did not come easily. In fact, they did not come at all. But this was enough. He left Nancy off at her house and went home. He took a shower and changed into some other clothes. Then he got back in his car and headed directly to the Sacramento County Sheriff's Department. At the front desk he asked to speak to someone to discuss a series of crimes. The receptionist was a little puzzled.

"Sir, it's Saturday and our normal crew is gone for the weekend. They will be back on Monday. Have you filed police reports on these crimes, sir?"

"Yes, I have. It's just that there are quite a few things to talk about. I am hoping that someone can put them all together and get to the bottom of this."

Mike knew that he should have tried to do something like this a long time ago. What was the matter with me? Why hadn't I done this before?

"Please take this form and fill it out as much as you can and I will see if we have anyone who can talk to you today."

Mike took the clipboard with an "Incident Report" form on it. Filled with expectations, he took a seat and began fill it in. It didn't take long to put down his personal information and a list of the unusual events in his recent life. Meanwhile he waited in the sterile reception area. It seemed longer but actually was only fifteen minutes. Mike checked his watch as a young man in coat and tie with short hair and a warm smile approached him.

"Mr. Zorich, I am Detective Adams. Why don't you come with me to one of our interview rooms?" Mike followed the detective down a glassy hall, green linoleum on the floors and lots of lights. "Here we go. Coffee?"

"No thanks, I'm good."

"Okay, let me see what you have written here." In just a few seconds, the detective looked up. "All right, Mr. Zorich, sounds like you have been very busy these days. Or, actually, it sounds like someone else has been very busy."

"These things just don't make sense to me. I am hoping that you can make sense out of all of it and figure out who is behind all of this."

"Not sure exactly what we can do, but let's start at the beginning. Why don't you tell me everything and I will follow along your report and make notes. I will ask you questions as we go along so that I can get the whole picture."

Mike immediately felt the frustration of having to repeat what he had just written on the report. The details of all of the events in his life were becoming more sickening with each rehashing. It seemed as if that was all he ever did, tell other people what had happened to him, as if that was going to solve the problem. He took a couple of gasps of air and gave the required information to the detective.

"I think I have given you most of the details. There probably is more that I just can't recall right now. But not a lot more. Oh, there is one other possible person. I tried a case a few months ago and there was a witness who wasn't too happy with me. His name is James Montoya and he is a parole officer with the State of California. I cross-examined him and I got the defendant an acquittal. Montoya told me that my guy was guilty. The reason I bring it up as that a few weeks ago I saw Montoya in my neighborhood at my grocery store. I don't think it was a coincidence. He might be carrying a grudge. Maybe you could check him out?"

"Yeah, we can check him out. At least ask him if he knows anything and see how he answers our questions. Hard to believe that some parole agent would be behind this, but you never know."

The detective looked back at his notes.

"You filed a report on the mugging on the bike trail and burglary of your home and one of our deputies came out that day, is that right? And that was Friday, September 17, right?"

"Yes, that's right."

"Okay, I will get that report.

"For the office break-in, you did file a report and that was on October 30?"

"Yes, that's right." Mike was getting a little annoyed. He already said all of this to the deputy. What was the point?

"The car ramming was in Yolo County on October 12 and you filed a report with the California Highway Patrol and the fire was in El Dorado County yesterday, November 12 and you filed a report with the El Dorado County Fire Department. Is that about right?"

"Yes, all of that is right."

The young deputy paused and looked over his notes.

"Just off hand, the problem I can see is that there are only two incidents that took place in Sacramento County, the mugging on the bike trail and the burglary of your home is one and the office break-in is the other. At least there are only two where we have reports. I will have to talk to the other jurisdictions. We don't have the authority to be investigating their crimes. Do you understand what I am saying?"

Mike could not contain himself. The minute he heard the word 'jurisdiction,' as in having no jurisdiction to look at the other crimes, Mike lost what little civility he had that day.

"For Christ's sake, what are you saying, detective? You can't investigate what has been going on? You can't try to put this all together? You can't help me, because something happened somewhere else? Just listen to yourself. This is absolute bullshit."

Mike's voice was getting louder as he spoke. In fact, he was shouting.

"What the fuck good are you? What's the point of a Sheriff's Department in the first place if you can't even try to figure out what is going on? What am I paying you for? Just to sit on your butts and tell people that you can't do anything for them?"

Mike regretted his choice of words the minute he said them. But he was too worked up to offer an apology. The detective's face betrayed his shock at the response from Mike. Fortunately, he was not defensive. He sat there quietly.

"Sir, I can understand your frustration. Really, I can. Look, this is Saturday. I am assigned to the burglary detail. What we need here is for the lieutenant to assign some detectives to get a handle on all of this. I am going to personally talk to my lieutenant and see that he gets back to you. But it won't be until Monday.

There really is nobody else here today, who is not working on something else like murder or something like that. Some sort of emergency."

"A lot good that does me. Whoever is behind this arson apparently didn't take the weekend off."

"I understand. I really do. We need to get more manpower on this whole thing and we will. I assure you."

Mike just looked at the young detective not knowing what to say.

"Fine. This whole thing is just beyond my comprehension. It seems as if all I get is the run-around. I tell someone what has happened. A report is filled out. It is filed and then nothing happens. There is some sicko out there who is trying to get me. Maybe two sickos. Now he is trying to kill me and my girlfriend. I think that this merits some attention."

"I understand."

Mike thought the deputy was becoming a bit condescending. Hell this kid was only twenty-five, at the most. It was clear that nothing was going to get done today. He took a couple of long breaths and put his hands to his face.

"Okay, I will wait for the call on Monday. Thank you, detective. Listen, my apologies for my outburst. You're just doing your job. I get it. I didn't mean any of it personally."

Mike shook his hand and left. He left and drove straight to Nancy's house. By now she had a chance to recover from the fire and was feeling better. She said that she had called her son to tell him what had happened. She also called Peter and told him. She figured that Mike would not have done that yet.

"Thanks. That was nice of you. I have not called him. I haven't called Denny or anyone else. I am just so pissed off. Nobody can do anything. It's Saturday. Wait until Monday.

They spent the afternoon at her house. Mike put on a basketball game. The Sacramento Kings were playing at San Antonio. Not that the Kings were any good. It had been a good six or seven years since they last competed at the top level. Since then they had come on some hard times. But watching a basketball game was a good diversion. It was Mike's favorite sport as a kid. As he watched, he drank a couple of scotches. Nancy busied herself in the bedroom, washing and folding laundry. She would watch some of the game but she liked to wait until the fourth quarter. "Why bother watch the rest of the game," she would say. "It all comes down to the last five or ten minutes." She was right most of the time. But still he loved to watch the full game.

On Monday morning, he was surprised to get a call from a Detective Sauer of the Sacramento County Sheriff's Department. He had just arrived at work and Alice put the detective right through.

"I've read your report and the report from Detective Adams from Saturday. Plus I have the other reports from our office and from the CHP. I hope to get something from the El Dorado County Fire Department, but they tell me that they aren't done yet with their investigation. So that might take a while."

"Detective, I can't begin to tell you how good I feel that you have done that," Mike said. "I have been so frustrated about all of this and that nothing seems to be happening to figure it all out. I'm afraid I might have been a little rough with Detective Adams on Saturday, but I hope you can understand my frustration."

"I do. No worry about Adams. He's a big boy. He's the one who lit a fire around here and why I am calling you first thing this morning. So, you can thank him."

"I will do that."

"At this point, we need to put together a list of the likely suspects. At the risk of repeating the question that I am sure you have heard before, who would you think is behind any or all of this?"

"I really don't have a specific person in mind. I'm a former public defender. So there are a lot of possibilities there. Maybe some old client who is still pissed off that he got sent to the joint. These days I am involved in a lot of litigation but it is civil litigation. I can't imagine that someone would be out to get me. At least it has never happened before."

"What kind of civil litigation? Any case in particular that you are working on now that might get someone mad at you?"

"I do have one newer case, a pretty big one. It involves the Darnoff family. They are big wine grape growers in Yolo County. The opposing attorney doesn't like me. We have a bit of history that goes back. But so what? A lot of lawyers don't like me, I am sure. When you are in the courts every day, you are bound to make enemies. It just goes with the turf. I don't have a problem with any of that. But I seriously doubt that anyone would want to get back at me personally. What they would want to do is to beat me in court. They would want to make my life miserable in court not outside of court."

"Yeah, I can understand that," the detective said. "But still, we could try and check on some possibilities. This lawyer in the Darnoff case. What is his name?"

"Robert Cannes. It is spelled C-A-N-N-E-S. Pronounced like 'can.' He is over in Woodland. But I can't believe that he is behind this. It doesn't make sense."

"Robert Cannes. It is a long shot and I have to say that I have never heard of a lawyer doing something to another lawyer just because he is pissed off as to how things are going on a case. It would be a first. Stranger things have happened, I suppose."

The deputy took another sip from his coffee.

"The Darnoff family itself is always a possibility. I have thought of them," Mike said. "The parents are going through a messy and complicated divorce. They are quite elderly so that is a little unusual. The children are in their forties and they are fighting each other. I represent one of them and the other two are aligned against him. So I thought that maybe someone associated with the other siblings or with the other side of the divorce might want to make trouble. But the thing is why would someone only want to do this to me? There are plenty of other lawyers involved in this case. Any or all of them would be likely targets, just as much as I am. In fact, my role in the case is relatively minor."

"Okay, that is worth checking out. What are some of the names of people involved in that lawsuit?"

Mike gave him all of the names that he could think of.

"All right, what about some of your former criminal clients? Any likely folks there?"

"I have a short list of possible clients. But that is all it is, just possible people, based purely on guesses, no evidence of any kind pointing in anyone's direction. I have asked my secretary to check with the Department of Corrections to see who has been released and to see if there is any likely person there. There is one who was recently released and then got arrested for a new beef. Johnnie Ray White. He is currently a guest in your hotel. But I have no reason to believe that he is out to get me. As far as I know, he is still in jail so he couldn't be doing any of this stuff anyway.

"I'll check him out anyway. See what he has been up to before he went to jail. Anyone else?"

"Two other options are Billy Wycomb and Arthur Scheffler. Both went to the joint under circumstances that could possibly lead to some repercussions down the road. I don't have any more specific information about them. I guess that when it is all said and done, I can't say that I have any great leads, detective. These are just guesses."

"I get it. Look, here's what I will do. I am going to check out these past clients of yours. I will see if we have anything current with the Darnoff family. I will grab these other reports from the other jurisdictions and then I am going to talk to my partner and see what he says. I'll see if the lieutenant will authorize me to do a little digging around. We have a funding problem here as you might have read in the papers. We can't always do everything we want to do. But if he gives us the go ahead, it is worth a shot. It can't hurt. But just don't get your hopes up. I seriously doubt that there is much we can do at this point. If we find something or get a lead, we will be in touch with you right away. How does that sound?"

"Sounds good. I guess I can't ask for anything else. Anything you can do is better than where I was when I walked in here. Thanks, detective. You know how to get a hold of me."

"Right."

He came out of his office and told Alice and Denny what he had just told the Sheriff's Department.

"I don't have my hopes up that anything will happen. They don't have any ideas and neither do I. But I just feel so helpless waiting for the next thing to happen. You would think that there would be something that I could do to get ahead of the game."

Neither of them had an answer for Mike. They were just thankful that he and Nancy escaped the fire with their lives and wondered what they could do to help. He called Nancy. She was feeling much better and was going to her office later in the morning. Then he called his son.

"Peter, this is the next chapter in the exciting adventure of your father and the bad guys."

"Dad, this is not funny."

"I know that it's not."

"Burning down the cabin is serious. It is very serious."

"Right."

"Someone trying to kill you is serious."

"Right again."

"It's beginning to sound like some reality show. Your life is becoming way too scary. I wish Mom were here. She would know the right thing to say and to do."

That brought Mike up short. After a pause he said, "I miss her too."

Peter said he wanted to go and see what was left of the cabin. They would also talk tomorrow. Mike spent the day in the office and tried to immerse himself in the appellate briefs for the hearing in December. He was tired that night. But sleep was not easy. He thought of Cannes again and that old case when Mike had not been the most gallant of victors after he won the arbitration award. But that was life. In the business of being a trial lawyer, you win some and you lose some. You can't take it personally. You just have to move on. But who was he to talk? He was taking this whole thing personally.

On the next Wednesday, he got a call from the El Dorado County Fire Department. They were all very fortunate, he was told, as this fire could have been a disaster for the neighbors and for the surrounding forested area. A couple of years ago, the authorities had started taken very aggressive steps in demanding that individual homeowners clear the space around their dwellings, for the purpose of isolating them from any forest fire. This had worked in reverse in containing the fire to the house and not the forest. Mike knew all of this but he waited patiently while the officer finished his spiel.

The main thing he heard that day from the nice Captain was that this was definitely arson. There was no question about it. This was not a news flash to Mike. There was too much happening in his life for this to be a coincidence. The Captain said it would be automatically referred to the Sheriff's Department. In any event, they would inevitably have more questions for Mike as they continued their investigation. They would cooperate with the Sacramento Sheriff's Department and see if any leads were developed. Mike asked them to contact Detective Sauer as he was trying to put it all together.

Mike also filed a claim with his insurance company over the fire. An engaging young lady stopped by his office on Friday morning. She was knowledgeable and somewhat helpful. They didn't know any more than he had already learned from the fire authorities for El Dorado County. Arson was the cause all right, based on finding the gasoline can some two hundred yards away beside the road and based on the way the fire burned from one side of the house inward in a very distinctive pattern.

She asked for a description of the contents of the house. This was relatively easy for Mike to answer as there was not much and it was old. Sheila and he had always looked at this as a rustic second home with the emphasis on rustic. On this trip he and Nancy had not taken much with them.

The insurance agent was optimistic that Mike could get full payment at replacement value within a few weeks assuming that everything went as it should within her company. That would give him the opportunity to rebuild or sit and wait. The latter choice seemed more logical for the moment.

FOURTEEN

It was a crisp morning, Monday, December 6. Cold did not exactly describe the weather. Fog and gloom would be more accurate. December through February in Sacramento were always the foggy months. Only rain seemed to dispel the fog. But there was no rain today just the deep coldness in the fog.

Neither the weather nor events in Mike's life could stop the court docket. It just keeps going one case after the other. It does not stop even for significant events in the lives of judges, lawyers, court staff, witnesses, jurors or the many other players. Unseen forces buried within each courthouse seem dedicated to ensuring that the docket will go on and on like a water wheel on a fast river.

Mike and Jim headed for the old Library and Courts Building at 9th and Capitol Mall in downtown Sacramento. Mike parked his car at 10th and L and they both walked the few blocks, their overcoats carefully buttoned to keep the heat inside. Mike held his head high attempting to place a look of sternness yet confidence on his nervous face. He even tried for a faint smile, the sure sign of a winning lawyer. With the help of a lightweight file cart, Mike lugged the two briefcases with lots of paperwork, mainly copies of cases that he wanted printed in full, so that Jim could make ready reference in argument.

On Wednesday, Mike and Jim had spent about three hours going through a mock question and answer session. They tried to anticipate all of the questions that the Justices might consider. Mike even took a rather belligerent and sarcastic tone with Jim knowing that such a tone would be unlikely in real life. It was good practice to be prepared for the worst. Preparation was the name of the game and there was no one better prepared than Jim Haggerty. Mike threw himself into the whole process hoping to keep his mind off of his narrow escape from the fire in Kyburz and the inability of anyone to figure out what was going on.

They walked up the few steps in front of the building and submitted to the usual search of his person and belongings by the State Police and an especially sensitive x-ray machine. They entered the Court and took a seat in the circular row on the right side. Mike took off his coat and laid it on the chair next to him. The seats resembled a "theater in the round," all grouped so as to face the justices of the court at the open end of a horseshoe. The courtroom was a sparkling reminder of a more opulent time long ago.

Glancing directly across the room, he could see that Cannes was already in the august courtroom, sitting on the other side and looking straight ahead. There was another attorney next to him, undoubtedly an associate from his firm who had assisted on the appeal. They weren't talking to each other. In fact, nobody was talking. The quiet added to the tension in the room.

Their case was the second one on the docket that morning so Mike would get a chance to hear others argue and allow him the opportunity to gauge the mood of the Court before they started. He could always use some more time to just settle down and focus on the task at hand. And settling down he needed.

Haggerty sat next to him and busied himself with his own papers. Mike placed his briefcases beside his chair while they waited. He took another quick look around to see what other spectators might be watching today's action. Most appeared to be lawyers also waiting their turn, but there were a few others who did not fit that role. Probably clients, he thought to himself. He was too nervous to pay more attention.

The first case was called and the usual presentations of counsel followed, interspersed with questions from the members of the particular panel of justices chosen to sit on this case. The Third District Court of Appeal consisted of ten justices, any three of whom would comprise a panel. Panels were selected at random and Mike had drawn a good group of Justices, all of whom he knew. At least he knew then enough to recognize them if he saw them on the street. But he did not know them so well that they would recuse themselves. He knew them as did most attorneys in town who attended bar events and ran into the Justices in a social setting. Recusal, when judicial officers voluntarily remove themselves from sitting on a case, only occurs when that officer feels that he or she cannot be fair or impartial or that the circumstances might allow for the "appearance of impropriety" under the circumstances. None of that applied here.

Then his case was called. They both took seats at the counsel table, Mike attending to the wealth of material that they had brought along and Jim taking out his notes for his presentation.

"May it please the court, I am James Haggerty and I represent Michael Zorich who has been found in contempt of court. This is a direct appeal of that contempt finding. The underlying matter is known as the Darnoff case. Mr. Zorich is the attorney in that case and he represents one brother, Brian Darnoff, who is involved in a partnership dispute with his brother Jason and sister, Linda. As you know, there is also a related marital dissolution case involving the parents of the three siblings."

There was a little stirring among the justices. Jim proceeded with his prepared comments. He had the burden of proof as he was the appellant on this appeal. He would have to convince the justices of the Court of Appeal of the merits of his cause. Of course the justices had already read the briefs of both parties and, for all he knew, had already made up their minds. It didn't really matter. Jim was going to take the time this morning to lay out his case in a passionate voice so that there would be no mistake as to his true feelings. He doubted that the justices would mistake his feelings no matter what he said. But this was personal for Mike and Jim was well aware of this. Spending time in a jail, even if only for a booking, was not the kind of thing Mike signed up for when he took the bar examination.

What was remarkable that morning was that Jim did not get even one question from a justice. Instead he just proceeded according to his outline and notes carefully quoting exact language from the cases that he thought were important. After his allotted time, just after the little red light came on in front of him, he sat down.

"Thank you, counsel," intoned the Presiding Justice.

Jim had not reserved any of his time for rebuttal and Mike wondered if he was now thinking twice about this strategy. Maybe he should have saved a couple of minutes, if the justices had a question. But he, along with several other attorneys who were far more experienced than he, probably thought that if any justice had a question of him, they would ask it, even if he had spent his time. After all, the justices were in charge and the limit on time was their rule.

Robert Cannes had barely started his prepared comments when one of the justices interrupted him, as justices are likely to do when they have something on their mind.

"Mr. Cannes, how do you explain the fact that counsel appears to have been acting pursuant to a lawful, valid order of the Superior Court of Yolo County. How can that possibly be contempt of court?"

It wasn't the question itself, but the strength of voice of the justice that caught Cannes off guard. He paused, giving the justice just the kind of opening that they like to have.

"Mr. Cannes, if you can't answer that question, please try this one. Why would any judge simply disregard a valid, lawful order of another court?"

"Mr. Justice, I can answer your question. I was only pausing for a moment. The fact is that Judge Thoreson issued a valid, lawful order and it is that order that should be the focus of our discussion today. It was that order that was disobeyed. It was that order that was so blatantly defied by counsel, in open court and without the slightest hint of apology."

"Mr. Cannes, are you telling me that if I issue you an order today that is in direct violation of another judge's order, you would disobey the first order and follow the second order? Is that what you are saying?"

"No, your honor. That's not what I am saying."

"What was Mr. Zorich supposed to do? Was he to risk violation of Judge Newman's order? And one more question, where were you in this whole thing? Why did you just remain silent? Don't you have an obligation to the court to stand up and say something yourself? You know that not everything that happens in court is part of some partisan game. You are an officer of the court, are you not, Mr. Cannes?"

"Mr. Justice, I can only say that I believed that Judge Thoreson's order was lawful and valid and I certainly could not stand there and tell Judge Thoreson that her order should not be obeyed."

Another justice decided to join the conversation.

"Counsel, I am having a very hard time understanding this contempt charge. It makes no sense to me at all. Why would any trial judge hold an attorney in contempt when the attorney is following a lawful, pre-existing order of the court? Am I missing something?"

The rest of Cannes' time before the court was pretty much the same. Mike could barely contain himself. Things were going a whole lot better than he imagined. They were not asking him questions at all. Of course, that was not always a good sign, as Appellate Justices were sometimes known to pepper the side in whose favor they would eventually rule. But Mike could see that this was different.

After a total of fifteen minutes spent arguing and pontificating, both by Cannes and the various justices, the Presiding Justice gaveled the case to a close and called the next one. Both counsel picked up various papers scattered over counsel's table and stuffed them into their briefcases. Because Mike was taking his time and Cannes was trying to get done very quickly, Cannes exited the courtroom first. That was fine with Mike. He had no desire to talk to the clown.

Cannes could not wait to get out of the courtroom and the building itself. He hurried along to his car which was parked nearby and drove away. Very quickly, he dialed and got the chambers of Judge Thoreson in Woodland. He had long since given up on the ethical prohibition of contacting a judge without opposing counsel present. He knew that it was important to Judge Thoreson. In fact, he knew that it was very important. He got through right away. He wondered if Judge Thoreson had interrupted her morning calendar to take his call.

"Judge, I am not sure things went all that well today. You never know, but I did not leave with a good feeling. They were all over me as to why Zorich was forced to violate another court order in order to follow your court order."

"Not happy to hear that, Robert. Not happy at all."

"Judge, I was prepared. They didn't have any case that I had not thoroughly researched. Nothing new in the legal area came up today. It was just the tone of two of the Justices that was rather obvious that has me concerned."

"Not happy with that, Robert. Something has to be done. This cannot go this way. Do I make myself understood?"

"Yes, your honor. But I am not the one who controls this. You issued an order and I have supported you to the extent of my ability. There is nothing more I can do."

"Nothing, Robert?"

Cannes paused as he had no idea what that meant.

"I think we have said enough, Mr. Cannes. Good bye," said the judge.

With that the telephone call came to a close. Cannes was left alone in his car driving through the streets of Sacramento to the freeway and heading over to Woodland to his office, totally bewildered. "What did she mean by "nothing" else he could do? What was she trying to say? His job was to argue cases. He couldn't force a judge to make a ruling in his favor. Judge Thoreson knew that, of course. So, she must be talking about something else. Robert Cannes had many thoughts on his mind that morning and he knew that he hadn't even begun to assess the full extent of the "roasting" he had received that morning.

Jim Haggerty and Mike returned to Mike's office where they assessed the situation. They were feeling good, actually very good. Both of them were happiest at the attitude of the Justices on the Court. They were clearly upset with the contempt order. Mike knew that they had to guard against overconfidence as you never knew how a case would turn out whether it was the Court of Appeal or a jury trial.

In about ten days the formal Opinion of the Court of Appeal arrived in the mail at the law offices of Robert Cannes. It was postmarked December 13. It was about twelve pages in length, having been printed on both sides of the paper as the Court of Appeal customarily did. Like all attorneys, Cannes skipped to the end.

"Therefore, this Court finds that the order of Judge Thoreson was in error and it shall be set aside. It is null and void. The appellant shall recover his costs."

Cannes' heart sank. He knew that Judge Thoreson, who was probably receiving her own copy of the Opinion at about this time, would not be happy. He did not want to call her. Instead he would wait. He would wait for a phone call that would not be good.

A few miles away, Mike opened his mail and reacted in a different way. So few words but such big impact. The Court of Appeal got it right, he thought to himself, as he quickly read the opinion.

"Time for champagne. We won. Hooray for the good guys," Mike yelled out to the whole office.

Grantham heard him just a few feet away and came into his office as quickly as he could. So did Alice.

"How about that? There's justice in this world after all," Denny added.

"I'll say. Take that Cannes. Take that Thoreson." There was a glow on Mike Zorich's face.

Denny retrieved a bottle of champagne from the refrigerator. After popping the cork he poured the bubbly into three glasses and Alice cleared a space on the table. Then he offered a toast to "God, Truth and the American way." Alice, who rarely drank, took a sip and offered her own toast. "You deserve it, Mike, you deserve it."

They celebrated awhile longer, Mike reading various parts of the opinion aloud as the small group reveled in their success.

"Okay, you've read enough. Let me have a look at it. Piece of art, I say," Denny said as he took the opinion and went back to his office.

Mike was on the phone to Peter as soon as he could. He needed Peter to know that his father was not a common criminal. He should not have been handcuffed and carted away. He was right and the judge was wrong. Mike called Nancy to tell her all about it. Later he went to her house where they celebrated the good news, with a toast to vindication followed by dinner out at a local restaurant specializing in steaks. It was one of their favorites.

Karen Thoreson read the opinion late in the afternoon. She pretty much expected the result, after Cannes called her to tell him how things had gone at the hearing. The reversal appeared to have little effect on her. At least there was nothing that anyone could see by looking at her. Underneath she was steaming. How could this happen? How could this little snot, Michael Zorich, win this case? She could see it now. Zorich would be back in court demanding this and demanding that just daring her to do something else. She was embarrassed. First there was the reversal of the criminal case that she had with Zorich and now this. The other judges were sure to take note of the coincidence. There were sure to be snickers behind her back. Maybe she wouldn't be offered a good assignment. She left the courthouse early telling her clerk that she had a headache.

After going home, she went to her living room where she sat in a large chair. For a long while, she just stared at the photos on the wall. There were photos of her husband and children and photos of her mother and father and her stepfather and her brothers. And there was a special photo of just her and her favorite brother, Steven.

FIFTEEN

"Well, I think that went well," Mike said.

"Except that you drank way too much and you managed to insult me, Linda and your partner. Not bad for one night's work. Here, give me that glass, you've had enough to drink tonight."

Nancy was mad at him. That much was clear. Mike was sitting on the sofa at eleven p.m., with yet another scotch and water in his hand. Now his hands were empty. Denny and Linda Grantham had just left. The four of them had enjoyed an exquisite dinner of Cornish game hens in Madeira sauce that Nancy had prepared. She topped it off with a scrumptious tiramisu. The wine and other spirits flowed liberally. It had been a special holiday dinner.

"I didn't insult anyone. I was just having a spirited discussion with my partner and his wife. We all had fun. Denny and I are always kidding each other."

"Well, let me count the ways. You told Linda that she came from a backwater state. You made it sound as if all Texans are red necks who have to prove their virility with a gun and a Stetson. Your comment about all of the men being 'all hat and no cattle' was a little too close to home. You were describing her father, in case you didn't figure that out. You know that she is very close to him. It's not her fault that he still lives there. Did you notice how quiet she got after you lit into Texas and all of its charms?"

"No, can't say I did. But it's true. They're nuts down there. They practically require everyone to have a gun. They are all rednecks, as far as I am concerned. That goes for a lot of other states in the South as well. I can't help it that she was born and raised there. At least she saw the light and came to California, even if it did take her 20 some odd years to finally make it here."

"Well, I can guarantee that's not the way she took it. And how many scotches have you had tonight, by the way? At least seven by my count."

Mike knew that she was wrong but he was not about to correct her because he knew that it was more than seven. In fact, he was just about to get another if he could manage to get off the couch without making a fool of himself. But then she resolved that by relieving him of his glass. He thought that he should just sit still for the moment rather than stumble and fall.

"And what about your partner? Did I hear you right that you told him he wasn't a real trial lawyer because he had never tried a criminal case? I'm sure that he loved that keen observation. Have you ever told him that before?"

"No, I haven't but it's true. He has only tried civil cases. I meant no harm. I was merely trying to point out that there is another whole side of trials in the courthouse. Besides, what do you care? Denny and I go way back. He's said worse about me, I'm sure. I just can't think of anything at the moment. But we're used to give and take. Tomorrow he will have some bon mot for me, I'm sure."

"Maybe, but I could tell he was hurt. You were way too direct and way too loud. And it didn't sound like good-natured kidding to me. It sounded serious. And it was loud. If you hadn't been drinking so much, you would have seen it for yourself."

"You drank your own fair share, Miss Nancy. Don't go Holy Mother of God with me. You're a lot smaller, so you should only be drinking half of what I drink. It's a known fact."

A smile crept over Mike's face. He knew that a good offense was the best defense. That should cool her for a while. But it didn't. The next sound he heard was her glass breaking against the door and falling in pieces to the hardwood floor.

"Why, you asshole. How dare you talk about my drinking? I hardly had anything. Meanwhile, you've been acting like a camel in the Sahara who hasn't had a drink of water in two months. How dare you!"

The sight of the broken glass and the vehemence in her voice brought him to a momentary silence. He didn't know what to say.

"And another thing, how can you possibly tell them that the dinner wasn't my best effort? What the hell was that supposed to mean? Do you have any idea how hard I worked to make dinner for your partner and his wife? Did you notice the extra decorations in the house, the flowers and the garland? Do you even know that it's the Christmas season? The potatoes au gratin were the best I have ever done. The asparagus were just right. The game hens were golden brown, each baked to perfection, with the most luscious sauce. The meat was soft and moist. And how many times have you ever had someone make tiramisu from scratch, like I did? I have spent the better part of the last two days on this dinner, just for you and your partner. I planned this meal to get your mind off all of your troubles and to have a little fun and all you can say is that it was not my best effort. Are you nuts?"

Nancy was in rare form. Mike wasn't sure that he had ever seen her like this before. But he was coming to the realization that he was not going to win any arguments tonight. Even in his drunken state, he knew that she was right. He knew that she was telling the truth about all of his comments even if it hurt to hear them. But he didn't want to admit it. He just stayed where he was, silent and staring at the wall.

"Well, what happened now? Having trouble talking? You didn't have that problem tonight. You were Mr. Talk-a-Lot all night long. Nobody else could get a word in edgewise. Now you can't say anything? Is it possible that you can't handle the truth? Huh? Huh?"

Nancy was in the kitchen putting dishes in the dishwasher while she was explaining the facts of life to him. In his silence, Mike realized that not only had he insulted her but he was not helping her with the clean-up. The old Catholic guilt was settling in.

"Look, you make some good points. Let me think about it. Let's not do the dishes tonight. I promise I will clean everything up tomorrow morning. Let's go to bed. I'm not in any condition to help you tonight and I'm feeling guilty watching you work."

"Well, that's the first coherent thought you've said all night. But if you think you're getting me into bed tonight after your sick performance, think again. You can sleep on the sofa right where you are. Just turn your head and go to sleep."

"Now is that any way to treat a friend and a lover? Look, I'm sorry for whatever I said tonight. This whole thing has been eating at me especially the fire that almost killed us."

"I get that part. I know that you have been under a lot of stress. So have I. But that does not excuse your boorish manners, if I can be so polite."

"But I am sorry. Really."

He managed to get up off of the sofa, surprising even himself. He made it to the kitchen without listing too much. She just glared at him, her anger only slightly abated.

"Tell me one thing specifically you are sorry for. Not just in general. What specifically did you say or do tonight you are sorry for?"

"For starters, I can't believe that I said your dinner was not your best effort. Believe it or not, I meant it as a compliment. I was trying to say that if they thought that this was good, they haven't seen anything yet. You have done even better."

"Oh yeah? That's a little hard to believe. That's not the way it came out."

"It's the truth. I meant to say that you are the best cook in the world, really. Your Cornish game hens were fantastic. But you've done Coquille St. Jacques and Beef Stroganoff that are even better. You are a great cook. That was all that I was trying to say."

Nancy eyed him suspiciously. He knew that she was considering the merits of his defense. He came closer to her and put his hands on her hips.

"Now, really, do you think I am so stupid as to actually put your cooking down, when you know how much I appreciate it? I may be dumb, but I'm not stupid, or however that saying goes."

He leaned forward and kissed her on the forehead and then he gently lifted her chin and kissed her on her lips. She did not reciprocate but she did not move away. He wondered if he should tell her that she meant the world to him but something held him back. This would have been the perfect time, he had to admit. They kissed some more. This time she returned his kisses. In a few minutes, she reached for his belt and undid it along with the button on top of his pants. She let them drop to the floor. Not to be outdone, he unbuttoned her blouse and reached for the snap on her bra. They were kissing harder and harder now. But then she pulled back and began laughing at the spectacle of him standing in the kitchen in his skivvies with his pants on the floor. He had to admit that he felt a bit awkward.

"Let's go to my bedroom, assuming that you can make it that far."

Her voice was decidedly softer. Love was in the air.

"Oh, I can make it to your bedroom, all right. Are you kidding me?"

When Mike awoke the next morning, it was already 8:30, according to the clock at the side of Nancy's bed. She was not there. He rubbed his eyes and then put his arms behind his head and just lay there, taking it all in. His head was throbbing and he felt thirsty. He knew that it was going to take some time to work off this hangover. But the memories of last night overwhelmed his mind. Someone once said that make-up sex was the best of all. Mike couldn't think of who stated this truism, but he concluded that it was a known fact. He knew that Nancy could bring the best out of him even when he was pretty drunk. Amazing talent she had.

Then he smelled the coffee. After visiting the bathroom and consuming a few aspirin and a lot of water, Mike made it to the kitchen. Nancy seemed very alert. She was right that she didn't have all that much to drink last night.

"Look, I am really sorry. I made an ass of myself last night. I have some apologizing to do today. But I have to say that last night ended with a bang. You were something else."

He was smiling at her and she was smiling at him. She said nothing.

Mike made it to work that day even though it wasn't until the early afternoon. After greeting Alice, he made a beeline to Denny's office. Closing the door behind him, he sat down in front of Denny who was finishing up a phone call.

"Hey, man, I've got to apologize for last night. Not my best performance. I don't know what got into me. Too much booze, I'm afraid. I am really sorry for impugning your trial abilities. It doesn't matter that you haven't tried criminal cases, you are a fantastic trial lawyer. I know it and you know it. I don't know what overcame me."

"Ace, it's okay. I understand. It's the truth. I haven't had any criminal trials. Let's just leave it at that and forget last night. Except that I cannot forget that dinner. Nancy outdid herself. I don't think I have ever eaten Cornish game hens that were that succulent. They were just out of this world. And that dessert. Wow. Linda told me on the way home that she has never had homemade tiramisu in her life. Same for me. I have always bought it at a bakery. Takes a lot of work. Tell you what, Ace, you've got a keeper there. And not just because Nancy's a great cook. She's a wonderful person in all respects. I haven't really known her before but she had such thoughtful comments on everything that was being discussed. Smart, beautiful and a great cook. I won't go any further with her many attributes, but I can only imagine. Am I right or am I right?"

"You're right, my friend. I know that I've got a good thing. But that's another topic for another day. Right now, I just want you to know how sorry I am for what I said. I would go into battle in the courtroom with you any day of the week."

"Enough said."

"Now, about Linda. How bad do you think I was with all my talk about Texas? Nancy thought I was out of line with everyone and that Linda might have taken what I said in a personal way."

"It's possible. She did mention it. But I wouldn't worry. Linda is tough. She knows what you have been through. She's probably forgotten it by now, anyway. I wouldn't worry about it."

"No, I will worry about it. I need to make amends. But thanks."

Mike looked right at Denny in a way that said way more than any words could possibly say. Mike knew that damage had been done but he hoped that the healing process had started. As soon as he got to his office, he called a florist in the neighborhood and had a large bouquet of yellow roses delivered to Linda. He paid extra for immediate service, which the floral shop was only too willing to provide. He dictated a note to accompany the flowers. "Linda, you will always be my yellow rose. Love, Mike." Then he went back to the front of the office and asked Alice what was happening.

"Not much. Your mail arrived. It's right there in your basket. I'm not sure you are going to like the order of the court."

Mike's heart sunk again. What's next? He removed the single page from the letter that Alice had already opened, read and calendared. After he received the Court of Appeal's decision in his favor, Mike had filed a motion to have the Darnoff case transferred to another judge. It was pretty straight-forward, as the law clearly required such a transfer when the original judge had been overturned on appeal. Mike had figured that this would be granted as a matter of routine, even if Judge Thoreson didn't like it. Mike had also asked for the case to be continued.

"Motions denied. Counsel has not demonstrated sufficient facts as to why the court cannot be fair and impartial in this matter, given the ruling from the Court of Appeal. Counsel has also not demonstrated sufficient facts to justify any delay in this matter."

"You're right, Alice. I don't like it. How can this judge not recuse herself? The law is clear. She has to be the most incompetent judge on the bench. It's pretty clear that she doesn't know what she is doing. She hasn't got a clue."

Alice did not say a thing. When Denny came out of his office, Mike gave him the order.

"You're going to have to file a motion to have her disqualified, Ace. You have no choice. She cannot possibly be fair and impartial."

"Yeah, one more thing to do."

The remaining days of December were quiet. Mike felt like he was a punching bag, one blow after another. Through it all, Mike could not wipe the memory of the booking at the county jail from his mind. It just stuck there, forever embedded. When he read anything in the paper about a jail, he immediately recalled his own experience. Whether it was jail overcrowding or a convicted felon being hauled off to jail or budget negotiations within the state over funding for the prison medical problem, Mike could not escape the raw wound that had been inflicted on him. For some people, jail was a way of life, but not for Mike. For him, it was a foreign place, as if visiting a country in Siberia. He had no idea. He could hear the clang of the cell doors and the bang of the large sliding doors between hallways, whenever a door slammed in any public building.

Occasionally he would think of the mugging on the bike trail or the ransacking of his house and the burglary of his office or the car smashing on Interstate-5, but there was one thought that even took precedence over all of this and over his time in the Yolo County Jail and that was the arson of his cabin in Kyburz. He and Nancy could have been killed. The anger was always there as was the smell of smoke. He could not even light a fire in the fireplace without thinking of it. Any smell that was remotely close to smoke always brought the same memory. He and Nancy were scrambling in the dark to get out of the cabin. They were looking for clothes and for the door and then the stairs and finally they were on the ground, watching the cabin quickly dissolve before their eyes.

Just before Christmas, Mike picked up Nancy to go to the theater. The storm from Nancy's dinner with Denny and Linda had passed. Mike knew that he had better slow down on his drinking and think a bit more before engaging his mouth. He was sure that he had heard that advice before, but he couldn't remember when. Probably Sheila. She was the source of a lot of wisdom.

They enjoyed a local production of an old standard by Tennessee Williams, "A Streetcar Named Desire." The local repertory did a good job. It was great fun as was just being with Nancy. After the theater they caught a quick bite at a popular restaurant on 26th Street. As they were being seated, Mike got a glimpse of someone he knew. It was James Montoya. What was he doing here? Was he tailing him? Montoya was leaving the restaurant by the back door at the time and Mike did not see him again.

After dinner they went back to Nancy's house. Mike was clearly distracted so there was not a lot of talk. Nancy knew that Mike had crawled back into his cave and thought she best leave him alone. Mike climbed into bed with continuing thoughts of trying to unravel the mystery before him. That was what it had become, a mystery.

Whoever was out to get him meant business. The more he thought of all of this, one new thought entered his mind. Nobody is going to solve this for me. "If you want something done right, do it yourself," as his mother would always say. He had to figure out a plan. The Sheriff's Department was cordial and professional but it didn't seem like much follow-up was going to happen. The California Highway Patrol just had one car smashing, undoubtedly one of many. It could not be a high priority for them. The El Dorado County Fire Department had a fire but nothing else and no incentive to spend much time finding out what Sacramento was doing with everything that happened in that fair city. In fact, they had told Mike to light a fire with Sacramento and get them to take charge. It was clear to Mike that night that if anything was going to happen, he was going to do it.

Nancy took her time getting ready for bed. She looked at Mike nestled in bed and wondered about their conversation when she had suggested that they could move in together. They had not touched it again. She knew that she needed to give him time and space and she had been very good at that. But that was not Nancy's style. It was taking all of her mental powers to insert a gag into her mouth and steer clear of talking about the future for the two of them. Even her son was asking about it, which was a little strange as Brent rarely asked about her life.

There were some changes. She saw that Mike left some clothes behind one time. A toothbrush and razor and a couple of other similar items had taken up residence in the second bathroom. She wondered if it were an accident or done on purpose. Nancy had reminded herself once again that morning that she was not getting any younger and that if Mike was not the one for the rest of her days that she had better get going on finding someone else. The suspense in not knowing was getting to her even though she had promised Mike and herself that she would give him all the time he needed. She had changed her mind.

"So I want to ask you something. Where do we stand, Mike? Like, where are we going?"

"If you are talking about the two of us as a couple, I thought we talked about this."

Mike was taken aback by Nancy's statement. He had gotten used to her direct approach but this was abrupt. Mike sensed that there was a lot behind it.

"We did talk about this, but we never came to a conclusion."

"I thought we had. We agreed that it would be a good idea if I spent more time at your place and that maybe we should move in together. But we have never finalized any plans. So much has been happening, it is hard to think about the two of us. I've got a lot on my mind."

"Mike, I know that. But we talked about having a discussion about doing something more permanent at some point in time. I simply wanted to know if that was on your radar."

"I don't know what to say. I just wasn't thinking this. I need some time to think it over."

That was Mike's way of ending the conversation and Nancy knew it.

"Can we set a date when we will discuss it?"

"Just give me some time. We will talk, for sure."

"Well, do what you need to do. I have to go to Anaheim anyway to help with my mother. I will get someone at the office to watch my business. I will leave right after Christmas, but I am probably going to be gone for a while."

"Sounds serious," Mike stated more as a question than a statement.

"It is serious. She is not able to drive so a neighbor lady has been driving her to her card games and to get groceries. But now she is out walking around. The neighbor found her a couple of blocks away but not before she had called the police. She left the gas on the kitchen stove the other day. I think I am going to have to move her somewhere."

Nancy's statement hung in the air. Mike barely knew her mother, Elaine. They had met a couple of times when she was visiting Nancy. Elaine seemed cold at first, then warmed up and then got cold again. It was hard to know what made that woman tick, he thought.

"So, are you thinking of bringing her here?"

"Not really. At least not as a long-term solution. My mother and I have a love-hate deal going on. We don't do well with each other over the long haul. I would rather find her a good place to live where her friends are."

"That makes sense. What about the cost?"

"That is the issue. She does not have a lot of money. Dad's pension won't cover it. Social Security is nice but not much. I don't think she qualifies for MediCal. And those places are just depressing. I don't know what I am going to do, but I am going to do something."

There was something in the way that Nancy made her last statement that Mike thought might have more than one meaning. He knew that Nancy liked to tie down loose ends. She much preferred making a decision, right or wrong, as opposed to letting something sit out there without answer. But the fact was that he just wasn't there yet. He hoped to be there at some point.

"I don't know when I will get back. I will talk to my brothers, but I am not expecting much help there. Maybe there is some money floating around and someone will be willing to step up but I doubt it. I will just have to assess the situation and decide what to do."

In short order the conversation was over. Mike knew that he had more things on his plate, maybe more than he could handle. And, like it or not, there was more to his life than the law.

The two of them had a quiet Christmas. Peter and Brent joined them for the day. Nancy then left for Anaheim. Mike knew that business was slow for her, as it always was at this time of the year before the good weather came and people began thinking of buying a new house. The young families wanted to be situated well in advance of the new school year so that the transition for their children would be smooth. April was the time when sales and purchases of homes really starting heating up. With their phone calls, Mike knew that Nancy was clearly worried about her mother.

No sooner had Nancy arrived in Anaheim than her mother developed a thrombosis in her leg and had to be hospitalized. Actually, Nancy soon learned that her mother had been diagnosed with this ailment quite some time ago, but her mother had suffered in silence. Mike and Nancy talked on the phone every other day or so, mainly just to catch each other up on what was going on.

"So, how's it going with your mother?"

"Not much different. I found a couple of places that look like possibilities, but until I get medical clearance from her doctor, there is not much I can do. Nobody will take her while her leg is in this condition. She has to be ambulatory."

Nancy had been with her mother in her house for two weeks. She told Mike that she spent her time reading and preparing food and tending to her mother. It was not the most scintillating time of her life but it was needed. Nancy wanted to feel needed, so it served both of them well.

"Any idea of when you are coming back?"

"Not really." Nancy said. "But I don't know what difference it makes."

"What?"

"As for us, Mike, what difference does it make?"

"A lot of difference. I miss you."

The change in the topic of conversation was jarring. He wondered if she was less focused on her mother and more focused on him, at least more than she let on.

"I miss you too. I will let you know as soon as there is a break. I am caught between my mother's medical condition and the rules for admission to any of these assisted-living facilities. The two do not meet together right now."

"I still miss you."

"Okay, but you need to figure out what you are doing, you know. What you are doing about us, I mean."

"I know."

"Mike, I miss you terribly. I...love you. You do know that, don't you? That isn't a surprise is it?"

Mike was taken aback. She had never quite said that to him before, at least not that emphatically. "I don't know what to say, Nancy. I really don't."

"Well, I had to tell you. You need to know where I am coming from and then you can decide what you want to do. I felt that you needed to know that."

Left alone, Mike could not decide whether he was ready to make any kind of commitment to Nancy. Moving in with her would certainly be that. And, inevitably, it would lead to something more. Was he ready? He honestly did not know and much preferred to just avoid the whole topic.

The next week Nancy phoned to tell him that she was coming home. She found a place for her mother. Plus she talked to her brothers and they agreed to help pay. On January 13, he met her at Sacramento International Airport where he had taken her just a few weeks ago. He immediately drove to her house. Nancy said that she had a couple of promising leads for some new buyers from out of town and she was anxious to get back to work.

SIXTEEN

NANCY WAS MISSING. Mike had called last night and only got her answering machine. She had not called back but that was not unusual. She would frequently get immersed with clients and not return all of her calls. Now he tried her again in the morning of Wednesday, January 19. Still no Nancy and no return call. That was odd, as they would normally check in with each other at least every other day. He knew that she was chasing these new leads with some buyers from out of town who were looking at property in south Sacramento.

Later that morning, he got a call from the office manager where Nancy worked. It turned out that a client was trying to find Nancy and her office had wanted to know if Mike knew where she was. Nancy was not answering her cell phone. Mike told the office manager that he had not heard from her in a couple of days. Now he was worried.

He called Nancy's son but it was all news to him. He had not heard from his mother since last Sunday, but they usually only spoke on weekends. Mike called one of Nancy's friends but only got voicemail. He called Nancy's office manager back and asked her who she had spoken to at the office. She said that she only spoke to the receptionist who said that a client had called, looking for Nancy. That was all. The manager did not have time this morning to follow up as she was attending a meeting downtown at headquarters. Mike thanked her and then called another one of Nancy's friends in the office, someone with whom Nancy usually spent time. He found Mary Spencer on her cell in her car while she was going on the weekly home tour.

"She told me that she was going out to Latrobe Road in the south to show some property to these new buyers. I knew that she had an appointment at six p.m. on Monday. I asked her if she wanted me to come with her since it is dark and lonely out there, but she said she had it covered. Now I wished I had insisted on going with her. I'm afraid something has happened, Mike."

"I am too, Mary. No idea if she ever checked back into the office, I guess?"

"No, I don't spend too much time there. Our manager might know, but I doubt it. We work pretty much on our own."

"Thanks, Mary. I really appreciate it."

"I'll give you a ring, the minute I hear something. What are you going to do, Mike? I think that this is serious, don't you?"

"I do and I'm calling the Sheriff right now."

Mike hung up and dialed 911. He explained the situation and left his number. Then he drove to Nancy's house. As he feared, she was not there. It didn't take long before he heard from Detective Sauer, the same detective who had called him in December after the fire in Kyburz. Mike explained the situation and they agreed to meet at Nancy's house that morning.

Two detectives, Sauer and his partner, Jablonski, were there in about 45 minutes. Mike told them everything he knew. They were veterans and they asked Mike a lot of questions about his relationship with Nancy and who they knew in common and who might be a likely suspect. They even asked if he and Nancy had been fighting. Mike told them that he didn't think Nancy had any enemies and that he had no clue as to why she was missing. He told them that this could be related to a client who was looking at some property on Latrobe Road in south Sacramento. Mike told him how to contact the office manager and Mary Spencer.

They took it all down and advised him to do nothing for now. They would contact Nancy's office and see what they knew and report back to him. According to protocol, they were not authorized to send out an all-points bulletin until she was confirmed missing for 24 hours. They didn't know exactly when she was missing at this point. He needed to be patient. They asked if they could take a look around her house and Mike agreed right away. They walked through the house and spent some time in the bedroom and told Mike that it didn't look as if she had packed for any kind of a trip. Then they asked if she had any kind of diary or calendar at her house. Mike told them that she put everything on her phone calendar and that there was no paper trail, as far as he knew.

"But you know, the receptionist at her office might have a record of who had called for her," Mike said. "She's a nice lady. That's the place to start. Plus, as I said, Mary Spencer might be able to recall something. I hope she can, at least."

"Thanks. We're on it and we will keep in touch."

Mike had another thought.

"Detective Sauer, I have a feeling in my stomach that Nancy's disappearance is something more. I think that this might be related to everything else has been going on in my life, all that stuff we talked about in December. I'm not sure I told you before, but Nancy's tire was flat one day and there was no nail. Someone deliberately let all of the air out of her tire. It happened some months ago. But I think it was meant as a message to me. Whoever is doing all of this knows about Nancy."

"That's certainly possible, Mr. Zorich," Sauer said. "I will get my file and all of those other reports and take a look at them. If this is connected with all of that stuff, it broadens our search considerably. But I think our best immediate lead is the buyer who was looking for property. I want to see if there is any record of who this is, if Nancy made any notes of this. If you find anything about that, let us know."

"I will, you can be sure of that. But please phone me, even if it is to say that you don't know anything. I need to know. This woman means a lot to me."

"Will do."

The officers left and Mike thought about Nancy and knew right away that she meant a lot to him, a lot more than he had admitted to himself or to her. The rest of the day was a complete waste. Mike went home but ate nothing. After a mostly sleepless night, Mike eventually nodded off around four a.m. or so. He woke up with a start only to be confronted with a horrible feeling in his stomach. Nancy was missing. It was nine in the morning. He went to work but just sat in his office waiting for the phone to ring. He left his cell in front of him on the desk and he would stare at it, willing it to ring, to tell him that they found her. Finally, he called Sauer who told him that they had a lead on someone named

Roberts but that they could find no information. Mike told them that the name meant nothing to him.

Friday was the same. He went for a run in the morning so he could work out some of the stress he was feeling. He went by Nancy's house again in the hope that some new clue might be there staring him in the face. But he didn't find anything. Sauer had nothing to report. They were at a dead end. Mike spent the rest of the day fiddling here and there, accomplishing very little, all the while trying her cell phone every hour, but he only got her voicemail. Eventually, he went home and ate something from the freezer. He phoned Brent to tell him what had happened. After watching some inane television, Mike tried to go to sleep but that didn't work. So he spent the night in his bed staring at the ceiling and becoming more nervous as the night wore on.

The next morning, Saturday, Mike woke, put on some clothes and was back at the office around 9 a.m. He had planned to meet Denny, although they had never agreed as to exactly why they were meeting. Mike knew that Denny was trying to be a good friend and right now Mike needed a friend. Denny was already there and he met Mike at the door, looking very somber.

"Didn't expect to see you here this early," Mike said.

"Do you know anything about this?"

Denny handed a piece of paper to Mike.

"IF YOU WANT TO SEE NANCY AGAIN, IT WILL COST $250,000. I WILL CALL YOU TONIGHT. NO COPS."

The writing was printed in large, uneven block letters, almost as if it was written by a young child.

"What is this, a joke?"

"I don't know," Denny said. "I found it under the door when I got here. So it could have been delivered at any time during the night. I haven't called anyone, figured that I shouldn't get anyone alarmed until you saw it and we figured out what to do."

"Right, I appreciate that," Mike said.

"So what to do?"

"We've got to call the Sheriff's Department."

Mike did and left a message for both of the detectives who came to Nancy's house on Wednesday. Detective Jablonski called back in about twenty minutes and Mike told him about the note. He said the he would be right out to the office. When he arrived he took the note. Mike figured as much and had already made a copy of it.

"We put the APB out on Thursday, so we have to hope that something comes up from that. You need to take it easy. I know that that is pretty difficult under the circumstances, but you have to leave everything to us. This is our job."

"Do you think that someone posing as a client lured her out to look at property?"

"Possibly. The one lead we had went nowhere. I am going to talk to my partner, but we need to be here when he calls back. He will probably call you on your office phone because he left the message here. I will call you in an hour or so, but for now, let's plan on meeting here at 6 tonight."

Denny said he would stay at the office with Mike. When the officers arrived that evening, they sat down in his waiting room and they all waited for the phone to ring. They explained how they would pick up on the extension at the same time he did. Mike thought this was right out of the movies. But he wasn't complaining. After an hour or so, someone suggested getting pizza and Denny ordered a delivery. The hours dragged on and by eleven, the detectives announced that it did not look like anything was going to happen tonight. They said they would call it a day. Mike tried to convince them to stay but all they could say is that the kidnapper just wasn't ready to act. We would have to wait for another call. They left and Mike looked at Denny.

"How do you like that?"

Denny had no answer. They decided to leave as well. On Sunday morning, Mike decided to drop by the office to see if there was a message. Nothing had been left under the door, but in his office he saw that the red light was flashing on his phone.

"I said no cops? Do you want her or not? Tomorrow night."

The kidnapper had phoned back last night after Mike and Denny left. He had to be watching and had seen the sheriff's detectives. The voice was hard to make out, but it sounded gruff and muffled. The words were clipped. It was definitely a male voice, but not one that Mike had ever heard before. Mike called the Sheriff's Office and asked to speak with Detective Jablonski, but he was not due back on duty until Monday. The same for Sauer. He asked to speak to whoever was in charge and was connected to Nick Cain, who, fortunately, had the report on his desk. Cain said he would be over in the afternoon in an unmarked car to listen to the recording. After he got to Mike's office, Mike played the tape for him a couple of times.

"I plan to be at my office tonight to see if this guy calls," Mike said. "Do you see any problem with that?"

"No, but we will be here with you. I'm going to try to get in touch with Sauer or Jablonski and see if they can pull some overtime."

"He said 'No cops.' Won't that be a problem?"

"No. We won't come in a marked car. We won't be noticed. Don't worry."

"You think he is watching us?"

"Could be, but I'm not sure that he would risk it. We don't really know. The timing of this call coming after eleven last night and before midnight, because he said tomorrow, is telling. And I've got to say that there are quite a few buildings and windows around here, so that it would be possible for someone to be watching. It could be him or even someone else watching. We don't know if this is a single person or two or three or whatever."

"Okay, what do you think I should do when he calls?"

"Don't know just yet. We'll figure out the best way to handle it and tell you when we get here tonight."

Mike sat down on the closest chair.

"What can I do?"

"Nothing. We'll meet you here around five. Doubt that he will call before then. We will check out the surrounding area before we come into your office, to see if anyone is watching. We will be very low profile."

That night Detectives Cain and Sauer arrived around five but it was not until 7 p.m. or so that the phone rang in Mike's office. Mike, Denny and two detectives were waiting. Mike picked up and the detectives were listening on the other phone.

"I said no cops. Got that?"

"Yeah, I've got that," Mike said.

"I don't think so."

"Yeah, yeah. I've got it. No cops. I've got it."

"Tomorrow."

"Listen, I've got to talk to her."

The voice on the other end hung up.

Mike looked at Cain and Sauer.

"That didn't work out too well," Mike said.

"Yeah, it happens. He will call back. We will have to figure something else out. He probably is watching your office. It sure sounds like he knows that we are here or at least that you have contacted us."

"Can't you put some kind of tracer on his call?"

"We can, but it wouldn't work with this guy. He gets off the phone right away. We need time. The thing is that this guy knows what he's doing."

Mike went home. He picked up the mail from his mail box in front of his house that he forgot to pick up on Saturday and sorted through the usual catalogues and junk mail. But there was one letter that was a bit odd. It was a small envelope with no return address and with Friday's postdate. Mike's name and address were printed in childish handwriting, large uneven block letters, just like the ransom note. Inside, there was a single piece of paper with the words, "PETER WILL DIE."

Mike had a terrible sinking feeling in his stomach as he read the words. This was getting very serious. Nancy had been taken hostage and now this clown is threatening to kill his son. Mike phoned Peter to check on him and everything was all right. Mike told him to come over to his house right away and to spend the night there. Then he called Detective Sauer on his cell phone with the latest. Sauer did not answer, so Mike left a message. It was not a nice message.

SEVENTEEN

ON MONDAY MORNING Mike picked up his newspaper from the front porch and saw the headline immediately. "Local Real Estate Agent Missing." The article gave a few details about Nancy, based mainly on interviews with agents at her office and a few comments from the Sheriff's Department. Mike wondered how this thing got leaked to the papers. He knew that someone from the press would be trying to contact him today for his comments. But Mike had other plans. The guy wanted money in return for Nancy. It was that simple.

Peter emerged from the bedroom where he was sleeping.

"You got the coffee going?"

"Yeah, it's right there. The newspapers have picked up on Nancy. Here read this."

"I guess you have to expect this," Peter said.

"I'm going out today. But I want you to stay right here. You don't go anywhere. When I talk to the detectives, I am going to be sure that they come by here and keep a watch on the house. You got that?"

"Yeah, I got that, but I don't like it. Can't I go with you? I'll go nuts in this place all day by myself."

"I guess that would be okay."

Around eight-thirty, he called a local agent of the mutual funds company that oversaw his IRA account and asked what it would take to make a significant withdrawal. He was told that it could be done, but it would be difficult, given the paperwork that would have to be completed and sent to the East Coast. Mike and Peter were at the company's office in about an hour and Mike filled out the forms. The agent asked if there was anything he could do to rearrange his investments more to his suiting but Mike told them that this was an emergency and had nothing to do with the types of investments that the company held for him. The agent advised him of the 10% penalty for withdrawal before age 59 and a half but Mike assured them that he was well aware of this rule and needed to make the withdrawal notwithstanding the penalty.

"Dad, are you sure this is the right thing to do? That's a whole lot of money."

"It is. But it is also the right thing to do. This guy knows what he is doing. He's watching me. He knows that I have contacted the cops. If I want to see Nancy again, I have to play ball. He wants money and I want Nancy. It's that simple."

Back at his office, Mike tried to hide out and avoid any media-type calls, but they persisted. He instructed Alice to tell anyone who called that he had no comment. Detective Sauer phoned around ten responding to Mike's call.

"What exactly did the note say?"

"It said that 'Peter will die.' I've got Peter with me right now. I am either going to keep him in my sight or have him stay at my house. I think he will be safe there. But I would appreciate it if you would have the sheriff's deputies take a look at my house and my neighborhood."

"Right. I will notify the patrol division and they will take special care around your house. But the best thing is probably to keep him with you."

"All I can say, detective, is that I am scared. First Nancy and now Peter. This guy means business. It's obvious that he is watching me. He knows that I have contacted you guys. I'm afraid that he is going to do something to Nancy."

"Well, I have an idea about that."

Sauer explained that they had some new technology that would allow them to listen to the calls coming into his office from a remote location. Mike would simply have to dial a certain number and it would simultaneously forward all calls to the Sheriff's Department while still allowing it to ring and be answered in his office. It was called a split router. Mike listened to the instructions, hung up and then dialed the number to forward his call. He used his cell and called his office, just as the detective said to do. Then he answered his own call. He asked if anyone was on the line and Sauer answered that he was. Darn, something works right, Mike thought to himself. He thanked Sauer and hung up. That was an improvement. At least there would be no obvious law enforcement types at his office tonight, assuming that the kidnapper was watching his office.

Next Mike called his bank and asked to speak to the manager. After pointing out that he had been a loyal customer for more than twenty-five years, Mike explained that he was expecting a rather large check and needed to know what had to be done to convert the check to bills. Naturally the bank officer was a little put off when Mike told him that he was talking about $250,000. The officer told him that banks don't normally keep that kind of cash lying around. Besides they had reporting requirements and this kind of transaction was going to require more paperwork, not to be done in one day.

Mike did not want to explain the real situation for fear that the bank might call the police or sheriff to check it all out. He explained that he was making a series of small cash investments and that the money was quite important to him. To be sure, Mike hinted that he could go somewhere else, if that would be more convenient, but that he always used this bank and thought that he should conduct all of his business at one bank only. The officer got the hint and quickly told Mike that it was not necessary to go anywhere else. The officer told him to check back in the morning and meanwhile he would do all he could to get the cash.

Around three p.m., he heard back from the financial company. Nothing had been confirmed today from the East Coast but they were pretty sure that they could arrange for the withdrawal by tomorrow afternoon. They didn't promise anything but the representative was most accommodating.

It was around five and Mike began getting nervous that the kidnapper would be calling. Peter and Denny stayed and Alice went home. Denny dialed the local pizzeria, a joint a couple of blocks away on Fair Oaks Boulevard and asked them to deliver a large combination pizza. It arrived about a half hour later and Denny paid for it. They were well into the pizza when the phone rang.

"I said no cops. Why don't you understand that?"

"I do understand that. You have my word that there are no cops. There's nobody here, just me and my partner. No cops, just like you said. Just tell me what to do. Oh, and I need to talk to her before I can do anything. I need to know that she is safe and in good condition."

"You must think I'm pretty stupid. I saw the cops. Now, listen carefully. Read the note and do what it says exactly. No cops. This is your last chance."

The caller hung up immediately. Mike held the receiver and looked back at Denny.

"He just told me to read the note and do what it says. He also told me again that there were to be no cops. But what note? I don't have a note and he didn't say how I would get a note. Do you figure that he plans on delivering a note?" And he didn't say a word about Nancy."

Mike phoned Sauer on his cell phone.

"Did you guys get all of that?"

"Yeah, we did. We are going to keep your office under twenty-four hour guard. He has to come there, the way I figure it," Detective Sauer said. "He probably plans on delivering a note there and maybe we can catch him then."

"That makes sense," Denny said. "This is where everything has been happening."

"We will be hidden, you won't know that we are there, so don't even bother looking. I suggest that all of you go home and get some rest. We'll get him, one way or the other. Leave it to us. One of us will be in touch with you in the morning."

"I'm not so sure this is a good plan, detective. The guy said no cops. He sees us."

The detectives tried to be reassuring but Mike could see that further arguments were a waste of time. Mike, Peter and Denny left the office. Mike could not help but be bothered by the turn of events. This is not going well. He got home and spent most of the night, tossing and turning, but he did get some sleep, probably more from sheer exhaustion.

On Tuesday morning, he got his paper from the porch, again, expecting to see another article with more quotations from office mates of Nancy. There was an article but that wasn't what caught his eye. Folded in his paper was a note just like the first one.

"$250,000 IN 100's AND 20's IN TWO SUITCASES UNDER THE BENCH AT THE PARKING LOT NEAR THE 13 MILE MARK AT WILLIAM POND PARK AT 6 TONIGHT. NO COPS."

Again, it was printed in a childish way, with uneven letters. The words "no cops" were circled in black. The note was on a letter-size piece of paper, folded twice, and placed inside the folds of the paper. It had to be inserted just a while ago, as the paper was normally delivered around five thirty or so and it was now seven. Mike shuddered at the thought that this guy had been at his home that morning.

Mike knew the location described in the note exactly. It was where he parked his car when he got mugged in September and this bench was the one where he sat and waited for the Sheriff's Department to arrive after the mugging. This guy is sending a clear signal that all of this is tied together. Mike immediately phoned Denny and told them about the note.

"Well at least you heard from him, Ace. I spent the entire night inside our office, waiting for something to be delivered. But nothing happened. At least nothing happened while I was awake."

"What the hell did you do that for? Were you going to catch the guy or something?"

"I don't know what I was going to do, but I wasn't all that sure that the sheriff's deputies were going to get him. This guy seems pretty slick to me. You know what I mean?"

"Yeah, I know what you mean. He is slick all right."

Mike and Peter went to the office around nine. Alice told them that a different detective came to the office when she got there and said that he and his team had been watching during the night and hadn't seen a thing around his office during the night. No notes, no visitors. They were reporting back to the detectives in charge, who would be in touch with Mike.

Mike phoned his bank and got some good news, the money would be available around noon. So around eleven, he and Peter drove to a Goodwill Store nearby and looked for some suitcases. They found two that he thought would be big enough, not knowing how much room was needed to carry the kind of money that Mike had in mind. Each was the expandable, soft luggage type. Then they went to the financial company where he maintained his IRA account. Mike had to wait for a while but eventually he got the check for $250,000 made payable to himself.

It wasn't until around two in the afternoon that Mike and Peter drove to the bank. They parked and walked in with the suitcases, trying to look normal, even though this was anything but normal. It did not take that long as the bank was prepared for him.

"Thanks for getting the cash. I know that it is not a normal transaction," Mike said.

"You can say that again. I have never done anything like this before. But first time for everything, I guess," the bank manager said. "Come back here with me. We have it in the safe deposit box room."

After counting the hundred and twenty dollar bills, mostly hundreds, which seemed to take forever, Mike and Peter loaded up the suitcases and were happy to see that it all fit. After signing off on some kind of form, they left the bank and placed the suitcases in the trunk of Mike's car, looking around all the time to see if anyone was watching.

"This is weird. Wouldn't it be ironic, if we were robbed while trying to get some money for a kidnapper?" Mike said.

"Totally. But you've got me. I'm a big strong brute, Dad. I'll protect you."

Peter was smiling. It was good to spend some time with his son, even if it was a stressful situation. They made a good team, Mike thought to himself. Around three-thirty, Mike got a call from Detective Sauer who suggested that they guy would probably call back again tonight. Mike told Sauer that that was unlikely as he got a note that morning. Mike explained what the note said, but did not give the location at William Pond Park. He told them that he was afraid that if any cops were involved that Nancy would be hurt or worse. He didn't want to take the chance. Mike made it clear to Sauer that he needed to take care of this himself. It was the only way. Mike hung up before the detective could say much of anything.

Mike had kept Denny in the loop with his plan, during the day. Denny had expressed reservations at first but eventually had come to Mike's conclusion that they had to do this by themselves. Denny asked Mike how he could be sure that the kidnapper would exchange Nancy for the money. Mike said that he didn't know that but that the only thing he had was faith. They really had no other choice. This guy was too smart.

"Look, Denny, think of all the crap that has happened to me. Nobody has a clue who is doing this. These people are professional. We are not going to get the bad guys tonight, but we have a chance to get Nancy. She is who is important. Agreed?"

"Yeah, you're right. But I still don't like it. You may be paying all of your money for nothing. Then what?"

"That's what I'm thinking, Dad," Peter said. "How do we get Nancy? Can't you tell this guy that this has to be an exchange, money for Nancy? That's how they do it on television. If you just give this guy the money, there's no saying he's going to give you Nancy."

"That is a risk that I have to take. I have no way of getting a hold of this guy. I either do it his way or I don't do it. I've got to take the chance. I have to do this, it's my only chance. And I have to do it without any cops. This guy is watching us."

"I'm getting cold feet, Mike. I don't like this idea."

"I'm with Denny," Peter said. "At the very least, you should have the sheriff's department alerted and ask them to stake out the place."

Mike looked at Denny and Peter with puppy-dog eyes, pleading for his supper.

"Oh, all right. But I have a bad feeling," Denny said.

Peter did not say anything.

By five that night, they were ready. Mike wanted to leave early to check everything out, before delivering the money. They waited awhile and then all three got in Mike's car. They left for the park at half past 5, arriving around fifteen minutes later. They waited in the parking lot with their eyes on the picnic bench that was closest to the parking lot at the thirteen mile mark. There was only one that fit this description. This had to be the one. Mike knew it well. None of them saw anything out of the ordinary.

At six, Mike got out of his car and took the two suitcases to the table and put them under the bench, looking around all the time. Meanwhile, Denny was standing by the car, looking in the opposite direction, looking for any signs of life. There were some bicyclists out that evening but not too many. At this time of year, it was still light at six, so they could see pretty far in any direction.

"Well, that went all right," Mike said.

"Yeah, I guess so, but I'm still worried about Nancy," Denny said.

"We are working on faith here. We don't know anything for sure, but we have to hope that things work out. Like I said, we really don't have any choice."

Mike tried to sound like the Rock of Gibraltar but inside he was feeling like a wet sponge. He had no guarantee that his plan would work. "Desperate times call for desperate measures," was the thought in his mind.

They left the park but not before delaying as long as possible in the hope that they might see who had come to pick up the money. Then they drove back to the office and the three sat there, pretty much in silence, thinking of Nancy. It wasn't long before Mike began sharing out loud Denny's doubts about what they did. Serious doubts. He should have told the detectives. He tried to calm his nerves by eating something but he really had no appetite. He turned on the office television and read the paper, more out of nervousness than any desire to be entertained. At about 8 p.m., the tension was interrupted by Detective Sauer who was at the front door. Mike answered the knock.

"Detective, I didn't expect you."

The look of shock on Mike's face brought a quick smile to Sauer's face.

"I know. We tailed you. We saw you leave the money and then our guys waited for it to be picked up. Some guy in a pick-up, big guy, blond hair, drove up and took the money. We followed him for a while and he went downtown."

"Oh, thank God Almighty. Thank you, thank you. I screwed up, I know."

"Yes, you did."

"So, what's happening now? Are you going to arrest this guy and get Nancy?"

"I don't know. I told you everything I know. I wasn't there. I'm waiting to hear from Jablonski right now. He was one of the guys. I can tell you this. We aren't too happy with you guys. Not the smartest move. You could have been killed."

Mike knew that Sauer was right. There were tears in Mike's eyes. It was going to work out. They were going to find Nancy and going to arrest the son-of-a-bitch who was behind all of this. Mike sat down and slumped in the chair, resting his head in his hands with his elbows on his knees. Peter walked over to Mike and put his hand on his back. Denny sat back and breathed a big sigh of relief.

At that moment, there was static on Sauer's handheld radio and he stepped aside to listen. After a couple of minutes, Sauer turned back to Denny and Mike.

"We followed the guy to an apartment house on G Street, between 15th and 16th, but there is nobody there. We have searched the place. Somehow, this guy must have gone out a backdoor and down the alley. He was carrying the money in the suitcases when he went in but there is no money in the place. We're not sure where he went."

Mike's joy was gone.

"You don't have Nancy?"

"No, we don't have Nancy. We have our guys, along with a couple from Sac PD, and we have the neighborhood covered. They can't go too far. We'll get him. We are doing everything we can."

"God, I hope so. This is too much. I don't know what to say. I know I screwed up."

"You can say that again. I thought we had made that pretty clear. Our plan was to wait for the guy and get him to talk and find out about Nancy, do an exchange. But you just short-circuited everything. I understand about your concern. But you should have left this to us."

Mike didn't know what to feel. Now he was out the money and there was no Nancy. The police had the guy and then they lost him. But how could he blame the detectives for losing the guy? He didn't even want them involved. He had only himself to blame. He screwed this up royally. He had counted on the kidnapper being true to his word.

Detective Sauer stayed until eleven, thinking that maybe the kidnapper might make contact there. Nothing like that happened. There were more reports through the night from Jablonski, but nothing positive to report and eventually Sauer turned to them and told them all to go home. He promised to phone Mike on his cell the minute he heard anything.

Mike and Peter went home. Mike tried to sleep but he only could worry about Nancy. The more he thought about her, the more he realized something that he had not yet quite put all together. He loved Nancy. He couldn't live without her. He needed her and he was a fool for taking his time in reciprocating her love for him. Now he may have lost her for good.

There was no sleep that night. Mike gave up around 2 a.m. and turned on the television, searching for some old movie. Escape what was he wanted. That and Nancy.

EIGHTEEN

MIKE AWOKE AROUND 6:30 and immediately picked up his newspaper. No messages. He made some coffee and ate some cereal. There was no real news in the paper. Peter did not get up until an hour later. Around 8, they both went to the office. They got there at the same time as Alice. On his way, Mike called the detectives to see if they knew anything but he only got voicemail machines. It wasn't until 8:45 that he heard from Detective Sauer. The news was not good.

There was no lead on the guy they tailed from the park. He must have gotten away. They still had some officers in the location but it would be a lot easier for anyone to get away in the daylight with a lot of people in the vicinity. They advised Mike to sit tight and hope that the kidnapper contacts him again. This time they were a little more direct.

"And look, Mr. Zorich, none of this Lone Ranger stuff, all right? We are working on it. You just have to be patient in these kinds of things."

"Yeah, okay," Mike said.

"I'm not sure you really understand how serious this is. You made a bad move last night. You have to understand that we know what we are doing and we will get the bad guy. You need to stay out of it. Am I clear?"

"Yes, detective, you are clear."

"If you get any message at all, whether it is a note or a phone call, you let us know right away."

"Yes sir."

Mike felt like he was back in second grade being reprimanded by one of the nuns who taught him many years ago. Those memories did not go away easily.

"I can tell you that we are tracking a few leads on some low-lifes in the area. This area downtown is a close community. We're betting that someone has heard something. We'll let you know."

The answer was not very reassuring. It struck Mike that the cops didn't really have any kind of a plan. They were just like him, waiting and hoping for something to happen. Mike knew that he had to do something and he had an idea.

As soon as Mike got off the phone, he called the office of Robert Cannes. He was betting that Cannes would not be there that early in the morning.

"Mr. Cannes' office, please"

"May I say who is calling?"

"Mike Zorich on the Darnoff case."

Many secretaries had the annoying habit of not only asking your name but what case you were calling about, as if their attorneys could only be bothered on some cases. Mike had gotten into the habit of giving the case name right away, to avoid all of this.

"One moment please. I am not sure that he is here yet."

In about a minute, Cannes' secretary picked up and told Mike that his eminence was not available.

"Say, Dorothy, I was just going to ask Robert if he knew of a good private investigator I could use. I have a case and Robert was talking about someone that he uses, but I just forgot his name. My regular guy is out of business. Retired for the good life, I guess."

Knowing his secretary by her first name did not hurt. She had to be more than a little surprised that Mike Zorich had such a friendly tone. After all, her boss had just squared off in the ring against him. Mike was sure she had heard all manner of bad things about him directly from her boss. But he also knew that she had been around a long time and knew that most legal business was just that... business. She probably had no idea of the extent to which Cannes or Zorich was taking this personally. And she probably did not care. Mike didn't think that Cannes was the kind of guy who inspired much warmth in the old law office.

"I don't really know, Mr. Zorich. But I think he has used Tom Summers a bit. He really doesn't get many cases where a private eye is needed."

"Oh yeah, Tom Summers. That was the name. Thanks loads. I appreciate it, Dorothy."

Not wanting her to think that this was any big deal, Mike figured the best thing was to get off the phone and hope that Dorothy, the busy secretary, would forget the whole thing.

If Cannes had anything to do with this, he would probably work through someone like a private investigator and Summers was his man. Mike knew Summers by reputation and it was pretty good. So he did not think this was going to go far. But it was something.

Locating a public telephone in Sacramento these days was not that easy. Seems as if they had all been removed or vandalized. Instead Mike went to a Radio Shack and bought one of their disposal phones and called Summers. He did not want Summers to be able to trace the call. He was put through right away.

"Mr. Summers, my name is Ken Johnson. I'm an attorney and I have need of your services. I am trying to obtain some information on someone in town. Can you help me?

"Well, that depends. Who is this again? I don't think I know you."

"Well, that's because I'm new in town. I am trying to help a client on a collection matter and I need to get some information on another attorney. His name is Michael Zorich. Can you help me?"

Mike figured that the mention of his name should do the trick, if Summers was already working on an assignment that was focused on him.

"Yes, I can probably help you, Mr. Johnson. There is a fee, of course. What kind of information did you want?"

"Anything. Anything at all. I am trying to find out whatever I can about the man. Just background stuff, like a credit report, rap sheet, lawsuits, newspaper clippings, that kind of thing. Oh, malpractice claims, if there are any of those."

"If what you want is background information, I can do that. What kind of time frame are we talking about here?"

"Here's the deal, Mr. Summers. I am in a big hurry, if you know what I mean. I need you to jump on this right away. Yesterday is too late."

"Got it. Actually, you are in luck, as I have some preliminary information on Mr. Zorich right now. It came from another case. There will be a charge, of course, but not a big charge as I already have this information. It should be something to get you started. Then I can go to work and see what else I can find. How does that work for you?"

"That works fine. How about if I send over a retainer of, say, twenty-five hundred? Would that be enough to get you started and to get my hands on what you already have?"

"Yeah, sure. That works just fine."

"I will have a runner drop by your place within the hour, then. Thanks, Mr. Summers. I look forward to a mutually satisfactory working relationship."

Mike hung up. He had the cash delivered to Summers office by one of the routine messenger services that morning, after instructing the young man not to divulge Mike's name under any circumstances, but rather to indicate that he was sent by Mr. Johnson, if asked. Mike was sure that twenty-five hundred in bills would impress Tom Summers. Maybe he wouldn't even bother to report it and could realize a hundred percent gain on the assignment in lieu of sharing any with Uncle Sam. Who knows?

That afternoon Mike called the Sheriff's Department again but they had no more information for him. Mike didn't know what to say.

About an hour and a half later, the young man from the messenger service came in the door with a fat envelope. Mike ripped into the package. Pay dirt. There were articles all about him for sure. There was even information on an old case when Mike had to sue a client for his fee. But there were also some of his files from the Darnoff case. He could hardly believe his eyes. There is only one way that Summers could have these files and that was through the burglary of his office. So Cannes had to be behind this. Hard to believe that Cannes would be involved in a burglary but he must have been. It was also hard to believe that Cannes had obtained Mike's files on the Darnoff case and used them in his own preparation for the court proceedings. If he did that, he probably was behind the fire at his cabin on Highway 50. Cannes had to be behind all of this. At the bottom of the pile of stuff on the last page, there was a cryptic note to Tom Summers from someone named Frank.

Mike ran into Denny's office.

"Look at what I got. I got a hold of some papers from Tom Summers, the private investigator. You know him, don't you?"

"Yeah, sure. He's been around for a while."

Mike explained how he got the documents. Denny was impressed with the ruse that Mike had used to get Cannes' secretary to part with Summers' name. He was even more impressed with the papers scattered in front of them. Most were not useful or relevant. But a few items were helpful.

"So what to do," Mike asked, more to the wall than to Denny.

"You could confront Cannes and see if he talks," Denny said. "I would think that he might be a bit worried about getting into trouble with the State Bar. There are a couple of ethical issues here, to say nothing of burglary."

Mike had to think. He rubbed his hands, almost as if he was in prayer.

"We could, but I doubt that he would talk. I'm not sure that we have real evidence of his direct involvement. We don't know for sure that this stuff was even given to him. We know that Summers has it and he gave it to us. That's all."

Denny was quick to respond.

"You're right, Ace. You can't just lay this at Cannes' feet and not expect some push back. Lawyers are like dogs backed into a corner. You know that. After all, isn't that what you are doing?"

Mike was day dreaming at this point. Then he picked up the last piece of paper that Summers had delivered to him.

"What do you make of this, Denny? Who is Frank? Was he the one who got the documents?"

Mike picked up the throw-away phone that he bought at Radio Shack and called Tom Summers' office and thanked him for the documents. It was a few minutes after three.

"I really appreciate the help, Mr. Summers. This will go a long way in our effort to resolve my case. By the way, who is this guy Frank? I see that he wrote you a note, telling you that this is all he could find," Mike said.

There was a pause on the line before Summers answered.

"Oh, Frank is a guy who helps me out from time to time. He is a free-lancer, you know. Lives downtown. I didn't know that his name was on anything."

"Yeah, his name was on some note. Just curious, that's all. Know how I could find him? I would like to thank him and see if he had any other ideas on what I could do? Always like to talk to the horse's mouth, you know."

"He's downtown and I don't use him all that much. I really would not like to get him any more involved, Mr. Johnson," Summers said.

"Oh sure. Listen, Mr. Summers, I'm not trying to go around you. I will pay you directly for any time that Frank works on the case. You can take it out of the retainer. Really, I just wanted to thank him for his good work. That's all. Maybe get a clue on something else."

"All right, I guess I don't have a problem with that, as long as I have your word that you are dealing directly with me on payment. Keep me posted on whatever he does for you, okay?"

"Yeah, sure," Mike said. "Do you have his last name and his address?"

"The thing is that I don't really have an address for the guy. Usually, I find him at the Pine Tree bar. He hangs out there a lot. Last name is Bolger. Bigger guy, but not really too tall. Been around, you know. I'm sure you could ask around for him at the Pine Tree."

"Thanks, Mr. Summers. Thanks a lot. I will try to find him and I'll give you a ring, one way or the other, just so that we can keep in touch. Okay?"

"Yeah, that's fine."

Mike hung up and called the Sheriff's Department. He talked to Sauer but he had nothing to report. Nancy was nowhere to be found.

"Listen, detective, I think I got a lead on someone. A guy named Frank Bolger. I saw his name on some papers that I have and I think he might be involved. Any chance you guys could check him out?"

"Yeah, sure. I can run the name. You don't have a date of birth or a social do you?"

"No, sure don't. But I would love to know where this guy lives and whether it is anywhere near where you saw that big blond guy go last night. I bet there is a connection."

"Worth checking out. So, tell me again, how did you come up with his name?"

"It was on some papers that I have in the Darnoff case and I think that he was working for Cannes, the attorney in Woodland. I think I got his name by mistake. It might not be anything, but if he lives anywhere near G Street, it would be a hell of a coincidence, don't you think?"

"Okay. I'll see who we have available to check it out."

Later that afternoon, Detective Sauer called back and said that Bolger was on parole but that the address from his parole officer was in the south area, not downtown. Sauer told Mike that it probably doesn't make much sense to follow-up, unless there is some real connection to what has been going on. Mike thanked Sauer for getting back to him so soon and hung up. He walked into Denny's office.

"The Sheriff's Department couldn't find any connection with Bolger, but there has to be something here," Mike said. "I think that we should try to find this guy, Frank Bolger. He may really lay something off on Cannes and might be willing to testify. Who knows?"

"That is a possibility, but I doubt that he is going to cooperate with you. Plus, if he was trailing you, he would be spooked if you came onto him, don't you think?"

"Yeah."

"Probably the same for me. How about Peter? He just might get a kick out of something like this," Denny said.

"Not sure about that. I don't think I want to get him involved in this whole deal. If Bolger is really involved with these guys, they are dangerous. Burglary, arson and kidnapping are not small potatoes, you know."

"I get it. But we don't know that. All we know is that Bolger has some connection to Cannes. The thing is that Peter is big and strong and can take care of himself and we can be close by, in case he needs help," Denny said.

Mike stared at the ceiling for a while.

"I guess it's worth a try. Nothing else is happening."

Mike went into the spare office where Peter had been hanging out. Peter had spent the day trying to do his real estate business from his phone. He was not happy with his confinement, even though he knew it was for his own good. Mike asked Peter to come into Denny's office. Denny explained everything and asked Peter if he was willing to help find Bolger and get him to talk. Peter was only too happy to become a junior investigator. Denny and Mike said that they would follow Peter wherever he went and would keep him in view at all times.

Peter went to the Pine Tree that night but didn't find anyone who fit the description of Frank Bolger. Mike and Denny were in a booth on the other end of the large room adjoining the bar watching Peter's every move. They didn't see any likely suspect either. They were about to leave around 10:30, when they heard the bartender yell to one of the customers.

"Hey, Bolger, you want this on your tab?"

"Yeah."

Peter was finishing up with a game of pool with a college guy. He spun around when he heard the name to see a heavy-set guy, not tall, balding and somewhat disheveled. Mike and Denny saw the same guy. He was carrying two beers and moving toward a table where another guy was sitting. Peter kept an eye on both of them, hoping that one or the other would be attracted to the pool table. When that didn't happen, Peter took up a seat at the bar, as close as he could to the table. The two were talking pretty softly and it was hard to make anything out.

A pool table came free and Peter thought he would give it a chance.

"Hey, you guys interested in a game of pool?"

Bolger and the other guy looked up with a puzzled expression.

"Nah, we're good," the other guy said. Bolger nodded without looking up at Peter.

"Right, just thought I'd ask."

They went on about their business and Peter pushed the balls around the pool table by himself, until someone else came up and asked for a game. After about forty-five minutes, the other guy who was drinking with Bolger left. Bolger stayed at his table, drinking his beer by himself and looking around the bar. Peter finished his game of pool and took his beer to where Bolger was sitting. Peter stood nearby, while looking somewhat disinterested.

"So, you from around here?"

Bolger looked up and studied Peter's face, trying to place it.

"Don't think I know you, do I?"

"Doubt it. I don't come here all that often."

"Yeah, I've been in this town for a while," Bolger said. "How about you?"

"Actually, I've lived here since I was born. Went away to school, but back now. Working for a construction company," Peter said. "Custom homes."

Peter figured that Frank might bite at that.

"Oh yeah? I've worked on homes before, a lot of them. I'm a good worker. If you ever hear of anything, let me know. Could always use the work."

"Yeah, what do you do?"

"Pretty much anything. Jack of all trades, I guess. I can pound nails, lay sheetrock, some landscaping, little electrical and plumbing and maybe something more heavy-duty, if given a chance. Usually, I just work with others and do what I'm told."

"Good to know. We are looking for just that kind of worker from time to time. How would I get a hold of you?"

"Let me give you my address and cell. You can call anytime."

Frank went to the bar and found a scrap of paper and a pen. He wrote his address and phone number and gave it to Peter.

"Okay, I'll call you if I hear of anything," Peter said. "Do you come here often?"

"Yeah, I'm a regular. Just about every night. Either here or the Rusty Nail down the street."

"Good to know. So, what else do you do to keep going?"

"Oh, here and there, know what I mean? Whatever I can get. Do a little work for a P.I."

"P.I.? You work for a private investigator? Sounds cool," Peter said.

"Actually, no, it's kind of boring. I just tail guys and try to find some information."

"Tell me about it, sounds a whole lot more exciting than anything I'm doing."

Peter flagged down the young lady serving drinks and asked for another round. He then sat down opposite Bolger.

"It's really not all that much. I've been tailing one guy, a lawyer in town. Trying to find out stuff and doing a few things."

"Yeah, like what?"

"Nothing, really. It's all confidential. So, I can't tell anyone."

Peter sensed that it would be best to back off. He had made progress and he would be back. Bolger would open up sooner or later. They drank their beers and talked a little baseball. Peter was a big San Francisco Giants fan and he could talk all day about them. Bolger followed sports and liked the Giants, also. After a while, Peter told him that he had to be on the road.

Peter left and Mike and Denny followed him out a couple of minutes later. They met in Mike's car and Peter told them everything. Peter figured that he could get more information from Bolger if he gave it another chance, tomorrow night.

NINETEEN

THE PHONE RANG at Mike's house at 3:30 in the morning. It was Detective Cain from the Sheriff's Department. They had found Nancy. She had been taken to Mercy General Hospital on J Street. He explained that she was pretty beat up and in the intensive care unit. They found her in Old Town near the Railroad Museum, on a side street. Some people who were leaving one of the bars came upon her when they heard some moaning. They called 911 and the ambulance took her to the hospital. They talked to her for a while but she was in pretty bad shape and she needed to rest. As soon as they had more information they would call back. Meanwhile, there was nothing that Mike could do.

Nancy was alive and back. Thank God. He ran into Peter's room. He was already awake from the phone call.

"They found her. She's alive. Thank God."

"That's great, Dad."

Mike was crying as he embraced his son.

"Dad, can I ask you something?"

"Sure."

"Do you love, Nancy?"

"That's a great question, Peter. It is one that I have been asking myself for a while. The answer is yes. I love her."

"Kind of what I thought."

"Are you okay with that?"

"Yeah, sure. It's been five years since Mom died. I know that she would want you to find someone. As long as you are happy."

"I am happy. And tonight I am doubly happy. She's alive and I have her back. And you are safe with me. Now, all I have to do is to hang on to her and to you. That will make me even happier. What do you say we go and see her?"

Mike and Peter put on their clothes as fast as possible and drove over to the hospital. Naturally, they wouldn't let them see her, not only because of her condition but because Mike was not a husband or even a relative. "Good friend" wouldn't cut it. They took up a seat nearby and grabbed some magazines. Peter went to the hospital cafeteria and came back with coffee and donuts. Mike hoped to grab a doctor who might have some information but that proved useless. At six, he called the Sheriff's Department but Cain had gone home and the other detectives working the case would not be in until later in the morning. Mike would have to wait. He called Denny and gave him them the news. He also called Alice at nine when he knew that she would be in the office.

When he finally got through to someone at the Sheriff's Department a little later, one of the detectives said he would be at the hospital by 10:30. Right on time, Detective Jablonski met Mike. The detective explained to the staff that he wanted an update and that Mike was with him. The report was that she had a couple of broken ribs, a broken left wrist and her face was not very pretty. A few cuts and there would be extensive bruising. She bled a lot but she was going to be okay. It would take time. She was lucky that it was not worse. The broken ribs could have penetrated her lung, for starters.

Nancy told the attending nurse that a big guy had beat her up and dumped her in Old Town around eleven last night. She said that he kicked her in the chest a lot. She broke her wrist when he pushed her down some stairs at the back of a house, where she had been held. That was when she suffered all of the cuts to her face. All of this happened last night.

Jablonski turned to Mike and said that Nancy had told the Sacramento Police officer who was called to the scene last night that the guy who beat her up was a big guy, scraggly blond hair and lots of tattoos. Bad complexion. But that was not all.

"You know, that kind of describes the guy we saw in the truck that we followed from the park to midtown," Jablonski said.

For the time being, the staff did not want anyone to visit her. She was heavily sedated and was sleeping, which was exactly what she needed. They told Jablonski and Mike that they should check back tomorrow around noon, at the earliest. It might be possible to allow them to talk to her then, but there were no promises. The rest of the day for Mike was one of relief, mixed with a healthy dose of exhaustion and anger. He tried to rest at his home but that didn't work out too well. It was broad daylight, for starters, but the thought of Nancy and what she went through was overwhelming. Who the hell did this? And why? The description did not fit anyone he knew, especially Frank Bolger. But there was something about the description that bothered Mike. He just didn't know what.

Peter stayed with him at the house and they agreed to try and meet with Bolger again. Mike eventually got himself put together around 6 and the two of them went to his office where they met Denny. Mike said that he had a new approach to Bolger. He figured that it was about time to get a little more serious. Nancy was back and they needed to get some answers now before anything else happened. Mike said he wanted to talk to Bolger himself.

They all went to the Pine Tree in Mike's car. As soon as they arrived, Peter took off for the pool table, so Mike and Denny found a booth and ordered beers, leaving Peter alone. It was a long evening and Frank never showed up. Around ten they decided to call it a night. When they left, Peter said that they might as well try the Rusty Nail which was just a couple of blocks away. Mike and Denny agreed. The Rusty Nail was noisier and catered to a younger crowd. It was also more crowded than the Pine Tree. Mike and Denny stood at the bar trying to order some beers. When they finally got served, Mike made small talk with the bartender, an attractive woman in her late thirties. The bartender was no help. Mike felt decidedly uneasy trying to fit in with a group that was at least thirty years his junior.

Peter went off by himself and soon struck up a conversation with a couple of cute women who were out for some fun. Mike and Denny found a table in the back. After about a half hour, their patience was rewarded. Frank Bolger entered and headed for the bar. He stopped at a table and started talking to two guys who were sitting there. Mike had to wait for Bolger to conclude his conversation and leave the table, but eventually Bolger went to the bar and ordered a beer. Mike took his beer and walked over right next to Bolger and asked him if they might sit down in the back to discuss the Darnoff case.

Bolger was a little put off by Mike, to say the least. "Who are you?"

"Oh, you know who I am, Frank. I'm Mike Zorich. You've been tailing me for some time."

Bolger was startled. He looked right at Mike and said nothing. He was definitely caught off guard. Mike couldn't tell if he was faking it or if he really did not have a good fix on what he looked like in person.

"Come on, Frank. Let's talk. I can guarantee you that this will be good for you."

Mike smiled and nodded in a confident manner at Bolger.

"Oh yeah, how so?"

"Well, for starters, I think that I have a job for you."

"What kind of job?"

"A job that pays money. That kind of job. Come on, we'll talk about it."

Bolger took his beer and followed Mike to the table in the back.

"Frank, this is my partner, Denny."

Frank was surprised to see anyone else with Mike and he didn't sit down at the table.

"Hey, what is this? What's your partner doing here?"

"Just take a seat, Frank, and I will explain it all. If you don't like what I am saying, you are free to go at any time. I am at least good for some free beers tonight. No charge at all. How's that sound?"

Frank sat down. He had a puzzled look on his face.

"There was a kidnapping, Frank, and a fire at a cabin that I own, up on Highway 50. There was also a break-in of our law office, Frank. There were a couple of other things. Like, I got beat up. And I just found out who did it all. Thought you might like to know."

That got Frank's attention. "Yeah, what's that got to do with me?"

"Well, I have been talking to one of my friends at the Sheriff's Department and he has been talking to a guy who has just been arrested. Guess what, Frank, he spilled the beans."

Frank looked at Mike and said nothing.

"I have no idea what you are talking about. Why are you bothering me anyway?"

"I'm bothering you because your name came up, Frank. Whoever it is that is talking has fingered you in this whole deal. The Sheriff is getting a warrant to search your place and you are in a shit load of trouble. Just thought you might like to know. You are probably going to be arrested at any time now."

"Really? How did you say that you know all of this?"

"I have my sources, Frank. But I came here tonight to make a deal with you. See, I'm a criminal defense lawyer and I figure that I can help you. But I also figure that you can help me. Make sense?"

Frank didn't say a word. He just stared at Mike. And he took another sip of his beer.

"Here's what I am saying. You tell me the truth, right now, the whole truth and I am going to do everything I can to help you get out of this, Frank. I know a lot of people in this town, starting with the D.A.'s office and the judges and other lawyers. But you already know that Frank. You got a lot of information about me. I know. I've seen it. I can help you, but I need to know everything. The way I see it, you need a friend. And you need a lawyer. I can't represent you, because you did some stuff against me. But what I can do is to find you a good lawyer, Frank. And I can put in a good word for you. Coming from me that ought to count, don't you think?"

Mike wasn't sure if Bolger was buying his bluff or not. If Mike was barking up the wrong tree, Bolger would just laugh at him, get up and walk away. But Bolger didn't do that. He was still sitting in his seat, studying his beer with intensity, as if he was some physics professor interesting in how bubbles formed on top of beer. So Mike thought he must have said something that hit the mark. Mike looked around and caught Peter's eye at the pool table and gave him a quick but tight smile. Only Peter would know that Mike was signaling that it was going well. Anyone else looking at Mike would have no idea what was going on at the table in the back, where three men were engaged in some serious talk.

"Frank, don't look a gift horse in the mouth, know what I'm saying? What my partner is saying is solid gold. You can bank on it," Denny said.

"I don't buy it. I don't buy anything you're saying. This guy in jail didn't say a thing to the cops. No way. If he did, the cops would have arrested me. Who is this guy in jail, anyway?"

"Look if you don't want my help, I'm good with that. No big deal. I'm out of here."

Mike didn't move. He sat there staring at Bolger. And Bolger didn't move.

"Okay, Frank, let's go over this again. I got a call an hour ago telling me everything this guy said. I don't know the name of the guy they have in jail. The Sheriff's Department called me because they wanted more information from me. They said that they were making great progress. They told me that they were going to arrest you but that they would need a warrant because they want to search your apartment at the same time. They obviously know where you are and they are not in any big rush. But that doesn't mean that they aren't hot on your trail, because they are. They know where you hang out. They told me. That's why we're here."

"How do I know that you're telling the truth and not just making all of this shit up?"

"Why would I want to do that, Frank? You have been responsible for a whole lot of trouble in my life. If I was mad at you, I would have already done something to you or just waited for the cops to do their thing. But I know that there is more to it than that. That's why I am trying to help you. I want to know the details. You scratch my back and I scratch yours. What do you say?"

"I'm not responsible for anything in your life. You are barking up the wrong tree."

"I don't think so, Frank," Denny said. "All Mike wants is a little talk, some information. If you aren't responsible for anything, then you have nothing to worry about, right."

"If I talk to you, what exactly are you going to do for me?"

"I am going to fight like hell for you, Frank. If you give me some good stuff, you can bet that I will be there in your corner. When you get arrested and go to court, I will be standing up in your corner. You can't ask for much more than that. That's a promise."

Mike was looking straight at Bolger when he said this. Mike was sure that he was scoring and that Bolger understood exactly what he was saying.

"Like I said, Frank, you need a friend. And I'm your friend right now. Maybe your only friend. And I'm a friend who can actually do you some good."

"Look, things got out of hand. That is all I have to say. I was just trying to do the right thing. Then one thing led to another. But I didn't do anything. That's the truth. I got out before I did anything bad."

"Okay, Frank. I get it. You were trying to do the right thing. Makes sense. Let's start at the beginning. You got a job from Tom Summers, right?"

"Yeah, Tom Summers. How'd you know about him?"

"Just say that I know and leave it at that. The point is that you were checking me out, right? You were doing some background on me because of a lawsuit, right?"

"Yeah."

"Then you say that things got out of hand. Tell me about that."

"Summers told me to check you out. I did that. He told me to give any information I got to this other guy. I did that. Next thing this guy has me do some other stuff. But he had some other guys do some things too. They did the big stuff, you know. I was just on the deal at your office. That was all. Swear to God."

"Okay, so what you are saying is that all you did was the burglary of my office, is that what you are saying? You got some papers from my office on this case? And you got my computer, right?"

"Yeah, that's what I'm saying. But I had to do it. After that I was done. I swear to God, I didn't do anything else."

"So who is this guy that's telling you what to do, Frank, the guy Summers said to give the information to?"

"I can't tell you that. You think I'm stupid or something? He's a big shot in the AB. I can't be talking about him."

The mention of the Aryan Brotherhood clicked in Mike's mind. He drank some of his beer as he looked at Frank. The description that Nancy gave of the guy who beat her up was like a guy that Mike knew who was in the AB. He knew the guy from a long time ago.

"AB, huh? I may know the guy, Frank. I think I used to represent him when I was in the public defender's office. Big guy, scraggly blond hair, bad complexion, right?"

Bolger said nothing.

"Name of Art Scheffler. Am I right, Frank?"

Bolger jerked his head up from his beer and looked right at Mike. Then he looked away. But it was too late. Bolger's actions said everything. Mike knew that Scheffler was the guy.

"No, you are not right. No way I know anything about him and I'm not saying anything about him."

"Tell you what, Frank. The way I figured it out, Scheffler is the guy that the cops have in jail who gave up your name. He's the guy who is fingering you. He's making his own deal to save his own butt. It's a little late for you to be trying to protect him. If you want to save yourself, it's time to help yourself."

Frank said nothing. Mike just sat there for a couple of minutes and looked at Denny, who turned toward Frank.

"Frank, let me ask you this," Denny said. "Who else was it who was working for Scheffler? What else did they do?"

The light seemed to out in Frank's eyes. Mike and Denny could see that he was very uncomfortable.

"They did everything else. The only thing I did was your guys' office, like I told you. They did the fire at the cabin and the bike trail and all the rest of the stuff. Everyone got paid pretty good. I never thought it would end up like it did. But I had nothing to do with any of that other stuff. You've got to believe me."

"So Scheffler is paying guys for all this stuff? Where did he get the money to do that?"

"All I know is that you don't fuck around with him. What he says to do is what you do. So I did my part, got paid a few hundred bucks and that was all. I don't think he cared all that much for me. I told him that I didn't want to do anything else, that I was trying to stay on parole and out of the joint. He was okay with that. He had a lot of other guys who were happy to get a few bucks, so he gave me a pass. The money came from someone else, don't know his name. But all the money added up. Somebody with some dough, for sure."

"Did Scheffler say anything about an old case when I was his lawyer," Mike asked.

"Okay. Here's the deal. He told me that you're a bad person. You screwed up his case and you got someone's brother killed. So, this other person isn't too happy with you either. I think this other person might have been the one with the money."

"Scheffler told you that?"

"Maybe. He said that you deserved anything that came your way and that his job was to remind you that you are not so tough, that you are not so hotsy-totsy. That's the deal."

"I got someone's brother killed? Did he say how I did that?"

"Yeah, he said that you represented the brother and did a shitty job and got him convicted, when he was innocent. So he went to prison and was murdered there, because he didn't know how to take care of himself. So you caused it all. And he said that you think you are the biggest thing going in this town and that you needed to be dropped down a notch or two."

"Scheffler said that, did he?"

"Yeah, he did."

"So, who is this guy with the brother?"

"Don't know. But I think it was some big shot. Like I told you, I wasn't involved in any of that other stuff. You've got to believe me. Swear to God."

"So, if I have this right, Scheffler is kind of a boss and he has a lot of guys working for him. And the money is coming from the guy with the brother who was killed in prison, right?"

"Yeah, pretty much. There was this one odd thing. Never did figure it out."

"What's that?"

"I got a call once from a lawyer in Woodland. Somehow he got my name and asked me what I could do for him. I didn't really know what he was talking about."

"You remember that lawyer's name."

"I don't. But it was a weird name. Couldn't figure out how he ended up with a name like that."

"Was it something like 'can'?"

"Yeah, that was it. Can."

"Okay, so this lawyer from Woodland phones you up. What does say?"

"Not much. He just wanted to know what I could do to help him out. Something about some appeal. That's all. I couldn't do anything for him. Actually, I didn't even know what he was talking about. Told him that he should talk to Summers and the guys working for him. I couldn't help him, whatever he wanted."

"Okay, Frank. You've done good."

"I don't know anything else, really."

"I believe you, Frank. Here's my card. If the cops come to arrest you, you tell them you want to call me. I can't be your attorney but I will talk to the Public Defender's Office. I used to work there and I will be sure that you get a good lawyer."

"You guys are sure that the cops have Scheffler all locked up right?"

"Right, but what difference does that make?"

"I was just thinking. Scheffler once told me that he would never be taken alive. He would never be arrested. If any cops came after him, he would kill the cops and anyone else around him. You have got to know this guy. He's crazy and he's serious."

"Okay, I've got it, Frank. Thanks."

They shook hands and left. Outside, Denny and Mike talked for a while in Mike's car. Peter came out in a few minutes and they told him what had happened. Mike took Denny back to the office to get his car and then Mike and Peter drove directly to Mercy General Hospital. This time Mike was greeted a little more warmly when he asked about Nancy. He knew that he was not supposed to come back until tomorrow but he asked if he could just have a couple of minutes with Nancy. They agreed because Nancy was awake, but only for two minutes. He had to promise that he would just go in, see her, say a few words and leave. He promised. The nurse opened the door to Nancy's room to let Mike enter before she left.

"Hi."

That was about all he could manage to say when he went into her room. Nancy was a bundle of bandages. Her face was all wrapped up, like a mummy, except at the mouth and nose and eyes. Mike could hardly believe what he was seeing. Her left arm was laying straight by her side, wrapped heavily, but not in a cast. She had various tubes hooked up and there was a constant blinking and beeping of a machine at her side. She seemed to be asleep at first but she opened her eyes when he spoke and looked at him. He thought he saw a bit of a smile but was not sure. He tried to hide his feelings of shock.

"Hi, yourself."

"Imagine you can't talk all that much."

"I can manage a bit. My mouth is okay. It's just that my face feels like hell. I've got this little push button here to make me feel better."

Mike looked at her right hand which was clutching what we figured was the control to a morphine drip. Then he looked back at her.

"This guy who beat you up. You told the cops he was a big guy, scraggly blond hair?"

"Yeah, he had tattoos and bad breath. Ugly looking-guy. And mean."

"Any particular kind of tattoos?"

"Nazi kind of stuff, I think."

"Did he do anything else to you?"

"No. He didn't do anything to me until last night."

Mike remembered that he only had two minutes.

"Just one thing I want to say to you and then I have to leave. But I promise I will be back tomorrow."

She looked at him but didn't say anything.

"I love you."

He looked right at her and she smiled back. There was no mistaking the smile. Mike waited a few seconds and left quietly.

TWENTY

THE FIRST THING the next morning, Mike and Peter drove to his office. Denny arrived about half an hour later and came right into Mike's office.

"So, what's up, Ace? How's Nancy?"

"Don't know for sure, but she smiled and said a few words. I saw her last night. I think I will know more today. What a relief. I tell you, it's the power of faith."

"Yeah, yeah," Denny said. He rolled his eyes.

"I've got to tell you, we got some good stuff last night, didn't we?"

"You guys were awesome. You got that guy to spill his guts," Peter said.

"We did," Denny said. "We got a lot of good information. But we have got to tell the Sheriff's Department right away. Maybe they can find Scheffler. Plus we need to warn them. Scheffler's a guy who could hurt some people, if and when they try to arrest him."

Mike called the Sheriff's Department and got put through to Detective Sauer. Mike told Sauer that an old client of his, Art Scheffler, fit the description that Nancy gave of the guy who beat her up. Mike was sure that Scheffler was their man. Mike said Scheffler was probably carrying an old grudge from when Mike represented him years ago. Mike also told Sauer that Scheffler is a dangerous dude and that he promised to take down anyone who tried to arrest him.

"So, how do you know all of this?"

"I've been talking to an informant. I'm trying to put it all together right now. But it's good info, detective. You have to watch yourself."

"This informant, is that someone that I should know about?"

"It's Frank Bolger, the guy I told you about. You said he lives in the south area, but I think he lives in midtown or at least that is where he hangs out."

"So, what's the connection between Bolger and Scheffler?"

"I'm not sure right now. I am still checking on a couple of things."

"All right, thanks for the lead. We will check Scheffler out. Actually, his name sounds kind of familiar to me. And we'll take another look at Bolger."

After he hung up, Mike turned back to Denny.

"I think I owe Mr. Cannes a phone call."

It was about ten in the morning when Mike called Cannes' office.

"Mr. Cannes, please. Mike Zorich, here, on the Darnoff case."

He was put right through.

"Yeah, what can I do for you?"

"Robert, so good to talk to you. I have been talking to a friend of yours, Tom Summers. Nice guy. Gave me some interesting stuff."

There was silence on the other end of the phone. Mike could only imagine what Cannes was thinking.

"So? What does this have to do with me?"

"Robert, let's not get testy. It has a lot to do with you. How about Frank Bolger? Does that name ring a bell?"

"Can't say that it does."

"Really? That's not what he says."

"I have no idea what you are talking about. Now leave me alone."

"Robert, I am only trying to give you a 'heads up.' That's all. Bolger says that you called him and asked him what he could do about my appeal of the contempt charge. I don't think you were calling him for legal advice. I think you were calling him to give me another headache. That's what I think, Robert. In fact, I think that you are behind a whole rash of stuff that has been going on, starting with mugging me on the bike trail. That's what I think, Robert. But that is only half of it. I have got the evidence to back up everything I just said and I am about to go to the Sacramento Sheriff's Department with what I have."

Cannes didn't say a thing.

"The deal is, Robert, if I got any of this wrong, now is the time to clean it up, before you get dragged into this mess. So, care to let me know what's going on?"

"No. Leave me alone."

Cannes hung the phone up. Mike smiled to himself.

"This guy is panicked. I can tell it in his voice. Dollars to donuts he is calling someone right now. Maybe he is calling the guy with all of the money, the guy who was paying Scheffler and his gang to do all of this stuff."

"Tell me about this guy with the brother who went to prison and was killed," Denny said.

"Yeah, that's what I want to know," Peter said.

"He was a client of mine when I was a public defender. It was probably about fifteen years ago. Can't really remember the exact date. His name was Steven Preston and he was guilty as hell. He told me that he was guilty and he wanted me to do everything I could to get him off. He figured I would go along. He told me that he had a couple of guys lined up to testify for him. They were some of his buddies who would say anything. But I told him that I could not help him with his story because he was lying. It would be best for him to make a deal with the District Attorney. I was pretty sure I could get him off with a couple of years in prison. But he said he couldn't do that. He was going to trial and he was going to beat the rap. He wasn't going to prison."

"Did you go to trial?"

"We did. I refused to call his alibi witnesses. I also told him that I would not call his mother. I told him that I couldn't call any witnesses to the stand who I knew were lying. Told him it was unethical. Then I told him that if he testified he was on his own because I was prohibited from even arguing his testimony to the jury."

"So, how did it go?"

"Well he fought me. Couldn't believe that I wasn't going to call his witnesses or his mother and that I wasn't going to argue his case. Called me a 'holy mother-fucker,' if I recall his exact words. Trial did not take that long, as you might imagine. He testified even though I told him that I could not argue anything about his testimony to the jury. All I could do was to argue that there was reasonable doubt in the district attorney's case, that their case was weak. But you know how those things go... not very well."

"Do you know if he had a brother who was some big shot," Denny asked.

"No, not a clue."

"There must be a way we could figure that out. Where's the file?"

"Good idea. I have most of my felony trials around here somewhere."

Mike walked into the reception area and asked Alice if she knew where the old files were.

"Sure, they're in the other office in boxes."

"Thanks."

Mike moved the boxes and started going through them. The Preston file was one of the last in the second box. It was not terribly large. Mike pulled it out and began reading the file and his notes and the police reports. He read for a good half an hour but couldn't find anything of significance.

"Good idea, Denny, but nothing there," Mike said as he walked back to his office.

Mike opened his computer and googled "Steven Preston" and, after discarding some other "Steven Prestons," he brought up a newspaper article about the Steven Preston who was murdered in prison. There were a few more articles, a couple dealing with his burial in Rio Linda. It took a while before he saw it. But there it was, in an obituary, the name of his mother, Colleen O'Leary Thoreson Preston. Mike stared at the name for several minutes. He couldn't believe what he was reading.

"Hey, Denny, come here. Look at this. Preston is related to a Thoreson. Wonder if it isn't my favorite judge?"

"You figure that Thoreson is a prior married name?"

"Yeah. That's exactly what I figure. And that Judge Thoreson is the sister of the guy I defended, Steven Preston. And that Judge Thoreson is the money behind Art Scheffler. That's what I figure."

Peter walked into the office when he heard the commotion.

"Did you say Judge Thoreson? The judge who found you in contempt of court?"

"Yes, Peter, that is exactly what I said. Judge Karen Thoreson. I think that Steven Preston, the guy I was telling you about, is her brother, actually half-brother, to be exact."

"This is unbelievable. Thoreson? That is too wild for words, Mike," Denny said. "What are we going to do now? You just don't start making charges against a sitting judge, a Superior Court Judge of the State of California, in and for the County of Yolo. We had better be pretty sure of ourselves."

"You're right. What is that old saying, 'if you are going to try and kill the King, you had better not miss,' isn't that it?

"Something like that," Denny said.

"We have to try something else and I think I have an idea. I'm due back in court in a couple of days on the Darnoff case. Thoreson refused to recuse herself. Maybe I can use that to my advantage. I need to bring a motion to disqualify her. I will put down everything that I know and ask for a hearing in front of a neutral judge, to determine whether Thoreson can be fair and impartial in this case. If nothing else, I should rattle some cages."

Mike knew that motions to disqualify could not be heard by the judge in question but had to be heard by another judge. It could be the Presiding Judge but it could also be some other judge from a different county to ensure objectivity. In any event, it was the perfect opportunity to lay everything out in front of God and the world.

"Now you're talking," Denny said.

He agreed to help with the supporting legal documents. Mike went back to his office and pulled out a yellow pad and started to make some notes. He carefully listed what he knew for sure, what was hearsay and what he could deduce from what he knew. Then he began drawing up a formal declaration.

"I, Michael Zorich, declare as follows:

"I am an attorney at law, licensed to practice in all courts of this state and I know the following to be true on the basis of personal knowledge or on the basis of information and belief, which I am informed and believe to be true."

He began filling in the facts just as knew them. He created separate paragraphs for each event that had occurred, starting with the mugging on the bike trail and ending with the kidnapping of Nancy. The declaration detailed the entirety of the conversations with Frank Bolger and explained how Bolger had told him that he was responsible for the office burglary. Frank said that he worked for Art Scheffler, who used other parolees, and was responsible for everything else that had happened to Mike in the last few months. Mike knew that he was using a heavy dose of hearsay and speculation, but he figured that it would get someone's attention.

Mike also explained the phone call from Robert Cannes to Frank Bolger about the appeal that Mike filed on the contempt of court finding by Judge Thoreson. He also explained how Frank said that someone that Mike represented had been killed in prison and that he was the brother of whomever was behind all of this. He explained how he had once defended Steven Preston and that Judge Karen Thoreson was his sister, based on information that he found on the internet. Finally, he pointed out that the appellate court's ruling should disqualify Judge Thoreson from any further involvement with this case, pursuant to current law.

Although some of the information was inadmissible in court, because it was hearsay and speculation, it could be used to establish the appearance of impropriety and that was all that was needed at this point. It would be enough to make anyone reading it stand up and take notice. The declaration was seven pages in length.

Meanwhile Denny was working on a document called "Motion to Disqualify Judge Karen Thoreson, Pursuant to Code of Civil Procedure Section 170.1" and another document called "Points and Authorities in Support of the Motion to Disqualify Judge Karen Thoreson." When Denny was satisfied that the package made sense, he gave the documents to Mike to review and Mike gave Denny his declaration for the same purpose.

They both made some corrections and suggestions and it took a while longer to get everything in good order. Finally, they agreed that they were done and gave all of the documents to Alice to put in proper format for court filing. Mike signed and dated his declaration and asked Alice to call their normal runner to deliver the declarations and the points and authorities. The runner arrived in about thirty minutes and Mike told him to file the documents with the Presiding Judge of Yolo County and to serve a copy on Judge Thoreson and Cannes at their offices. He waited for phone confirmation that it was indeed filed. At about 3:30 he got the word on his cell phone.

Mike knew that once the papers were filed that they would take on a life of their own. The papers would be routed through the channels to all interested parties, including the judge hearing the actual motion, as well as opposing counsel. But to be sure, he wanted Cannes and Thoreson to have their own copies right away.

Now he sat back in his chair and he allowed himself a moment of reflection. Mike tried to imagine what was going on in the chambers of Judge Karen Thoreson as she read the declaration. She would be the first to get it. He tried to imagine what was happening in the law office of Robert Cannes.

Mike also mailed a copy of all of the papers to the Sacramento County Sheriff's Department, the Sacramento City Police Department and the Sacramento County District Attorney's Office. If nothing else, he wanted all of law enforcement to know exactly what he knew.

Meanwhile, Mike headed over to the hospital to see Nancy. She was a little more alert but still hurting. He could barely see her face through all of the bandages. She was having trouble talking but she said enough. He saw her each morning and afternoon for the next few days and saw that she was making progress. In fact, the nursing staff told him that the physician on his rounds had said that she might be able to go home in a couple of days.

It did not take long to find out how the declarations and points and authorities had been received by the Presiding Judge in Yolo County. The answer came in a white envelope just a few days later.

"The motion to disqualify Judge Karen Thoreson for cause is GRANTED. By law, she has been disqualified from any further involvement with this case because she was the trial judge of a proceeding that has been overturned by the Court of Appeal. As to the allegations of bias, no actual bias has been shown, but there exists in this case the perception of impropriety and bias by Judge Thoreson against counsel for one of the parties. A copy of this order as well as the motion and declaration from counsel will be sent to the Attorney General of the State of California and to the Commission on Judicial Performance for further proceedings. The underlying case and all related matters are hereby stayed, pending an assignment of a new and different judge to hear this case."

Mike read the ruling a couple of times as did Denny. They had won a small but important victory. Finally, Mike thought that he might get some justice.

After the ruling disqualifying Judge Thoreson was issued, someone from the Yolo County Superior Court Clerk's office alerted the local newspaper, which was pretty typical for any significant case. In fact, there were plenty of reporters snooping around any courthouse at any time and news of this type would not remain hidden for long. Mike soon got a call from the Sacramento Bee, asking for further information. Mike obliged the veteran reporter with answers to her questions, being careful not to stray from what he had written in his declaration.

Mike then called Detective Sauer at the Sheriff's Department and told him that Judge Thoreson had been disqualified. The detective told him that the department had already concluded that they had sufficient probable cause to arrest Frank Bolger and Arthur Scheffler. They wanted to take it one step at a time and to conduct more investigation before they took any action as to Robert Cannes or Judge Thoreson. It didn't take long for a couple of Sheriff's Deputies to find Bolger. After trying his apartment, they found him at the Pine Tree Bar. Frank Bolger went quietly. That was not the case with Arthur Scheffler.

TWENTY ONE

ARTHUR SCHEFFLER AND Karen Thoreson made an unlikely pair. If anyone saw them in public, it would be obvious that they were cut from different cloth. Scheffler was big, broad-shouldered, with scraggly blond hair and plenty of tattoos. His eyes were downright scary. It seemed like they could pierce steel. Overall he was an ugly, mean-looking guy. Scheffler dressed in whatever he could find. Nothing matched and he didn't care. Only his thick leather jacket was a constant. It was his trademark.

Karen Thoreson was usually dressed in a suit. She was very attractive with straight blond hair to her shoulders. As a Judge of the Superior Court, she maintained a certain dignity, even if it was learned and not natural. She was proper and righteous and ambitious. She was above the kind of life that Arthur Scheffler led. But the main difference between the two individuals had nothing to do with their appearance or with the obvious fact that one was a man and the other a woman. Arthur Scheffler was a bad guy. Karen Thoreson was not. At least she was not until she met Scheffler.

They never met in public, only in private, like today. Judge Thoreson was sitting in her car at a rest stop along Interstate 5, half way between Woodland and Sacramento. She was waiting for Scheffler. Their common thread was the judge's brother, now deceased. The memory of her brother just did not go away. It was many years ago, but the events of those days were emblazoned on her mind. She did not go to court to see his trial, as she was too ashamed of her brother and did not want anyone to know that she was related. After all, she had her career to consider. She had worked hard in college and law school and she deserved a chance to grab the brass ring. Having a brother who is a convicted felon does not exactly make for good press coverage.

But every night during the trial, she got the report from her other brother. Steven was charged with armed robbery. The trial lasted about two weeks and the jury came back with a guilty verdict. The case had then been continued so that the probation department could prepare a formal report and recommendation to the judge as to the proper sentence. Steven was sentenced to prison for six years.

But those were not the facts that Karen Thoreson cared about. She cared about what did not happen. Steven's public defender did not call any witnesses. Not one. Not even their mother, who told Karen that Steven was home with her that night. No way was he guilty. Without witnesses, without evidence, there was not much chance that the case could be won. The jury spent little time in deliberation. Karen's other brother told her that the jury asked the public defender why he did not call other witnesses. If he was at home, as Steven said he was, why did he not call someone to back that up? But the public defender had no answer.

There was no way that Karen Thoreson could make sense of the case. She knew that if she had been the defense attorney, she would have called witnesses. She knew that Steven would not have been found guilty. He would not have been sent to state prison and he would not have been murdered in his cell. He would be alive. And their mother would not have died with a broken heart. And she would not have died knowing that her son had been murdered in prison. And all of that because of Steven's public defender, Michael Zorich.

Judge Thoreson had been waiting for over thirty minutes. Scheffler was never late for their meetings. She wondered if something had gone wrong. Scheffler had phoned her at her chambers that afternoon, something that she told him never to do. Scheffler explained that they needed to meet right away and that he would be waiting for her at 4:30 that afternoon at the rest stop. Scheffler was not asking her to meet him, he was telling her. She left the courthouse at four and drove directly to the rest stop.

The rest stop was nothing special, just a lot of marked parking spaces, women's and men's facilities and a big map protected by a strong plastic sheeting, designed to help the lost traveler figure how where he or she was or where they were headed. The parking spaces faced the freeway on one side of the parking lane and faced away from the freeway on the other side.

But Scheffler was not there and she was the one waiting. She had more time on her hands, sitting there, to think about this whole mess. To think how she let herself get caught up in such dirty business. Scheffler was too smart for her. That was the simple truth of the matter. He knew what he was doing and she didn't. All she wanted to do was to teach Zorich a lesson, to put him in his place, to shake him up a bit. That was all.

She did not want to be there, but she had no choice. She was completely terrified of Arthur Scheffler. He had demanded that she show up at the rest stop. Finally, she saw Scheffler's car drive into an adjoining parking spot. He got out of his car and got into her car on the passenger side.

"Sorry, got caught up in some stuff. Hope you haven't been waiting long, your honor."

The words "your honor" were not said with any kind of respect.

"Whatever. What's so important that you have to phone me at my chambers? I told you not to do that."

"Look, Karen. You don't mind if I call you, Karen, do you? Somehow, 'your honor,' or 'judge' just doesn't do it for me anymore. We're buds now, right? You and me. Got it?"

She sat there staring straight ahead. She did not say a word. Her hands were trembling. She kept them together in her lap, one clutching the other. She hoped that her face didn't give away any other signs of her fear.

"Karen, here's what's happening. You are going to get me $250,000 in hundred dollar bills and get them to me in two days. I want the dough by 5 p.m., day after tomorrow. Got it?"

She just sat there behind the steering wheel of her car, not knowing what to do or to say.

"Karen, look at me. You got it?"

Karen Thoreson was afraid to speak, lest she would betray herself. Finally, she had to break the silence.

"There is no way I can get you that kind of money. What do you take me for? I'm not a rich person I shouldn't even be here," she said.

She kept staring ahead and did not dare even look at Scheffler.

"Yeah, but you are here. You haven't much choice now, do you? We've been over all of this before. If you want your career, if you want to still be a judge, if you care about your husband and children, you are going to do exactly as I said. Hell, if you care about yourself at all, about your body I mean, you are going to do exactly as I said. Now that's not too hard to understand, is it?"

His words were chilling. She knew that she had to be brave.

"What is all of that supposed to mean? Care about my body? Are you threatening me?"

Her words registered with him. He was thinking and looking straight at her. Suddenly he leapt at her and tore open the top buttons to her blouse and ripped it open. He pulled on her bra.

"Open it up and turn around. I have to check to be sure you're not wired. Do it."

Karen knew that he meant business. She undid the clasp to her bra with her left hand and slowly took her bra down, so that he could examine her back and her breasts. There was no wire of course. He looked her over, thoroughly enjoying the moment. She felt dirty.

"Okay. Leave your clothes the way they are. Let me see your purse."

His voice was gruff and loud. Mostly his voice left no room for discussion. It was a hard voice that demanded action. She handed him her purse, which she kept on her left side next to the door. There were tears in her eyes. Her hands were beyond trembling, they were shaking. Her lips were not working in unison. She sat there terribly mortified, her breasts exposed to anyone who came by.

"Do you have a wire? Are you wired, Karen? You wouldn't have gone all holy on me would you?"

"No, I don't have a wire. You can search me all day long. There is no wire."

The words were not said with any sense of strength.

"If I find out you have a wire, you are going to be in a lot more trouble than anything you have done until now. You can write off your husband and kids. Then there is your clerk, the gal who answers your phone at the court."

He paused and stared at her.

"Nice boobs by the way. Can't say that I have ever seen a judge's boobs before. He reached his hand toward her chest and cupped her right boob.

"Oh, feels good. Now, let's get back to why we are here. We are here to do business. Are you ready to do what I told you?"

"No, I am not here to do business. There's no end with you. Even if I did, then what? How do I know that it's over?"

Karen surprised herself with the strength of her voice.

"Well, you've got my word for it, sweetie. I've never let you down before, have I? I have always done exactly what I said I would do, exactly what we agreed I would do, even if you didn't like what I did. You know that you can count on me."

"I can't go on with this. It's gotten out of hand. It's time for me to stand up and take my punishment. I don't care anymore."

"Oh no you don't, honey. You're not going all goody-goody on me. You know it and I know it. If you want tomorrow's newspaper to read 'Local Judge Behind Attacks on Attorney,' then have at it. If you want to read about yourself as the person behind an arson and a kidnapping, that's your choice. But you're not going to do that. You can keep everything you have. Life goes on just as it is for you, minus a couple of bucks, of course. You just have to keep playing the game for a bit longer."

She said nothing and just stared straight ahead as she cried softly. Their cars were parked facing Interstate-5 and she could see an endless stream of motorists, passing by. They were oblivious to what was happening at the obscure rest stop. Little did they know that a judge was being shaken down by a thug.

Scheffler had first contacted her three years ago when he was released from prison. He told her all about her brother, Steven Preston, how he was killed and how he was framed in the first place. Her brother had decided not to become a member of the Aryan Brotherhood, the AB. Preston always told him that he was innocent, that his public defender, Michael Zorich, had sold him down the river. Zorich had not even called one witness on his behalf. Instead, he just let him go to trial and get convicted for some crap that he didn't even do.

But the way Preston told him, he held his sister just as responsible. He was mad that his own sister did absolutely nothing for him, even though she was a prosecutor and could have helped him. She did not even come to his trial. So when Scheffler got out, he came to see her. He shared with her their mutual dislike for Zorich, the public defender who screwed up Scheffler's case and Preston's trial. Judge Thoreson, for her part, found the idea attractive. There would be a little payback, just to help make Zorich's life a little uncomfortable, like Karen Thoreson's life. Make him suffer a bit, maybe let him feel a little bit of pain, even though it wasn't like losing a loved one, murdered in cold blood in his prison cell. And it was all Zorich's fault. He was the one who got her brother sent to the prison in first place.

When she said she couldn't commit right away, Scheffler told her how her brother died. It was not pretty. He and a couple of the boys invited Steven into the Aryan Brotherhood but Steven would have nothing to do with it. They told him that it was for his own protection. But Steven refused. So they roughed him up a couple of times on the playing field. Smashed a thirty-pound barbell into his head but that didn't work either. So they arranged for a couple of visitors from the Black Guerilla Family to pay him a visit. They figured that Steven would come running to them, begging for protection.

But the BGF got a little carried away. They had their fun with him at first and then decided that they needed to finish him off. It was bloody. Naturally, there were no witnesses. Scheffler claimed that he and the rest of the AB were shocked. They never intended for Steven to be killed. They only wanted him to be scared. But the fact remained that Steven had screwed up. He hadn't joined the AB when he had his chance. Karen was not sure that Scheffler was telling it straight. He was smiling at her all the time he was giving her the gory details.

"We don't like it when people don't treat us with respect, you know. We just don't like it. Like your brother, he made a big mistake. He should have joined us when we invited him. But he was a little too good for us. He wouldn't have anything to do with the AB," Scheffler said.

The message was clear. She had better treat Scheffler with respect. She had better go along with Scheffler. The plan at first seemed simple and so harmless. For a few bucks, Scheffler would see to it that Zorich suffered a bit, not too much, just enough. She liked that part of it. Scheffler could easily hire a couple of parolees, who were only too willing to do anything within reason for money. It was amazing how a few hundred dollars for a thug, and a few more for Scheffler's cut, would do the trick. She figured that for three hundred dollars she would do a little pay back and have Scheffler out of her life. But then things went bad.

She financed one and then another and then found out that she didn't have much choice as to what Scheffler wanted to do. She had paid Scheffler knowing that she couldn't back out. At any time, Scheffler told her that all he had to do was to tell the newspaper about her brother who had gone to prison and that she had done nothing to help him. By itself, that wasn't all that much. But when Scheffler started going after Mike and she was paying Scheffler off, it got a little dicey. Soon, she knew that there was no way out. Maybe Scheffler would make a deal with the cops and turn on her. Anyway, it was not going well.

Now she knew that she had to pay off or risk everything. Maybe this time it would be all over. Maybe Scheffler would go away, like he said he would. Maybe her life could return to normal. Maybe it would work out in the end. She just stared straight ahead, tears running down her face, her right hand clutching her torn blouse. Scheffler said nothing. He just stared at her with the most salacious grin. She expected him to jump on her and rape her at any moment. She knew there was nothing she could do.

"Okay. I'll do it. But I've got to know that this is it. I'm out of it. This has to be the last time, ever."

"Oh sure, boss, you're out of it. Nothing more. Well, nothing more with you. I still have some business with Mr. Zorich, but that is not your concern. I am about to wrap that up in a day or two."

"What kind of business do you have with Zorich?"

"Whatever it is, it's none of your business. You just concentrate on getting me the $250,000 by 5 p.m. day after tomorrow. I'll call you on your cell and tell you when and where to deliver it. Simple as that and then I'm gone. You will never see me again. You can count on me, just as you always have. Got it?"

"Yeah, I've got it. But I am not sure that I can get the money by then. I may need some more time. If I need another day, will that work?"

"No, it won't, Karen. Day after tomorrow it is. That's plenty of time. No money then and the world will know who you really are. You will be in jail. So will I, if they can catch me. But so what? I've been there before, no big deal. I'll work out some plea bargain, my testimony for a deal. The D.A. will be overjoyed to get the goods on you, to get you convicted. It's not too often that a big fish like you comes along. Can you imagine that guy's career? It will take off like a rocket. And all at your expense. I'll do a little time. But you will spend a whole lot of time in the joint. Maybe some of your old friends will come and visit you. You know, someone you sent there as a D.A. or as a judge? They would just love to drop by your cell and pay their respects. And let me tell you, the women can be just as rough as any man. You won't ever get a decent night's sleep. But that will be the least of it. Face it, Karen, you have a whole lot more to lose on this deal that I do. Got it?"

She nodded.

"You get the money and everything will be just fine. And don't get cute by calling the cops. In the end, it will work out just as I said."

TWENTY TWO

EVERYTHING WENT WELL for Arthur Scheffler. Karen Thoreson paid off like a slot machine. It took another day but Karen came through with the dough. Added to the $250,000 he got from Zorich, Scheffler was now half-way to becoming a millionaire. Not bad for an ex-con with little likelihood of ever finding a good-paying job. Arthur Scheffler was sitting pretty.

The beauty of it all was that nobody knew a thing. The guys that he hired for his work wouldn't talk if they were tortured. Karen was good as gold. There was no way she would tell anyone what they had done. All Scheffler had to do now was to get out of town and head for Mexico, probably Cabo or Acapulco. He could lose himself there in a New York minute. There were plenty of drifters who looked just like him. That he knew. With his money he could get by for a long time. Something else would turn up to do if he wanted. Life was good.

For Robert Cannes, life was not so good. The phone call from Mike Zorich was unsettling to say the least. He did not like Zorich's tone and he certainly did not like the idea of Frank Bolger talking to anyone. Cannes figured that he had better ask Tom Summers if he should be worried about Bolger. So he gave Tom a call, but Summers was out of the office and his secretary said she would have him phone back as soon as he got into the office. Tom called back the next day.

"What's up, Robert? Got any new work for me?"

"No, Tom. Nothing new. Wanted to know about your work with Bolger. I got a call from Mike Zorich. Seems that he has been talking to your guy, Bolger, and he was threatening me with something bad. Not sure what to make of it. You know anything?"

Tom hesitated. His mind was in overdrive. He thought of Bolger and he thought of Scheffler.

"Bolger was just one of the guys, Robert. That's all. I got a lot of guys. What can I say?"

"I don't know what you can say, Tom. Something is not right here and I don't want to go down for anything. I just hired you to do some background work for me. Next thing I know, Bolger is talking to opposing counsel. Doesn't sit right, you know? You said you had other guys, what does that mean?"

"Some other guys who worked with Frank, that's all. One of them was in charge and oversaw everything. I think the guy actually knew Zorich, so he helped Bolger get the information for you, I think."

"Yeah, who was that?"

"Nobody special. Just a guy. Name is Scheffler."

Cannes hung up but he knew that all was not well. He had no idea who Scheffler was, until he spent some time on the internet and then he knew all that he needed to know about Arthur Scheffler. He had to decide whether to cast his lot with the Tom Summers and Frank Bolger and Arthur Scheffler or to try and cut his losses. And there was Judge Karen Thoreson. Robert Cannes knew that he was in way over his head. He figured that he had better sleep on it. As it turned out, his decision came earlier than he expected.

The next morning at about 9:30, two Sacramento Sheriff's Deputies drove up to the office of Robert Cannes in Woodland. They had cleared their mission with the Yolo County Sheriff's Department ahead of time. The secretary buzzed his office.

"Couple of police officers out here for you, Mr. Cannes."

"Okay, be right there."

Cannes walked down the corridor to the receptionist's desk. He was puzzled as to why cops would be at his office.

"Mr. Cannes, would you please come with us to Sacramento? We would like to ask you a few questions."

Cannes stopped and looked at the officer. He face turned white and his heart was pounding.

"What's this about?"

"It's about Mike Zorich and a certain Frank Bolger who has been telling us about some stuff he has been up to. He says that he has been doing work for Tom Summers and that you might know something about that."

Cannes blinked a couple of times and did all he could to retain his composure. He looked down at the ground for about ten seconds.

"Do I have a choice in going with you or not? Am I under arrest?"

"Mr. Cannes, don't make this hard on yourself. We want you to come willingly but if you don't we will have to take you in for questioning. Call it a detention. Do you understand?"

The magic word 'detention' resonated with Cannes. "How about if I make a call or two?"

"You can do that at the police station, if you like, sir. Right now, we need you to come with us."

Cannes knew that he had no choice. A bead of perspiration formed at his forehead. He did not like this situation at all.

"Okay, let me grab my coat, will you?"

"Sure."

Cannes was back in a couple of minutes, but not before having taken a few deep breaths. He grabbed his cell phone, in the hope that he could contact a few people if things went bad.

At the Sheriff's Office, Cannes was taken to a rather sterile interview room consisting of three chairs and a table. After reading his Miranda rights to him, a detective asked him if he wanted to talk. Cannes didn't know what to do.

"What happens if I do or if I don't?"

"Well, depends on what you tell us and how it compares to what we know. Best case scenario, Mr. Cannes, we get your cooperation and we go to bat for you. We talk to the District Attorney and do our best for you. Especially if you help us with the rest of our case. Worst case, you are going down for a whole lot of stuff."

Like many lawyers, Robert Cannes figured that he was his own best lawyer. Maybe a big ego comes with the turf. But Robert Cannes was not a criminal defense lawyer. If he was, he would know the golden rule. "Never talk to the cops. Never, ever." This was the one piece of advice that gets quickly discarded in the heat of the moment. And this moment was very hot.

"I'll talk to you. But I am banking on you guys helping me out. I really didn't do anything wrong."

"We're listening."

"I hired Tom Summers to snoop around a bit on the Darnoff case and to get me some information on Mike Zorich. Thought it might be useful. But the thing about Zorich was that Judge Thoreson told me he was a bad actor."

"Oh yeah? How was he a bad actor?"

"The way I understand it, Zorich was responsible for getting Judge Thoreson's brother into prison. I don't know the details. But Judge Thoreson was sure that Zorich did a lousy job when he was a public defender. Never called any witnesses. Long time ago. I never much questioned her about it, to tell you the truth."

"How do you know this?"

"Judge Thoreson told me. See, after the Darnoff case was assigned to her, she called me into her chambers one day and told me all of this stuff about Zorich. She told me to press the case and not be worried about how it would go and that she would take care of everything. I wasn't about to look a gift horse in the mouth, as they say, so I was game. I knew Zorich from another case, years ago, and I knew that he was a jerk. So I figured out the best way of getting him into a little trouble was to demand some documents from him when I knew that another judge had ordered all of us to not disclose the documents. I figured that Judge Thoreson would just push him around a bit and scare him and back off. But then she found him in contempt of court and threw him in jail. She really surprised me. I had no idea that she would go that far. But not much I could do at that point."

"This talking to the judge about a case, you lawyers aren't supposed to be doing that, right?"

"Right. But what was I to do? She's a judge, for God's sake. She's the one talking to me."

"So you are settling your own score and doing her bidding, all in one little court motion. Is that it?"

"Yeah, I guess. Look, I did what the judge told me. I acted within the law. I simply filed my motions and made my arguments. I didn't do anything wrong. I got some documents from Summers on my case that were from Zorich's office. Can't say they helped me much. But that's all, honest."

"Sounds a bit like receiving stolen property to me, wouldn't you agree?"

Cannes did not say anything.

"So, is that all?"

"One time I called Frank Bolger, the guy who got the documents. He worked for Summers. I asked him to help me out. Judge Thoreson called me and wanted to be sure that I won an appeal on her contempt order. It was all crazy. I don't know why I called Bolger, but I did. Bolger couldn't or wouldn't do anything for me. He tells me to call Summers. So I do. Summers just tells me that he has some guys working for him, off and on. So that's the deal. Nothing happened from that. There's nothing else."

"Okay, let me ask you again. Is that all?"

"That's all."

"Who do you think might have burned down a cabin in Kyburz? Or kidnapped Nancy Richards, Mike Zorich's girlfriend? Or burglarized his house and office? Or mugged him on the bike trail or rammed his car? Any ideas, Mr. Cannes?"

"I don't know. I didn't do any of that. Maybe Summers or Bolger knows something."

The room was silent. The deputies left him alone in the room but returned in ten minutes.

"All right, Mr. Cannes. You are free to go for now. We will give your statement our review and consideration. Can't ask for more than that, can you? Just don't leave town."

The detectives next called on Tom Summers. He was cooperative, mainly because he feared what Art Scheffler had been up to. Summers simply told the detectives that Scheffler acted as his right hand man and did whatever needed to be done. The detectives left his office not knowing whether they were getting the straight scoop or not. But, then again, that was usually how they finished a lot of interviews. That was the nature of police work.

During the rest of the day, the detectives reviewed Mike Zorich's declaration and compiled all their information and concluded that the Honorable Karen Thoreson was probably guilty of several felonies. So they scheduled an evening meeting with the Yolo County District Attorney's Office to review the case. Bringing charges against a sitting Superior Court Judge does not happen every day and they wanted to be sure that there were no holes in the evidence. Everything seemed to make sense. The officers obtained an arrest warrant the next day and went to Judge Thoreson's house early in the morning, but she was not there. In fact, nobody was home. So they headed over to the Yolo County Superior Court, but she was not there either.

That morning Mike had driven to the bike trail to go for his usual run. Karen Thoreson had driven to the same bike trail, only Mike didn't see her. Instead Mike was out running on the trail feeling satisfied, maybe smug, from knowing that things were about to get better. He ran four miles and worked up a good sweat. After Mike returned to his car from his run, he saw her right away. Judge Karen Thoreson was waiting for him, standing next to her car. She was dressed in a typical business suit. Her arms were crossed and she was staring at him. Mike pulled his keys from his pocket.

"Judge, what are you doing here?"

Karen Thoreson approached slowly. Dressed as she was, she didn't exactly fit in with the morning running crowd.

"I've come to apologize, Mr. Zorich. I'm hoping that we can work this out," she said.

"Work what out, judge? And how did you ever find me here?"

"You know, this stuff with the case and everything. I could have handled things better, but things just got out of hand. I never intended for there to be anything bad happen to you or to your girlfriend. It's all about my brother and my mother. It was a lot for anyone to take."

"What about your brother?"

"You defended him and did a poor job. You have to admit that."

"What the hell are you talking about?"

Mike could see that her face was getting redder.

"My mother died knowing that her son was convicted of a crime that he didn't commit. He should never have gone to prison in the first place. And he was killed because he was in prison, all because you screwed up the case. That's what I am talking about. You know exactly what I am talking about."

The tone in her voice had changed, slightly. She was trying to contain herself but the anger was there. Still, she thought that this could all be worked out with him, that all she had to do was to apologize and it would all go away.

"Look, Judge, the party's over."

Mike said the word "Judge" with particular emphasis and with disdain.

"I know it all, so do the cops," he said. "It's just a matter of time. They have Bolger and Cannes for starters."

"Cannes isn't going to say anything. He's too smart for that, Mr. Zorich."

"Okay, you tell me what happened. Start with Art Scheffler."

"You know about him, huh? Scheffler is a bad person. I don't think anyone is going to believe him." she said.

"Maybe. Maybe not."

"Scheffler did tell me that you screwed up his case. I figure that you have some explaining to do. So, I can help you. I'll say that he is a bad guy. I can help you. You can say that everything was all a misunderstanding and that you do not want to press charges or anything. That way we can all go back to the way it was."

She looked right at him. Her eyes were wide open and her face was lit up.

"That's not happening, Judge. Besides, it's too late."

She looked at him and then turned away. When she turned back there were tears in her eyes. She was looking at the ground.

"Honest, I never meant for any of this to happen to you. I just couldn't get out of it. You've got to understand.

"Oh come on. You never meant to hold me in contempt of court? You never meant to throw me in jail? Who are you kidding?

Judge Karen Thoreson looked down at the ground. She had no words.

"Tell me about the mugging and the burglaries and the car smashing. Tell me about the arson at my cabin and the kidnapping of my girlfriend. Tell me you have never meant any of that to happen."

"No, I swear to God. I never knew about any of that stuff, until after he did it. I just gave him money to shut him up. He shook me down for a whole lot more money the other day. Now he's gone. If all of this stuff gets out, I'm ruined. I am so sorry. But will you help me? If this stuff comes out, I will lose my judgeship. Can't you see that I had no choice? He was calling the shots. He did everything."

Mike stood there in his running shorts, hands on his hips, just looking at the woman.

"I don't think so. Look, I don't know if this helps, but let me explain something. I defended your brother and he admitted to me that he did the robbery. He wanted me to call some witnesses who were going to make up some story to give him an alibi. You know that I can't do that. It's against the ethical rules. I couldn't call your mother when I knew that she was lying. You brother wanted to testify and tell his story. That's his right, his constitutional right. I can't stop that. He was found guilty for one reason and for one reason only. He was guilty."

"That's not true. He was home with my mother. She told me he was there and he was innocent. You didn't even call my mother or any witness. You could have done something. You didn't do anything."

"Judge, you don't know what you are talking about. You've got your facts all wrong. And you're nuts if you think I can just forget all of this."

He looked at her and she looked at him. They both realized that there was no more talking to be done. After a minute, Mike went to his car and drove away. He did not look back. He couldn't believe the conversation he just had with Karen Thoreson but he knew that it was useless to talk to her anymore. He figured that she must have learned from Scheffler that Mike liked to run on the bike trail most mornings. So she just came here hoping to find him.

Karen Thoreson got back in her car and headed for the Yolo County Courthouse. It took about an hour and when she arrived, there were two deputies from the Sacramento County Sheriff's Department, along with two more deputies from the Yolo County Sheriff's Department. They took her to Sacramento and soon found out all about Arthur Scheffler. She couldn't keep it bottled up any more. She had to tell someone. She begged the detectives to keep it all quiet and that she would cooperate in any way she could, but the detectives were non-committal.

An APB was put out for Arthur Scheffler with a special alert for the border crossings into Mexico. Later that afternoon, the authorities in San Diego called to say that they had stopped Scheffler at the border trying to cross into Mexico. They had him in custody. And they had half a million dollars that Scheffler was carrying with him. They would hold Scheffler and the money for pick-up by the Sacramento authorities.

When Mike got home, he showered and ate breakfast. Then he went to his office. He called Detective Sauer and told him all about meeting Judge Thoreson. Sauer told Mike that they had just arrested her at the Yolo County Courthouse that morning.

They had spoken to Bolger, Summers and Cannes. Scheffler had been found at the San Diego border. The case was falling into place. Sauer was appreciative of Mike's help and told him that they would get his money back to him in a couple of days. Sauer asked about Nancy and Mike told him what he knew.

Mike then went to the hospital. Nancy was released with a lot of pain medication and with a happy smile. There were fewer bandages on her face, only some on her cuts. But the rest of her face was black and blue. Her left arm was in a cast and her ribs were heavily taped. She walked unsteadily on Mike's arm. He took her to her house and she picked up some clothes and toiletries and they went to his house. She would stay there while she recuperated or maybe longer. It was not all that clear. They enjoyed dinner together that night, just like the old times. Nancy went to bed on the early side saying that she was tired. Mike sat in his living room with a glass of wine. It had been a hectic couple of months.

He was up the next morning and retrieved the paper. The Sacramento Bee carried the story on the front page, complete with pictures of Judge Karen Thoreson, Robert Cannes, Frank Bolger and Arthur Scheffler. According to reports from the Sacramento County Sheriff's Department, Judge Thoreson's brother was killed in prison and the judge had held Zorich responsible. She had then embarked on a campaign to either scare or injure Zorich. A local guy, Frank Bolger, was involved and another ex-con, Arthur Scheffler, was the one who actually did most of the stuff. The article explained about everything that had happened to Mike and to Nancy. Scheffler had been arrested in San Diego and was on his way back to Sacramento. Judge Thoreson was being held in jail, pending a bail hearing. Bolger had been released on his own recognizance at the request of the Public Defender's Office and the Police Department. Witnesses were cooperating with the authorities.

The reporter had contacted several local judges and lawyers for their comments and they were all completely shocked by the turn of events.

"I've known Karen Thoreson for a long time and frankly, I just can't believe what I have heard. There has to be more to this story," said one Yolo County judge who asked that his name not be used. An anonymous deputy district attorney from Yolo County added that he was shocked at the charges.

That morning Mike dabbled at the egg on his plate and put the newspaper down. He rocked back in his kitchen chair, the coffee now growing colder as the minutes passed. He put his hands behind his neck and closed his eyes. He could hear Nancy stirring in the bedroom. He tried to take it all in, but there was just too much. None of it made any sense. The only thing he knew for sure was that he had no regrets

ACKNOWLEGEMENTS

To THE TRIAL lawyers, those champions who labor in the trenches for their clients. You work at one of the hardest and least-appreciated jobs in a free society. To Laura and Mark for your love and support, as well as your significant input on my budding manuscript. You kept me going. Thanks to Jennifer Fisher for your very valuable editorial comments. Thanks also to Rich Fathy and Jerry Scribner for your overwhelming generosity and honesty. Your critical comments were a great help. To my father, Kenneth R. Malovos, and to Ken Wells, former Public Defender of Sacramento County, you were my models and my mentors. Your inspiration is never-ending. And to Michele, there are no words that could ever express my gratitude for your constant encouragement, keen eye and countless hours reading, editing and suggesting. You are my love.

Made in the USA
San Bernardino, CA
15 August 2018